MEDUSA:

HER STORY

CHERYL L-G TRENT

Paperback ISBN: 979-8-9893170-4-2

Ebook ISBN: 979-8-9893170-3-5

Hardback ISBN 979-8-9893170-5-9

To all who stand up against oppression and inequality.

Let us be Gorgons.

TRIGGER WARNING

This story deals with SA. These sections will be marked. While these scenes are graphic they are written with care to shine a light on these atrocities without glorifying them.

CHARITABLE DONATION:

To help fight for a better future a portion of the proceeds of this book will be donated to human rights advocates HRC and the anti-sexual violence network RAINN.

PROLOGUE
THE MYTH

Mehdi started looking for shells in the sand. The tide was receding, so she hoped to find scallops hiding in the exposed shoreline. Unlike in the shallows where they often lay on the ocean floor, their pink hulls softly glistening and their mouths half open, waiting to gather food. They had to sink deeper here, remaining in wait and safe from danger.

She walked along the water's edge, seeking the tell-tale sign of bubbles burping in the sand. Spotting a bubble burst and a small hole beneath, she dug up the earth with her toes, flicking the shell free. The scallop fluttered and tried to bury itself again, but she was faster.

Her braid worked its way loose, freeing her hair to dance in the wind and snap at her face. The netted bag held plenty for her offering, but she wanted one more. It almost got away when her toe flicked it into the edge of a wave. Lunging after it, she smiled, her prize trapped between palm and fingers. "Ha!"

Light glinted off the water's surface. Glancing at the sun setting in a sky streaked in pinks and blues, her mind swam with thoughts of joy that slipped into sadness. She slumped onto the beachy shore, wallowing in memory and sorrow. Hot tears stung her eyes as she sighed, finding no strength to wipe them away.

After a few more deep breaths, she exhaled and said, "Pink with long orange streaks. The top of the clouds are brilliant white and deep purple on the bottom." Her heart lifted a little, and she smiled.

Her peace faded and she fell into a sour mood as the silhouette of a man encroached. Wet and covered in mud, Mehdi stood, ignoring him, as she cleaned off her hands.

He tsked, "You are dirty. Perhaps you can take a swim and wash away the sand?" He offered.

She grimaced, not making eye contact. "No, thank you. I am avoiding the water presently."

"Shame, it is quite beautiful today."

"I will be fine. It is just sand." Mehdi then turned and walked away.

He followed and quickly caught up. Walking beside her, he asked, "Where are you off to?"

"The temple," she replied.

"For?"

"What else? To make an offering."

"To Poseidon?" he asked with glee.

Stunned at his audacity, she uttered, “No…Athena.”

“And what do you ask of her?”

“Patience.”

“Patience?”

“Yes,” she replied through gritted teeth.

“Patience for what?”

Stopping, her hand curled tightly around the bag. “Against men like you?”

“Men like me?” he asked, shocked. “What have I done?”

“Done?!” She glared at him incredulously. “You ask me that?”

“Why? Because I would like to know you better?”

“Did you even ask if I wish to know you?”

“No, but,” he stammered.

“Did you introduce yourself?”

“No,”

“Did you ask if I needed help? Or merely start helping?”

“You were muddy, and the water was right there.”

“You were inserting yourself into my life because what? You found me pretty?”

“Well, yes,” he said with obvious admiration.

She scoffed and quickened her pace.

He matched her step, keeping the distance between them small. “I came to see you.”

Her previous anger faded as ominous fear took its place. She could not stop the waver in her voice. “Perhaps you can meet me later.”

“But we are both here.”

Mehdi peered over her shoulder and could see the lights of the temple just over the hill. "Why me?" she said, slowly stepping further down the road.

"Your beauty," he cooed.

Mehdi rolled her eyes.

"The legend of your beauty has crossed mountains and seas. Skin smooth as a pearl, hair long and so dark you could get lost in it, and eyes," he moved closer, his voice dropping low, "that pierce the soul."

Cautiously nodding, and sensing imminent danger, she stepped back, but her foot slipped, causing her to stumble and fall against a tree.

In an instant, he pressed up against her, his breath quickening with anticipation.

Terror roiled inside her, but her voice remained calm as she stated, "I am a daughter of Athena."

His hand entwined in her hair. "That is fine."

She cringed, as his lips ran across her neck. "My duty is to her and no other gods."

"She isn't here." Crushing her against the tree, he grabbed her face, as his mouth groped for hers.

She fought his kiss, smelling his sweet, sticky breath, and spat at him.

Furious, he growled and tried to kiss her again.

Mehdi struggled under his great strength. Her hand, still clutching the bag of scallops, swung at his head with all her strength. When his hold loosened, she ran.

Fear-filled tears streaked down her cheeks as she stumbled down the darkening path, pushing her way towards the temple. Without looking over her shoulder, she knew he was behind her.

Her body slammed against the temple doors. Hands shaking, she rattled the handle, yanked it open and scrambled inside. Shutting it behind her, she lowered the heavy board, locking him out.

Sliding to the ground, she took safety within the sacred walls. If the door did not keep him back, the wrath of Athena would. He would not dare desecrate Athena's temple. Body trembling, she released the bag and walked over to the altar to give thanks.

Her knees buckled when a great explosion hit her in the back. The force blew her body up against the feet of Athena, tossing her into the raised stone. A sickening crack rang in her ears and pain seared her skull. Shards of wood rained around her and embedded in her skin from the explosion. Trembling from pain, she turned back toward the entrance.

A massive horse stood in the doorframe. Light sparked from its hooves and the earth shook with each clop as he walked towards her.

Her body froze in fear. Unable to move, her lungs fought intense pain as she drew in ragged breaths.

Hovering over her, the horse's head lowered and exhaled hot humid air onto her face.

His voice boomed from all around her. "You cannot deny me and what I want." The horse slowly transformed back into human form.

"Please, don't," she croaked. "This is the House of Athena. I am a daughter of Athena. Would you anger the Goddess of War?"

He grinned, grabbing her legs and pulling her closer. "She'll forgive me. She always does."

CHAPTER 1
FROM FATHER TO HUSBAND

Mehdi walked down the market street of the island village as she had done most of her life, but today felt different. Something in the manner of those around her changed. Unsure what was different, her eyes flitted about nervously, feeling simultaneously exposed and isolated.

Swallowing down her growing wariness, she spoke to a vendor, exchanging a portion of her daily collected eggs for some bread, before moving onto the other items on her list. Picking through the seasonal vegetables of another vendor, she sensed a presence behind her. Turning around she gazed up at the rotund Alcibiades hovering over her.

"Good day, Mehdi," he said with a toothy grin. "Shopping?"

"Yes..." Mehdi replied puzzled, obviously doing exactly that.

"You should have some figs."

"I cannot afford them today." Looking back at the seller, she offered him eggs. "Can I have some asparagus?"

The seller nodded and bundled the asparagus into a tight clutch when Alcibiades interrupted. "Let me pay." He handed the seller a drachma. "Add some figs too."

Shock sent a shiver down her spine as she fumbled together the words to protest. But the vendor snatched the coin before Mehdi could say anything. Unable to refuse, she smiled politely and slipped the items into her basket. Nodding, she attempted to walk away, but Alcibiades followed.

"How old are you, Mehdi?"

"My Twelfth summer has just passed," she replied.

"You have grown up over the past year."

Unsure how to respond, she cast her eyes down and away from him, focusing on milling through an open barrel of olives.

"Is your father home?"

"Yes..."

"Let him know I will see him later today."

"Okay."

His eyes twinkled with eagerness as he plucked a fig from her basket and bit into it.

She stared in confusion as he wandered back to his usual seat outside the taverna.

After he left, she finished collecting the items on her list and returned home to the rest of her duties. With no mother and her grandmother recently passed, Mehdi was self-reliant.

Her father was a sailor and spent months at sea to come home and sleep most of the day away.

Her father's snores resonated from his bed, as she checked the baking bread and put away the items she gathered from the market. Putting the asparagus in a tall container with a little water, she placed it in the center of the table as a decoration until dinner time. Rummaging for a bowl for the figs, she set them on the table too. They appeared out of place, but it would only be polite to display the gift when Alcibiades came to visit.

That complete, she started on her daily chores. Most days she enjoyed her solace and the sound the wet brush made when washing the floors, but today her mind raced over the events in the market.

Why did Alcibiades pay for their food? Why did his gaze linger on her? What business would he have with her father? Normally, she would not notice these things, letting the thoughts dissolve into the swish swash of the brush, but today, something changed and worry filled her.

Alcibiades visited Mehdi's father and discussed her future long into the night. Mehdi was not allowed to be present at the table as the men spoke, but she could hear everything from her lofted bed.

"She is still a child," her father argued.

"But my offer is sound," Alcibiades retorted.

"So, you think I will take the first offer?" her father asked.

"Do you think she will have more?"

"Look at her. She is blooming, give her time to grow. If

she is plucked too soon, she could wilt and die before she can bear full fruit."

Mehdi puzzled over her father's words. Why was she being compared to fruit?

Alcibiades, fully entrenched in the argument, pressed his commitment. "Then a payment for future betrothal. How long must I wait?"

"At least four more summers," her father retorted with an unusual calm, considering he was negotiating Mehdi's future.

"Sixteen?" Mehdi whispered to herself.

"Four years?" Alcibiades balked. "One."

"Three," her father countered.

"Two!" Alcibiades snapped.

"Three," her father replied firmly, "And you must match any other offers."

"Fifteen?" she whimpered. Overwhelmed by emotion, she rolled over, burying her face into the bed.

Alcibiades grumbled but submitted. "Fine. We have a deal."

Mehdi laid in her bed listening to the men share a drink and seal their contract. Staring at the stars through the cracks in the thatched roof and she wished to be among them.

The next day at the market, when she offered her eggs for barter, the shopkeeper refused and informed her that everything she chose from now on was paid for. Shock was her first response, confusion her next, then she saw the seller nod to someone behind her. Peering over her shoulder, Alcibiades raised a glass to her and drank. Mehdi suddenly felt like one of the goods in the crates. Bartered and traded with no say in the matter.

Emotionally disconnected and lost over the next few weeks, she went through her daily motions, conflicted over her fate. Alcibiades' offer was putting food on the table. It also made it possible for her to barter and trade for other needed items that improved their life. She tried to be thankful but knew the cost of comfort was her own future.

Chores became a solace. A way to escape the impending future. Since Alcibiades' constant gaze in the market made her dread shopping, she dove into daily tasks that he could not survey. Like the peace and quiet at the local well.

Drawing the water from the deep shaft, she lost herself in the sound of the rope rubbing against the beam and the bucket gently knocking the sides. Her hands crossed over each other, lowering the rope in a steady descent. She sighed with content when the rope slackened and the bucket as it hit the water. Moving the rope to and fro, she encouraged the bucket to tip and fill. Water flowed into the bucket slowly at first, then whooshed in as the weight of the water forced the bucket to drop under the surface and fill completely. Her muscles ached in a good way as she drew it back up and set the bucket on the edge of the well.

"Mehdi," Alcibiades called her.

Broken from her trance, her eyes widened, then dulled. "Hello, Alcibiades." She replied in a resigned tone, upset that even this place was no longer safe from his gaze.

"Mehdi," he said again, "Are you well?"

"I am fine," she replied, not looking up and taking her drawn water back to the house.

"You seem sad. Is there something I can do?"

"No."

"Let me walk you to the market. The figs are ripe and sweet. Perhaps some dates?"

"I am not hungry."

"How about a new shawl?"

"The one I own is fine."

"But this one," he replied, picking the shawl off her shoulders. "Is old and worn. You need something bright and new."

Mehdi's eyes flared, as she snatched back the shawl.

He chuckled softly. "Is it sentimental?"

"No," she snapped. "but it is not yours to take."

"Oh, don't be angry with me. I want to buy you something pretty."

"Thank you, but no," she continued up the path, an unusual anger stoking in her chest.

He followed. "Do you not like my gifts?"

"I did not ask for any."

"But a pretty girl like you deserves pretty things. I am merely trying to be nice."

Mehdi hung her head, partially in shame and partially in defeat. He was only trying to be nice. Lifting her head, she presented a polite smile, "Thank you for your kindness, Alcibiades. I do not deserve it."

His grin grew wide as his chest swelled with pride,

causing his round belly to protrude out further. “See, you are prettier when you smile. Let me buy you that shawl.”

“Of course, Alcibiades,” she replied, powerless to refuse.

“Please, call me Alci.” He leaned down and kissed her softly on the cheek.

Mehdi relented to the kiss but kept her eyes downward so he could not see her discontent.

At the market, she realized why people always stared at her. It was her appearance and the way others looked at her. Men would stare, forgetting what they were doing to leer at her. Women turned away from her, focusing on their tasks rather than make eye contact.

The sensation of her every move being watched, but feeling utterly alone, washed over her again. It was becoming too common a feeling, and she wished it would go away. She went through the motions of propriety, as Alcibiades showered her with gifts.

He paraded her around the market, insisting she try some sweets and adorned her in fine cloth and jewelry. Studying her face in the polished mirror, she felt like a sacrificial goat adorned with flowers ready to be slaughtered on the hill.

“Smile, Mehdi,” Alcibiades encouraged, placing another kiss on her cheek.

All eyes were still on her, as Alcibiades staked his claim. Mehdi’s heart pounded and her stomach churned. In her politest tone, she stated, “I need to go home...”

CHAPTER 2

THE PATH WE TAKE TO OUR FATE

Before he could object, she walked away, holding back rising tears. Compressed emotions bubbled to the surface, as her pace increased. Heart pounding and chest heaving, her feet carried her out of the marketplace and down to the shore. Without hesitation, she rushed into the sea until the waves crested at her waist. They crashed against her over and over, numbing her body and washing away her tears.

The waves tugged at her shawl. Its bright newness disgusted her. Tearing it off her shoulders, she tossed it, allowing the tide to draw it out to sea. Twisting and writhing, she forsook the shawl to the abyss.

Brushing back her hair, her fingers tangled in the jewelry Alcibiades bought. She tore it all off and watched them dance in the water and light as they sunk into the sea. The sand gladly devoured the metal and stone, showing only a glimmer of their new treasure.

"You can keep it," she said to the sand.

Sitting down, a calmness swept over her. The worries on shore disappeared into the crashing waves and soothing waters. The sea beckoned her to lay down and let the tide drag her away too.

The call tempted her, but feeling more herself, she stood and waded back out of the water. Thwamping onto a rock, she splayed out and allowed her tears to fall as her clothes dried.

"Well done," cheered the voice of a unknown woman.

Mehdi turned toward a woman standing behind a makeshift frame, pulling a net taut. It was Danae, a fisherman's wife, but not just an ordinary fisherman's wife. Stories said her husband found her drifting at sea.

Mehdi wiped the snot from her nose and brushed away the tears. "Pardon?" In her haste to get to the water, Mehdi had taken the first path she saw, which apparently led to a personal lot.

"I said, well done," replied Danae, as she pointed towards the water. "It might come back, but you were right to toss it in." She reached down into a basket and drew out a large needle and fresh twine.

"Really?" Mehdi asked, already regretting the bold action. Rising from the rock, she wrangled her wet chiton into a presentable state, but her unruly hair refused to cooperate, happily dancing in the ocean breeze.

The woman affirmed her summation, as she threaded her needle. "Men think they can decide our fate, but we do have some control."

"How?" she inquired, edging closer to watch Danae's nimble fingers as they moved the needle in and out of the aged net. "My father has agreed. The contract is made."

Pulling the fresh thread tight and sealing up the hole, she answered. "Your father may think he has the right to decide your fate, but you choose whether to agree."

"I can't refuse. He's my father. To do so will dishonor him."

Danae nodded. "But how does he honor you? Giving you, his child, no say in your future?"

Was she already the talk of the whole town? Did everyone know she was set to wed Alcibiades? "Perhaps this is my fate?"

Danae put down her needle and put out her hands. Mehdi took them hesitantly but felt a sense of calmness as their clasp tightened.

"My father also thought he had ultimate power over me. When the sages of Delphi told him a future he did not like, he locked me away."

Her brow furrowed in disbelief. "He locked you away?"

She nodded. "Yes, I was forbidden from seeing any man, for fear I would give birth and my child would kill him."

Mehdi gasped.

Putting away her tools, Danae continued her story. "It was awful. I was so lonely. Yet, despite my father's attempts, I still got pregnant and bore a child."

"How?"

The woman waved away the question and sat down on a stool next to a small table. "The how isn't the issue presently, but the truth is. Despite what they believe, men do not control our fate." She lifted a lid off a dish and offered it to Mehdi.

Mehdi selected a slice of pasteli and took a bite. The crunchy and chewy texture soothed the tension in her jaw. "You believe I have control over my fate?"

Danae poured them both watered down wine and took a sip from her cup. "Each of us has a part to play, but we choose what it will be. Prisoner? Servant? Wife?"

"Are those my only choices?" Mehdi asked, taking a sip to wash down the sticky confection.

Danae laughed and surveyed her little realm. "Typically, but perhaps you can find another path."

"I don't know... How can I defy my father? And even if I do, what else is there for me but to be a wife? If not to Alcibiades, then another."

The woman set down her cup and leaned forward, gently brushing back Mehdi's drying tresses. "Your end may be certain, but how you get there is your decision."

The statement sent a fateful chill down her spine, but before she could speak, she saw Danae look past her shoulder towards the water.

"Mother," called a young man's voice, as he and an elderly man pulled a small boat onto the shore.

"Yes, Perseus?"

"I hope you finished fixing that net, because this one is bad luck." He motioned behind him.

"Hush," grumbled the elderly man. "The fish weren't biting."

"They don't have to bite if we have the net," Perseus retorted with a giant grin.

Danae gave her son a half-hearted glare, then rose from her chair and slipped into the older man's arms. "Do not listen to him, Dictes. I am sure his incessant talking was the real reason."

Dictes nodded. "I agree. I couldn't even get a decent nap." He tilted his head, looking past Danae and onto a nervous Mehdi sitting in front of his house. "Hello."

The tenor and tremor of Dicte's voice disarmed Mehdi. "Hello," she answered back. Despite his welcoming nature, she felt a need to stand and exit. "I'll be going."

Danae reached out to her, "No, stay and have dinner."

"No, my own is surely expecting me. They likely think I have run away."

Danae grinned and approached her once more. She drew Mehdi's hands into hers and repeated, "You choose."

Mehdi smiled and squeezed back. The rays of the setting sun peeking from behind Athena's temple at the top of the hill caught her gaze and made her think of Danae's mention of Delphi. "Perhaps the Goddess of Wisdom can help?"

Danae smiled. "Perhaps."

CHAPTER 3

HER OWN PATH

Completing her farewells, she wound up the path toward the temple. The road was rocky and steep, but she kept a steady pace with all her focus on reaching the top.

Her whole life, Athena's temple watched over this land. A massive complex with huge pillars encasing the inner shrine and inside was a giant golden statue of Athena. Mehdi reverently gawped at the effigy. Strong and beautiful, Athena brandished her spear and shield and was adorned in the Aegis with a death mask affixed to the chest. Snakes coiled around the mask's visage and wing-like horns sprouting from the crown. Draped around Athena's golden shoulders was the ritual peplos that the people of her island made as a gift to the goddess.

Mehdi felt a deep connection to Athena, almost as deep as her connection to the sea, which she always found strange.

Poseidon, as the god of the sea, was chaotic in nature, while Athena was direct and true.

Kneeling before the magnificent statue, she prayed. "Goddess of Wisdom." She spoke in a voice soft and lost. "Why do I not want to marry?" Her tears found their way to the surface again. She brushed them away. "Alcibiades seems kind and wishes nothing but to shower me with affection and gifts, but…I feel nothing. Should I be grateful that I am pretty enough for a man like him? Marrying him means my family will want for nothing, but,"

As her unspoken words hung in the air, a line of priestesses entered the room. They paraded in, slow and rhythmic. Kneeling around her, they also prayed to Athena. Warmth and peace emanated from them, as a sensation of oneness filled her.

Prayers complete, each one stood, touched Athena's spear, and then exited.

Compelled to follow, Mehdi stood and fell in line behind them. When she touched the spear, a sense of clarity pulsed through her body. She followed their procession deeper into the temple grounds. They didn't seem to notice or care as she entered the inner sanctum.

Inside, she found an open courtyard where women sparred, grappled, and wrestled, throwing each other to the ground, then getting up and doing it again. Others fought with swords, either practicing drills or fighting with each other. The sound of the striking metal thrilled her ears.

Beyond them were others shooting arrows at targets. Some

wore chitons that were dropped to their waists, exposing bare chests, while others wore close fitting armor. Her heart thumped in time with the thunk, thunk, thunk of arrows striking in unison. One archer noticed her and offered the bow.

Mehdi allowed the woman to show her how to shoot. The tension of the bow was immense and took all her strength to draw it back. The arrow floated around aimlessly, until the archer positioned Mehdi's fingers, and balanced the arrow.

"Now take in a breath and release the arrow as you let it go," the archer instructed.

Mehdi inhaled, then exhaled. Unfortunately, when she released the arrow she let go with both hands. The bow snapped and everything fell to the ground.

The woman giggled. "It is okay. That happens." She picked up the bow. "Care to try again?"

Mehdi could hardly breathe. "Yes!" She spent the next half hour trying to shoot. Finally, her muscles jellied and she could not pull back the string. The instructor assured her this was normal and to come back tomorrow to practice again.

Her arms ached, and her pulse pounded in her ears. She did not want to leave.

Massaging her weak muscles, she wandered into a covered atrium where several women were in deep discussion over a map, while others were lost deep in thought reading from scrolls.

A woman approached her. "Can I help you?"

Mehdi's heart fluttered. "Can I speak to the Head Priestess?"

"Why?" one of them asked, taking in her still wet hair and excited state.

"I wish to be one of you."

~

"MEHDI, WHAT HAVE YOU DONE?" her father cried out.

"I have listened to my calling," she shouted back.

"But you are betrothed. You cannot do this."

"Why not?" she protested. "You did not ask if I wished to be married."

"You are a woman. You grow up, marry, and have children so they can grow up, marry and have children."

"But I choose not to marry."

"Why?"

"Because I do not like being sold like a goat." She saw the words slap her father hard in the face.

He sighed. "You are young, Mehdi. Do not make such a decision so lightly."

"At least it is mine to make. You sold me to Alcibiades without even asking me."

His shoulders slumped in shame. "You are right. I am sorry, but the contract is made."

"I think a pledge to a god outweighs a mortal contract."

He nodded again, unable to make eye contact.

"Perhaps," interjected the High Priestess Stheno, "we can find a middle ground. When will she be married?"

"No later than her sixteenth year."

"Then let her join us till then. Her virtue will be protected, and she will have a place to grow and learn."

Mehdi looked hopefully at her father.

"But if she refuses to marry after that time?"

"Then the temple will pay for any monetary loss."

Both Mehdi and her father looked at the priestess in awe. The temple offering to pay her dowry was unorthodox. What did the priestess know that they did not? For a moment Mehdi wondered if this was the priestess that visited so long ago?

Her father spoke, "I cannot agree without Alcibiades' approval as I said we have made a contract."

Stheno nodded. "Bring him here. We will come to an agreement."

MEHDI STOOD OUTSIDE THE ROOM, once again listening to others argue about her fate. She wrung her hands and paced back and forth, stopping when another priestess entered the room to fetch a scroll.

The priestess paused. "Are you well?"

Mehdi stared at her, unsure what to say.

The priestess smiled and approached. She was tall and

aquiline like Stheno, with the same dark olive skin and amber eyes. Mehdi recalled her name, Euryale.

Euryale's head quirked to one side. "Perhaps some wine?" She poured Mehdi a cup and offered it to her.

Mehdi silently thanked her and sipped.

"Better?"

Mehdi nodded.

Euryale jerked her head toward the loud arguing, "Why are they so mad?"

Mehdi sighed. "I'm...trying to choose my own path."

"Good for you!" Euryale declared.

Mehdi blinked in surprise. "Truly?"

"Absolutely. Let me guess, the really loud one wants you for his wife?"

Mehdi's head drooped, and she nodded lightly.

Euryale encouraged Mehdi to take another sip. "Men. Always thinking they can decide our fate."

Mehdi swallowed. "I've been through this. Danae said our fate may be certain, but we can choose the path."

"Even better, we can decide how the story is woven."

"Woven?"

Euryale nodded, gesturing to a wall-hanging, "Our fates are woven together in a great tapestry," Her fingers ran over the threads, "There is a warp and a weft, but what strands we add, what choices we make complete the story."

Mehdi gazed at the tapestry. The story of Athena's birth played out in connecting panels, each one describing a story in a tableau. It began with Zeus coupling a woman adorned in a tusked helmet and a spear much like Athena's. She also stood with an owl and a snake entwined around the spear. It was not Hera, Zeus' known wife.

In the next scene, the woman stood at odds with Zeus. They fought. Then the woman was gone, and Zeus was snatching a flying bug out of the air, swallowing it. In the last image, Zeus crouched in pain as Hephaestus cracked open his head to reveal Athena fully grown and adorned in the first woman's armor. Mehdi peered closer to this panel, noticing that as the owl alighted on Athena's shoulder, the snake slithered off the tapestry. She puzzled at the serpent, curious where it was going.

Euryale gently touched Mehdi's shoulder. "Not a common story."

Mehdi shook her head. "No, who is the woman?"

"Metis, a titan and first wife to Zeus."

"First wife?"

"Few speak about her. She married Zeus, hoping to solidify ties between the Olympians and the older gods. Zeus betrayed her."

"But she is the mother of Athena?"

Euryale grinned. "You keened that?"

"Athena is wearing her armor in this image, but the helmet Athena wears now is different."

Euryale nodded. "Athena felt it wise to fashion her armor to that of the people, so they know she is their ally."

"Where did the snake go?"

Euryale smiled. "She has other work to do."

The yelling in the other room ceased, and the group emerged.

Mehdi held her breath as her fate walked into the room. Hope flitted in her chest, seeing the scowl on Alcibiades' face.

Stheno gave her an affirming nod. "It is decided. You will remain with us."

Alcibiades bristled. "Until her sixteenth year."

Stheno gave a polite bow of acknowledgment.

"And I have visitation rights," he affirmed, striding over to Mehdi. "It is important I check on the progress of my bride."

As he put his arm around her, Mehdi's skin crawled, but she remained polite. Keeping her gaze lowered, she repeated inwardly to herself, *I choose my path.* Alcibiades nodded curtly to everyone, then gazed at Mehdi with desire and dissatisfaction. Bidding her farewell with another nod, he left.

Mehdi's father approached her. "This is your wish?"

Her mask of demureness vanished. Squaring her jaw, she asserted, "It is."

With a gentle touch, he patted her hand and then let it go. With no obligation remaining, he left without a second thought.

CHAPTER 4
SCRIMMAGE

Mehdi immediately felt at home in the temple. Surrounded by women, she spent most of her days learning to read, fight, and engineer. Unburdened by societal expectations, she grew strong in body, mind, and spirit. Mehdi discovered great kinship with her fellow priestesses, especially Stheno and Euryale. She grew to understand the bonds of sisterhood and the power that comes with working together against other forces.

Mehdi enjoyed combat and tactics. In particular, fighting in a group. She loved the feeling of working as a team. Today was field combat. All around her, swords clashed as one side fought against the other.

Hefting the sword in her hand to judge and regain balance over it, she swung up her shield in defense and blocked the incoming blow. Blow deflected, she thrusted her sword forward, but her opponent dodged.

Her opponent, Euryale, pushed off Mehdi's shield and

back into a fighting stance. They circled each other, their eyes focused on their opponents next move, while their other senses accessed the battle around them.

Hoofbeats pounded behind Mehdi, triggering her to ready her stance and mount a moving target. A flash of metal in the sunlight brought her back to the combat at hand, forcing her to block and parry. The horse rushed past her, an opportunity missed.

Euryale stopped and shouted, "Again."

Mehdi threw down her sword and shield in frustration. "I can't do it."

Stheno walked up. "I know this is a hard maneuver, but you will get it."

"I can't do it while holding a sword and shield."

"Then what should you do?"

"She's attacking me!" Mehdi claimed. "If I put them down to grab the horse, she can hit me."

"If you get on the horse, what advantages do you have?"

"Speed, force, height."

Stheno nodded.

"But I leave myself open for attack as I mount."

"When you hear the horse, get your opponent as far from you as possible and use your fellow soldiers."

She looked back at the team she was leading.

Hot, sweating, but fierce and ready, they tipped their heads to her in support.

"Battles can be unpredictable, but you can prepare tactics to use. You have 15 minutes to recoup, and then we go again."

She stepped back over to her team.

"Euryale is tough." Aikaterini huffed.

"And strong," Mehdi said, panting. "Any suggestions on how I fight her off and still get on that stupid horse?"

"I do!" Cassia declared. "We will make you a ramp." She motioned to Myra and placed her in a crouched shield position and then took her own shield and locked it into place between the shield and Myra's shoulder. "Now lean back as much as you can, Myra, without losing balance."

Mehdi studied the makeshift ramp, and an idea popped into her head. "Okay, Tana, when I signal you will toss me a spear."

"Yes, Captain!" Tana responded.

Mehdi felt exhilaration run through her body. She bounced up and down, loosening her muscles, and waited for the battle to commence.

The horn sounded and the two teams clashed, as they had several times today. Bolstered by confidence and the support of her team, she readied her stance.

Euryale came for her, and they battled. Swords and shields clashed and clanged, then Mehdi heard the hoof-beats. She glanced back quickly and saw her team protecting Myra and Cassia, who moved into position.

Euryale's blade came down again. She blocked it between her sword and shield. Euryale shifted her weight and pushed into the attack, exactly as Mehdi calculated.

Mehdi relented to the push, causing Euryale to falter. Mehdi quickly shifted her feet and lifted her leg, bracing it against Euryale's torso. Crying out with determination, she kicked Euryale with all her force. Euryale flew backwards and tried to regain her ground.

Mehdi threw down her shield and sheathed her sword as she turned and commanded. “Now!”

Tana tossed her a spear.

Mehdi bounded up the shield ramp, catching the spear midway. As she leapt off the ramp, she slammed the base of the spear into the ground. The wooden weapon bowed and vaulted her into the saddle as the horse passed.

Still holding the spear, she repositioned it in her hand and thrust it into the ground right next to Euryale. Smiling in victory, she sped past her opponent.

Her team roared in triumph. Mehdi pulled the horse to a stop and turned it about.

Stheno walked onto the field and helped Euryale to her feet. “Impressive. What made you think to use the spear?”

“Getting into the air was fine, changing speed and direction, so I was going the same way as the horse. That was tricky.”

“You could have just grabbed the reins and swung.”

“But then I would have no weapon.”

Stheno nodded. “I like that. We will add it to practice for everyone.” She looked at Cassia. “Excellent technique with the shields.”

Cassia beamed.

As THE DAYS and years passed, her beauty bloomed and its reputation with it. However, the temple was not self-sustaining, so trips into the towns and other harvesting chores were necessary. She felt uneasy outside the temple, for each day the men would stare. Weekly, one among them would be brave enough to approach the procession of priestesses. No matter who it was, the conversations were all eerily familiar. A man would see Mehdi, and with a little encouragement from friends, they would break from the group and approach.

"You sure are pretty."

Mehdi would smile politely and continue walking.

Sometimes they would ask, "Are you a priestess of Athena?"

"Yes," she would reply.

"Can priestesses marry?"

"If they wish, they can leave to marry."

"Do you think you will ever leave?"

Stopping, she glanced at the man, annoyed, but worked to remain polite. "If I do, it will be my choice."

A few men boldly continued this conversation day after day. Some priestesses liked the compliments, some played with them, and some even confronted men for daring to approach an Athenian priestess. They were sacred and were not to be touched without consent.

Despite being reminded of this daily, many men still pursued. Mehdi tried to go down with the other priestesses, but this only deterred some. The more she refused to pander their advances, the more insistent they became. Some eventually gave up, some pined and others sneered when she passed, blaming her for their unhappiness.

On a particularly tedious day after several men harassed her on her way to Danae's, they breached her limit. Breaking free of their solicitations, she cursed and mumbled to herself, trying to devise better things to say the next time, hoping it would stop them. As she trounced down onto the beach, she started picking up flotsam and tossing it back into the sea.

"So stupid," she mumbled and slung a piece of driftwood into the crashing waves.

"It will just come right back," Perseus said from behind her.

Mehdi pivoted at his voice, to see him sitting on a rock sharpening a fishing spear. Still irritated, she rolled her eyes at him, then flopped next to him on the rock. Staring up at the sky, she griped, "One day! I would like just one day to walk outside the temple without being harassed."

"Harassed? Who's harassing you?"

Her hands flew upward and spanned the sky. "Men!" Digging her palms deep into her eye sockets, she mocked. "Mehdi, you are so beautiful, the gods certainly smile down on you. Mehdi, may I walk behind you to bask in your presence? A woman such as you should never walk alone."

Slivers of wood curled under his knife as he shrugged. "They are complimenting you."

She gawked at Perseus, "Complimenting? They sound more like threats."

"Gods smiling down on you is a threat?"

"Gods noticing mortals rarely turns out well. Especially women."

This comment sobered Perseus, and he put down his knife. "Good point."

Sitting up, her hands dropped between her knees, and she slumped forward. "And why can women never walk alone? Why do we have to feel threatened every time we walk outside?"

Perseus scratched the beginnings of an adolescent beard, "You know, I really don't know. Because you need protection?"

"From men, right? And to be protected from men, you're expected to be protected by men, but if men are the attackers and the protectors, how can a woman ever feel safe?"

"You don't need a man to protect you, Priestess of Athena."

The compliment took her by surprise, but a dreadful thought washed it away. "But what about others?"

He drew his arm around her in a familial hug. "Maybe you can protect them?"

His tone put a grin on her face. "Certainly better than you can."

"Care to wager on that?" He hopped to his feet and brandished his spear.

She popped up on the stone, while still smiling, and shouted, "You draw a weapon on me? I'm unarmed!"

He curled a brow. "Are you?"

Smirking, she pulled back the folds of her chiton to

expose a sheathed knife. "But what good will this do?" She watched his eyes flick to her movement and leapt over him, grabbing the spear with two hands.

Off-balance, he had to decide whether to hold on to the spear or keep his footing. He chose his footing.

Mehdi followed through with her action, landing on the sand behind him, spinning around with the spear at the ready. Perseus advanced as she thrusted the spear. He ducked, grabbed the spear, and attempted to jerk it free.

Mehdi held on and let out a breathy laugh, "Hey that's my move." The two tugged the spear back and forth, both calculating a move that would disarm, but not harm. Mehdi dug the back of the spear deep in the sand and kicked a leg upward hard into Perseus' chest. Perseus lost his footing and fell to the ground.

She quickly rushed a prone Perseus and pointed the spear at his throat. "Do you concede?"

Spitting sand from his mouth, he raised his arms in surrender. "You're smiling, so yes."

She dropped the spear and put out a hand to help him up.

"Are you two quite finished?" piped up Danae, coming around the path from the market.

The two laughed and went to help.

"I thought you were with your father," Danae stated.

"He had a meeting with his brother," Perseus replied.

Danae glowered. "What does he want now?"

Perseus popped an olive in his mouth. "I don't know, but you can't refuse the King."

Dictes' relationship to the king was a tenuous subject. He was the younger brother, and had no desire to claim the throne, so instead he chose the simple life of a sailor. Then one day he fished a beautiful woman out of the water, who many considered a gift from Poseidon, causing the king to envy him more.

"It is probably nothing," Danae replied, but the quiver in her voice exposed her uncertainty.

Mehdi hugged Danae, unsure why she was worried, but wanted to make her feel better.

Danae wrapped her arms around her and kissed the top of her head. "Thank you."

Grinning back, her hand snuck a piece of pasteli off the table. Danae raised her brow at the impish act.

Mehdi gave her a peck on the cheek. "I need to go fish."

"Do you need to take Perseus?"

Mehdi looked over at Perseus and grinned. "No, I should be fine on my own."

CHAPTER 5
THE REAL BATTLEFIELD

TW: SEXUAL VIOLENCE

Despite Mehdi's hesitations, Alcibiades also continued his adoration of her. Her pledges to Athena did not sway him and he made regular visits. A peculiar relationship developed.

Alcibiades would take her on long walks and flatter her. He would talk about their future, their home, their children and often coax affection from her.

The requests at first were small. A kiss on the cheek or to stroke her hair, though uncomfortable she would oblige. Then it was kisses on the mouth and just like when she was a little girl she found the touch itself pleasurable, even if she found him undesirable and didn't want to marry him. Each visit he would persuade more, reminding her of their betrothal, pushing and urging for a little more, but always stopping when she asked. Mehdi felt in control.

One afternoon tucked away in a grotto kissing, he was very hungry and kept reaching to touch her breasts and between her thighs, but she held him in line without making him angry.

It was a tiresome game, but she managed it well.

His mouth groped along her neck and he asked, "Where is the necklace I bought you?"

"Which one?"

"The one with the pearls."

"I gave it away."

He stopped kissing, astounded. "Gave it away?"

"Yes, I give away all the items you give me."

"Why?"

"I have no need for them."

"Those gifts were for you!" he shouted, his passion turning to anger.

"If they were mine, then I can do with them as I wish," she snapped back.

"They are for you to enjoy."

"I didn't enjoy them."

"Then why didn't you refuse them?"

"Because when I do refuse your gifts, you don't listen and make me take them, anyway."

He ran a hand down his face and inhaled sharply as he paced back and forth. "Why do you not want my gifts?"

"Because..." She adjusted her chiton, "I don't wish to marry you."

He stopped and stared at her in shock. "What?" He spat.

Straightening her posture and jutting her jaw, she

announced. “I do not wish to marry you. I am pledging fully to Athena and staying at the temple.”

“Mehdi, you can worship Athena and still marry.”

“I don’t wish to marry at all.”

“At all!” He clutched at his hair and looked around erratically. “Three years I have waited. Three years and you tell me this now.”

“I told you three years ago, and you did not listen.” She yelled, “I told you over and over that I did not wish to marry you or anyone and you did not listen.” She glared at him. “I told you no, and you did not listen.”

“You were a child. I expected you to mature and understand.”

“Exactly, a child that you wished to marry. Taking my life without a word from me. This is my life and I wish to have nothing to do with you.”

He reached out and grabbed her by the shoulders. “That is not your choice.”

She broke free of his grasp and locked eyes with him. “Yes... it... is.”

Thrusting his hands at her again, he beseeched, “I want you. Don’t you understand that? You are mine to have.”

She moved out of his grip. “I understand, but I don’t want you.”

Furious at her words, his hand flew out to strike her.

She blocked his blow and stepped back. “Leave!”

“I will not.” He rushed her and pushed her against a tree. “You are mine.” Grappling at her shoulders, he stole a kiss.

“I am not!” she shouted and broke free of his grasp

again. She turned to run away, but he knocked her to the ground. Before she could get up, he was pinning her to the floor. “Alcibiades, stop!” The lust in his eyes terrified her.

“I’ll make sure no one wants you and I get what I deserve.” He went to hit her again, but she blocked it, only enraging him more.

He struck again. She failed to defend the fourth blow, leaving her dazed. Alcibiades pinned her arms down with one hand, while pushing away her chiton with the other. She felt his sweaty flesh against her skin and terror ran through her whole body.

Grabbing her, he shoved his fingers inside. Images of the man touching her as a child came rushing back. Alcibiades gave her the same grin as he pushed inside her. It did not feel good, and she did not want this.

Enacting years of training in Athena’s temple, she shifted her body and wrestled free.

Alcibiades grappled her back to the ground, but her strength and agility surprised him. His brutish force kept her pinned, but she knew how to fight a larger opponent.

Landing a few precise blows that weakened his grasp, she wriggled free, scrambled to her feet, and ran.

Racing out of the grotto, she rushed toward the temple grounds. She crashed through the gates into field warriors. Nearly every priestess in the temple was in formation practicing drills. They all stared at her in curiosity.

Out of breath and trembling, she braced her hands on her knees and gasped, “Alcibiades, he...he...”

"He what?" Stheno asked, leaping off her training pedestal and running to her.

"He..." She kept looking over her shoulder, expecting for him to appear, but he never broke through the trees. Mehdi hesitated.

Did she speak about what had just happened? They were fighting. They had fought before, but something about the way he looked at her, the way he touched her, was different. Confused and afraid, she wavered. "He...nothing." Gesturing that she was fine, she flashed a weak smile. "Alcibiades and I just had a fight...I will be fine."

"Mehdi..." Stheno persisted, "You're bleeding." She wiped the blood from Mehdi's cheek, then noticed the scrapes and red marks on her arms and legs. Her tone became very serious. "Mehdi, what happened?"

Mehdi dropped her eyes in shame. "I told Alcibiades I did not want to marry him."

"And?"

"And..." She sniffed, as the shock from fighting and fleeing dispersed. "He didn't like hearing that."

"Did he hit you?"

She nodded reluctantly.

Stheno paused and then carefully asked, "Anything else?"

Mehdi struggled to speak as the attack flashed across her mind again. She could feel his hands grope her flesh as he wrestled her to the ground. Her chest tightened and she couldn't breathe. She looked everywhere but at the Stheno.

It took great strength to muster the slightest nod of affirmation.

Not pressing any further, Stheno took Mehdi's hands and led her back to the temple.

A FEW DAYS LATER, mostly recovered from the incident, Mehdi strode down the path through the village towards Danae's. She noticed people were staring at her, not an unusual occurrence, except today there was something different about their looks and murmurs.

One woman was bold enough to step in front of her. Mehdi stopped suddenly in surprise and stared at the woman who grimaced at her, then spat at Mehdi's feet.

Mehdi stumbled back, then quickly moved past the woman, very confused.

Perseus, who was nearby filling water buckets, came over. "Are you okay?"

"Yes…but that was…strange."

Perseus surveyed the market, also noting how the townsfolk were glaring at Mehdi. "You go on. I'll see what I can find out."

Mehdi headed down to the water. She was worried, but found some peace in her task. There was rhythm and grace in casting a net. Her fingers gathered around the edges of the circular net in measured pleats. Twisting at the toros, she drew the net behind her, then swung it into the air. Spinning, the net splayed out and landed with a thunk in the water. Mehdi tugged on the attached rope, forcing the weighted edges to close the open end, capturing its prey within.

Her mind cleared, and her body relaxed from the repetition. Swish, Thunk. Swish, Thunk. She was picking the latest catch from the net when Perseus returned. The look on his face was serious, and Mehdi's heart raced.

Perseus kneeled, helping her clean the net. "I spoke to the villagers. They say Alcibiades has called a counsel. He claims your virtue is in question and is claiming breach of contract."

She stared at him. "My what?"

"Your virtue. He says he found you with another man."

"What? I..." she sputtered, astonished at the accusation.

"What happened the other day? Mother was expecting you for dinner, but you never came."

"I..." The violent memory flashed across her eyes, tightening her throat, and quickening her breath. "I... He..."

Her fingers curled around the net, and she clenched her teeth in a combination of anger and shame. She didn't want to talk about what happened, but if she remained quiet, others would believe his lie.

As she mulled over what to say, she saw another figure approaching them. It was Stheno and the look on her face was grim.

Mehdi leapt to her feet and rushed towards her. "I didn't do anything wrong. I already told you what happened."

Stheno took her hand with assurance and replied, "And I told you before. I believe you."

Danae came out of her cottage, wiping flour from her hands. "Stheno, what brings you here? Is everything okay?"

Mehdi held back a flood of emotions. She looked at each face, seeing their apprehension, and it unsettled her to the core. She grabbed the net and walked back into the sea. Mehdi could sense them talking behind her, but she did not want to hear their concerns, doubts, and fears. She bore enough of her own.

She heard feet step into the water behind her and knew who it was. "Perseus, please don't ask."

"Okay."

She pulled the net in to toss it again, but her hands started shaking. Perseus reached over to help, but seems to only make it worse. Mehdi threw down the net in frustration and let it sink to the sand.

"Mehdi." Perseus said softly and reached out for her hand.

She flinched at his touch.

"It's okay. I won't hurt you."

Tears bursting, she reached for his hand. He took it and pulled her into a tight embrace.

"I didn't do anything wrong." She sobbed into his chest.

He held her and said, "I believe you."

CHAPTER 6
A WOMAN'S VIRTUE

Mehdi's heart raced as she stood before a council of elders. They stared back with sagging disapproving jowls. Among them was Dictes. The King sat behind them, watching over the trial. Her eyes ran over the crowd seeing Perseus, but no Danae. In fact, no women at all in the main crowd. Where was Stheno? Stheno promised she would be here and help her through this.

"Mehdi," one elder addressed her, "are you betrothed to Alcibiades?"

"I am," she tentatively replied.

"You are also a postulate of Athena?"

"I am."

"Did you become a postulate before or after the betrothal?"

"After."

"Despite your time as a priestess, have you continued to accept visits from Alcibiades?"

"I have."

"Since your betrothal have you accepted the advancements of other men?"

"No."

"Have other men given you gifts?"

"Well, yes..."

A murmur of disapproval rolled through the crowd and across the aging faces of the council.

"And you have been seen conversing with men as you walk through town."

"I suppose. I'm not sure how speaking-"

He cut her off, "But you say that you have not accepted the advancements of other men. I fear you are lying."

"I am not," she stammered.

"Alcibiades states he found you with another man in a secluded grotto."

"It is a lie. I was in that grotto with no one but Alcibiades."

"You were alone with him?"

"Yes."

"A man you are not married to?"

"You know I was betrothed to him."

"But not married?"

"What is your point? I wasn't with another man. I was with Alcibiades. Yes, we were alone, but it was because I wanted to tell him I didn't want to marry him."

The surrounding audience began to mutter amongst themselves.

"You were breaking your betrothal?"

"Yes."

"But the betrothal agreement is not between you and Alcibiades. It is between your father and Alcibiades."

"I'm the one getting married," she said, raising her voice in frustration. "I should be able to decide who I marry."

The noise of the audience grew. The rapping of a staff called them back to order.

Annoyed by the disruption, the elder glared at the crowd before returning to her. "You have no say in the manner." He flippantly turned away from her to Alcibiades, "Alcibiades, is it true that Mehdi requested an end to your betrothal?"

"Only after I caught her with another man," Alcibiades proclaimed.

Mehdi gawked at Alcibiades. "There was no other man!" She looked back at the elders while pointing at Alcibiades. "I was alone with Alcibiades and we were fighting. I told him I didn't want to marry, and he attacked me."

"Now you are claiming he attacked you?"

"Not claiming. Stating." Anger replaced Mehdi's previous fears and shame of the attack. "Alcibiades attacked me and tried to violate me."

Another elder pointed out, "You were the one alone with a man, not your husband, in a secluded grotto."

She stared in utter shock at him, "I was the one attacked and you are telling me, it's my fault?"

Another nodded. "A woman such as yourself should not be alone. It's dangerous."

"A woman such as me? What do you mean?"

"You are too young and beautiful to be alone with a man that isn't your husband. To do such can at the very least damage your reputation and value, and at the most, bring you harm."

"So...I'm too pretty to be left alone."

He smiled a nearly toothless grin. "Yes."

Mehdi was beyond confused. Her head spun from the accusations. She rubbed her temples. "He attacked me."

"Alcibiades," an elder asked, "did you attack Mehdi?"

"Yes, as is my right. Since I found her with another man. Three long years I have waited. Three long years and she denies me what is mine by law."

The elders nodded, and the audience murmured in agreement.

"I wasn't with another man," she stated firmly.

"Perhaps we need to confirm her virtue."

Her eyes narrowed. "What do you mean, confirm my virtue?"

"If you were, as you claim, not with another man. If you have maintained your chastity as a postulate and as per agreement under your betrothal contract, then your virtue will be confirmed, and your word believed."

"Why is my word in question and not his?" she demanded, pointing at Alcibiades.

"Alcibiades is a well-respected member of our community."

"And I am not?"

"No." He clasped his hands and calmly asked, "Now, do you have a man to attest to your virtue?"

"It is my virtue. Should I not be able to speak for myself?"

"Of course not."

Finding herself panicked and desperate, she pointed towards Dictes. "He knows me. He can attest for me."

An elder looked over at his fellow council member, "Dictes, you know this woman."

"I do."

"Can you attest to her virtue?"

"I...cannot."

Mehdi's heart sank. "I have sat at your table. Your wife is like a mother to me, your son a brother."

Dictes' eyes dropped. "And this is where I cannot attest, because I have seen you with my son and you show no decorum."

The crowd became unruly now, spitting and jeering at Mehdi.

Mehdi investigated the mob of angry men for Perseus.

He was shouting too, but it was unclear what he was saying.

She dropped her head in utter hopelessness.

The elder rapped his staff again, demanding calm.

Mehdi's voice was tight with tears, but she croaked, "How exactly do you expect to confirm my virtue?"

"You will be examined."

The statement hung in the air, allowing Mehdi time to hear it and understand. They meant to check her virginity through physical examination, but Alcibiades had violated her. She was still sore and bruised from his attack. Any examination would show that she was not, by their definition, virtuous. Against her will Alcibiades had violated her and now she would be condemned for it.

Hanging her head in defeat, tears welled in her eyes. She steadied her breath, trying to hold them back, but failing.

"There is no need for an examination." Stheno's voice broke through the crowd.

Mehdi lifted her head discovering Stheno approaching her and the elders.

"Yes, there is," an elder replied, wary that a woman dare stand equal to the council. "How else will we know?"

Stheno lifted a silver girdle into the air. The audience audibly gasped when the girdle moved and slithered to wrap around Stheno's wrist. "Since this council decided to question the word of one of Athena's daughters, I felt it fitting to bring a gift from the Goddess of Wisdom. It can only be worn by those who are honest and true. If you lie while wearing this girdle, it will squeeze you and you will suffer."

She walked over to Mehdi and motioned for her to raise her arms. Mehdi complied and the silver snake slithered from Stheno onto Mehdi's waist. Cool to the touch, it made her skin tingle as the etched scales writhed, then stilled, turning into a mundane belt of a snake biting its own tail.

"Mehdi, were you with another man in that grotto?" Stheno asked.

"No," Mehdi replied. The snake remained still.

"Have you ever willingly laid with a man?"

"No!" Mehdi declared, shocked by the question.

"Did Alcibiades attack you?"

"Yes."

"Did he violate you?"

Mehdi shuddered softly, but the snake remained dormant. "Yes."

Stheno caught Mehdi's unsure gaze and gave her a warm smile. She then slowly pivoted on her feet and addressed the council. "Her virtue is intact."

The group of elders glared back, all wearing scowls.

Alcibiades blustered, "How are we to know that girdle even works!"

With a mere glance from Stheno, the belt whipped off Mehdi and towards Alcibiades.

He let out a yelp in fear and tried to paw the snake away, but it slithered around his rotund belly with lightning speed and stilled.

With a glint in her eye, Stheno grinned broadly, "Alcibiades, did you lie to this council?"

Alcibiades' pulse quickened, and sweat beaded on his brow, but he did not answer.

"Alcibiades, did you lie to this council?"

"No," he replied through clenched teeth. The belt tightened around his waist. He grabbed at the restricting coil, trying to get it off. The girdle squeezed, causing him to release a desperate yelp in agony.

"Alcibiades, did you lie to this council and tell them Mehdi was with another man?"

"No." The snake wrenched its head and sunk its teeth into Alcibiades' side. He groaned, falling to the ground wallowing in agony.

"Simply answer the question truthfully, and the pain will stop."

"Yes! Yes, I lied. It was all a lie." He bellowed. The snake released its grasp and slithered back to Stheno.

"You should not have lied," Stheno spoke in a smooth tone.

The only sounds that came out of Alcibiades were gurgles.

Stheno surveyed the elders. "Athena has spoken." Taking Mehdi by the hand, she proceeded to lead her out.

Groaning on the floor, Alcibiades spat at Mehdi, "It should not matter if I lied. There is a contract, and she broke it."

Stheno stood over Alcibiades. Her presence grew menacing as she gazed down at him. "A contract we agreed was null if Mehdi was unduly persuaded or pressed. A contract that gave Mehdi the right to choose devotion to the goddess rather than devotion to a husband. A contract, which is now broken due to your actions, not hers."

Alcibiade's hair stood on end.

Mehdi glanced at Stheno, curious what would cause him to be so terrified, and saw Stheno's eyes change for a moment. Mehdi realized Stheno was not entirely human.

Stheno's eyes adjusted back to normal, and she squeezed Mehdi's hand in assurance. The sea of men parted in stunned silence, watching the women exit. Alcibiades began to stammer and protest, but no one was listening to him now.

As they walked back to the temple, Mehdi asked, "What will happen to Alcibiades?"

"If they stop the bleeding, he will recover, but..."

"But?" Mehdi asked.

"He can never lie again."

"Stheno..." Mehdi began, "my virtue..."

"Is no longer in question."

"But Alcibiades..."

"No one can take your virtue. They can violate you. They can hurt you, but virtue is about your actions. Not what is thrust upon you."

Mehdi stopped walking, absorbing what Stheno was saying.

Stheno presented the girdle and slipped it on Mehdi's waist, "Wear this so that you know, and others can see how honorable you are."

"But I did let Alcibiades do things."

"By choice or by coercion and obligation."

She felt terribly guilty for allowing Alcibiades to coerce her, and more so when her body enjoyed it, even if she didn't. She hung her head again and tears started to fall.

"You don't have to speak, Mehdi. The girdle reveals the truth. See how it doesn't move." She pulled Mehdi into her arms and let the girl cry. They stood there tightly woven as the older woman passed her strength onto the younger. "Soon all of this will be a fading memory."

"Mehdi!" a voice shouted.

The women turned to find Perseus running up to them.

Breathless, he reached out to Mehdi. "Mehdi, I'm so sorry."

She pulled away from him, clearly angry.

"Mehdi, what my father said."

"Yes, what he said. How dare he. What exactly have I done to deserve that?"

"I don't know."

"You were no better. Shouting and jeering with the crowd."

"That's not..."

"No," she shouted, knocking his hand away again. "I loved all of you and...and...that's the way you see me?" She was now shaking with fury. "No, I won't be treated like that." She turned toward the temple.

"Mehdi, please."

"Leave me alone, Perseus. I will never cross your father's threshold again."

"I told you I believed you," he implored.

"And what is that worth? The word of a man?" She started walking backward up the hill. "No, I will never trust another man again."

CHAPTER 7
CASUALTIES OF WAR

Six months after the trial, Mehdi stayed inside the temple walls. No Danae's. No Fishing. No Market. She kept herself occupied with mastering her skills and daily practices.

Cassia was a formidable tactician and opponent, so Mehdi found any excuse for them to collaborate. She decided keeping her mind distracted would help her forget the outside world even existed.

Presently, they were theorizing ways to confuse the enemy.

"Perhaps smoke," Cassia suggested. "I can never think clearly if it is foggy. You lose your bearings."

"Great, but what happens if the wind changes direction?"

Mehdi watched her slip into deep thought but was personally focused on her lips. Their soft lusciousness entranced her. Cassia liked to stain them pink with pomegranate and Mehdi wondered if they tasted like pomegranate. The need to kiss them surged through her and the thought frightened her. Could she want to touch someone again, after everything? Would Cassia want to kiss her back?

"Mehdi," Cassia called, snapping her fingers. "You're doing it again."

"Oh..." she replied and bowed her head.

"It is okay. I do it too."

Mehdi looked at her, confused.

"Slip into my imagination. I think best when I shut out the world. Can you see the design in your head?"

"The design?"

Cassia lightly laughed. "Yes, the contraption for creating the wind."

"Oh! We could.... get some Palm leaves and fan the fire."

"How do we get it to go in the desired direction?"

"Hmmm, the easiest way would be to have a troop fanning the smoke in the desired direction." Mehdi drew out little stick figures with giant leaves. "This will still only work if there is no wind, or the wind is with us."

"And they would need to carry leaves and not shields."

"Shields! Yes, they could use those to fan the flames. Swinging in unison."

"What if we have five fanning the smoke down and the other five away, taking turns?"

She nodded. "But then that is fewer soldiers that could be fighting."

Cassia slipped into thought again.

Mehdi went back to staring, this time at the curve of her

arms. She followed the round of her shoulder down to her bicep, then forearm. She jumped when Cassia lifted her hand up then slapped it down.

"That's it." Cassia proclaimed, "We get something we can slam down, that will push the wind with such force that most breezes would fail to compete."

"Great. How do we do that?"

Cassia grabbed Mehdi's hand in excitement, "Come with me."

The two girls laughed as they ran.

The exhilaration of holding her hand made it hard to breathe. Nothing compared to when Alcibiades would grab her hand and force her to keep holding it. They arrived at the blacksmithing station where the sounds of hammering and hissing filled the air.

Stheno insisted all the priestesses know how to make their own weapons, so Mehdi immediately knew what Cassia was thinking. "The Bellows!"

Cassia nodded in excitement. "Grab the biggest one."

They entered and started searching. Mehdi spotted the bellows for the main fire, but that one was too big to move.

"What are you doing?" Stheno asked.

Stheno stood behind her covered in soot, sword and hammer in hand. Her skin glistened from sweat.

"I...."

"Head Priestess, we have an idea," Cassia said as she hurried over. "Permission to make something?"

"Is this going to be like last time?" Stheno asked.

The two girls glanced at each other, recalling the catapult incident.

"We honestly did not know it would go that far and are very sorry about the dead sheep!" Cassia blurted.

"What do you wish to do now?" Stheno asked.

"We want to see if we can create a fog of smoke," Mehdi declared.

"Burn a fire?" Stheno asked, her eyes narrowed in concern.

"No, Cassia has an idea to push the smoke in one direction."

"Using the bellows." Cassia beamed.

Mehdi glanced at the giant bellows again.

"No," Stheno replied to Mehdi's silent thought. "Start small."

"But small might not account for wind!" Cassia implored.

"Execute a single person fire and small bellows. Successfully." She asserted, "Then we will talk."

THREE MONTHS and three builds later, the girls stood on the training field. Troops gathered at each end. Mehdi and Cassia stood next to their giant bellows and a stack of straw covering wet wood.

Not only did they have to figure out how to direct the smoke, but make the best smoke. The bellows were the size of a cow and required both of them to pump it.

Mehdi looked at Cassia, brimming with excitement as she lit the fire.

Cassia's eyes sparkled back. She grabbed Mehdi's hands. "Are you ready?"

Mehdi nodded excitedly.

Together they pushed down on the bellows.

The bellows groaned as air expelled down the narrow neck exploding past the wooden flap and out the wide mouth that angled upward.

It hit the smoking fire and pushed the growing plume into the opposing troops.

Since this was for training purposes, time was allowed for the smoke to cover the opposing troops completely.

When Medhi and Cassisa noted a shift in the wind they directed the two other soldiers to lift and move the bellows into a new position.

The tactic was slow and exhausting, but quite effective.

As they pushed down again, Cassia said, "Imagine if we could do this with real fog?"

Mehdi released a grunty laugh, "I think that would require more bellows."

"Oh, or on a ship!"

"That's a lot of weight on a ship."

The horn for the attack sounded.

They watched their side rush forward with ease. Scarves wrapped around their head to protect from the smoke.

The other side did not advance at the same pace and

when they emerged they were completely out of formation, coughing and wheezing. Some did think quickly and use their cloaks as masks, but were intentionally ill prepared.

The opposing side was quickly defeated.

Mehdi and Cassia hugged and cheered when victory was called.

They hurried over to the commanding officers and discussed tactics.

"In a real battle I would suggest a volley of arrows first," Eurayle commented.

"I'm still concerned with the smoke after the initial direction. It will move," Myra noted.

"But it will thin out, so it shouldn't be too bad, if you wear a scarf over your face," Mehdi suggested.

"It's a usable tactic. If not a bit cumbersome. How does one carry around a large bellows?" Stheno mused.

"In a wagon?" Cassia offered.

"A large wheelbarrow?" Mehdi offered. "And that way the people pumping the bellows can also shift it. Requiring fewer soldiers."

"Excellent idea. Congratulations to you both."

Everyone cheered. "Let's clean up and eat."

Mehdi and Cassia carried the bellows back to the weapons stockade, giggling and hooting with triumph.

"Think she will let us try the catapult again?" Mehdi asked.

Cassia laughed. "Wouldn't hurt to ask, but..." Her laughter stopped.

Mehdi let go of the bellows as they set it in place and wiped sweat from her face. "But?"

Cassia looked away. "I'm leaving."

"Leaving?" Mehdi exclaimed.

Sighing, "I didn't know how to tell you." She wrung her hands. "I'm to be married."

"Married? No!"

Cassia sighed again, "Yes..."

"But...your life here."

"Was always temporary. My betrothed went to sea to gain riches. He was gone for so long... I thought...but he has returned and is claiming his reward."

"No! I won't stand for it. Surely Stheno can do something?"

She shook her head. "No, if I don't go, my family will be dishonored." She squeezed back tears.

Mehdi reached out and hugged her. "I'm so sorry."

Cassia hugged her back.

She stroked her hair. "It's so unfair. I hate men."

She sniffed. "Me too."

They pulled apart slightly and Mehdi stared in awe. She was so beautiful and smart and now Mehdi was going to lose her. "Can I ask you something before you leave?"

Cassia sniffed. "Sure."

"Can I kiss you?"

Cassia blinked in surprise.

Mehdi immediately let her go. "I'm sorry. I just. I've wanted to say something for months, but I didn't want to scare you."

Cassia stepped forward and planted a kiss directly on Mehdi's lips.

It was shocking, but felt good, "Again." she replied. Mehdi shivered when Cassia reached out and stroked her hair. Their lips touched again and this time she could taste her. Definitely, pomegranate and smoke. Her heart started beating faster. She slipped her hand into Cassia's hair and the two intertwined, locked in kisses growing more passionate with each pass.

Finally, Mehdi broke the embrace and panted, "I didn't know you felt the same, or…that we should."

"I know, but if men can take lovers, then why can't we?"

"Men take lovers?"

"Oh yeah." Cassia laughed. "My brother has had many." She started kissing her again.

The touch of her hands exhilarated Mehdi, and she wanted more. This time, the pleasure mingled with want and desire. She followed Cassia's lead and brushed her hands over Cassia's waist.

Cassia softly moaned into the kiss and Mehdi felt it deep, deep down. Her knees weakened as she broke the kiss again.

Cassia was glowing and Mehdi could feel her own flesh was hot and flushed.

"But you are leaving?" Mehdi said with great sadness.

Cassia touched her face again. "Not for three more months."

"Then we…we have till then?"

Cassia nodded.

Mehdi kissed her again, hungry for more. A floodgate

opened. She felt safe and free. Her hands roamed, searching and seeking bare skin to caress.

Cassia moaned in her arms, but broke the kiss this time. "Later, right now we have a victory to celebrate."

The two shared three months of unabated passion. Cassia was sweet and gentle and knew how to make her feel pleasure with no guilt or fear. She taught Mehdi to not feel ashamed and to explore. They spent their days and activities as before, close and full of fun, while stealing kisses behind trees and buildings. Every free moment they had, they would sneak away and spend it intertwined in utter bliss.

~

TIME PASSED TOO QUICKLY, and Mehdi was a blubbering mess the day Cassia had to leave.

"Stay!" she implored.

Cassia wept. "I can't. I have a duty to my family."

"What will I do when you are gone?"

She kissed Mehdi one last time. "Keep on your own path."

Mehdi snuffled, annoyed that Cassia was using her own words against her.

"And don't give up on finding someone else." She said sternly, "I can't think of you all alone." Cassia brushed her hands through Mehdi's thick curls and kissed her one last time, then left.

When Stheno and Euryale found Mehdi hours later, she

was under their favorite tree and still crying. Stheno picked her up with ease and carried her back to bed.

"Why? Why must men have power over everything?" Mehdi sobbed.

"Because women created the world and out of envy, men have been trying to control us ever since."

Mehdi pulled the sheet over her head and cried into a pillow. "I hate men."

AFTER CASSIA'S DEPARTURE. Mehdi became more reclusive. She participated, when required, but often focused on tasks that demanded silence and seclusion.

Another fall and winter passed. Today, she was in the forge, molding metal into weapons. Losing herself in the rhythmic sounds. The whoosh of the bellows, the sound of the hammer, and the hiss of hot metal in water blended into a song of solemnity. Lost deep within the melody, she didn't notice the visitor until his feet came into view.

She looked up and found Perseus. It appeared to be Perseus, but he was taller, thicker, and older.

He smiled softly.

She hefted the sword off the anvil and asked, "What are you doing here?"

His smile faded.

She turned away from him and put the sword in the fire again.

He inhaled deeply. "I came to invite you to dinner."

"I told you I would never cross your father's threshold again."

"My father wants to apologize. He has seen the error of his words."

She ignored him and worked on the sword.

"Mother misses you terribly." He drew closer. "I miss you."

She didn't let him see her face, but it reflected her own thoughts of missing them and the water.

The only true drawback to her solitude within the temple walls. Sitting high on the hilltop, there was no sand, no waves, no water, no sea. No Danae, no Perseus.

"Mehdi, I am so sorry if you ever thought I didn't believe you."

She sighed, "I was angry and the things your father said. Did you..." She began to ask then stopped.

"Did I, what?"

She put down the anvil. "Did you ever think I was inappropriate with you?"

Walking over, he took her hands. "Never."

"I mean. He is right. We are not siblings."

"No, but he's not my father, either. It doesn't mean I don't love him like one." He squeezed her hands again. "Nor does it mean I don't love you like a sister."

Swallowing hard, she grinned weakly.

He beseeched, "I'd rather love you like a sister than never see you again. You are part of my family."

Wrapping her arms around him, she choked. "And you are mine!"

Relieved to be forgiven, he tightened his squeeze.

Exhaling, she firmly nodded. "I'll go, but I can't go through the marketplace."

"We'll take the alternate route!" he excitedly declared.

Out the backside of the main temple, they journeyed down the hilltop. The route was less traveled and more perilous for the average person, but Mehdi and Perseus were reaching their prime.

In the year and half since they last spoke, he was no longer a gangly teenager, but strong and bristling with muscles that many gods would envy. Perseus picked up speed as they descended, bounding down the path with the agility of a goat. He glanced back at her with a playful smile, challenging her to keep up. It worked.

Despite not wearing a fighting chiton as short as his, she matched his skill and speed with ease. He leaped a great distance to a jutting rock and then another. She followed. By the time they reached the bottom, they were no longer on the intentional path, but one of their own.

He landed in the sand, and she alighted next to him. Both panting from exertion, they took a moment to catch their breath.

Hearing the crash of a wave, she looked up. The water instantly called to her. Mehdi glanced at Perseus, giving him one chance to guess, then bolted for the water. He stumbled for a moment, then raced after her.

She beat him to the water's edge and threw her hands

into the air in victory. He caught up to her and grinned softly at the cheering victor.

Kicking the waves with her feet, she walked in the shallows, enjoying the sand and sea. He patiently let her play in the waves, then showed her the rest of the path to Danae's.

When they arrived, Danae rushed out the door and pulled Mehdi into her arms.

Mehdi buried herself deep into the hug. Never meaning to hurt Danae, in her anger she had robbed them both of time together.

Danae broke the hug and examined her. "Look at you! Have you gotten taller?"

She nodded.

"You're nearly as tall as Perseus!"

"I think she is as tall as me," Perseus replied.

In motherly fashion, she compared her two children in stature, "I think her strength might rival you too, Perseus."

He sighed. "It always has."

Mehdi laughed, then noticed a shadow in the doorway. It was Dictes.

He hesitated to come closer, shame in his eyes. Finally, he approached and solemnly addressed Mehdi. "I humbly ask for your forgiveness. The words I spoke that day were...unintentionally cruel."

"No," Mehdi said softly but sternly, "They were intentionally cruel. You discredited me and your son."

"You are right. I spoke from ignorance and assumption and in doing so, I deprived us all of the joy you bring into our home."

Mehdi bowed her head. "Then I will forgive you, if Danae will forgive me for staying away."

He agreed, and Danae started crying.

"Of course, I forgive you," she said, pulling Mehdi into another embrace.

"Good!" Perseus declared, clapping his hands together. "Can we eat?"

Danae sighed, "Always hungry. It's like feeding an entire army!"

"I fear, I am no better." Mehdi chuckled.

"And don't forget, Alexios. He eats just as much."

Mehdi's brow furrowed. Just as she was about to ask who Alexios was, they entered the house and, sitting at the table, was another man. Mehdi stopped walking.

Danae took her hand and squeezed it in reassurance. "It is okay. This is a friend."

Mehdi hesitated. She had forgiven exactly two men and had no desire to deal with any others. She studied him and noticed he remained unmoved by her arrival.

He was alert to people entering, but paid her no special attention.

"Alexios, this is Mehdi."

"Pleasure, Mehdi," he replied in her direction but did not really look at her.

Perseus whispered in her ear, "You're safe. He's blind."

She glanced at him, uncertain.

Perseus slowly mimed by pointing at Alexios, then his own eye, then making the shape of a curvy woman. *He can't see you.*

In one singular moment, their sibling rapport returned. She wrinkled her nose at his teasing. He silently laughed. Then they both got smacked by Danae.

Mehdi helped Danae put the food on the table then sat down next to Alexios and across from Perseus. Her thought was it would be easier to talk to Perseus and avoid talking to Alexios if she wished.

Instead, it was worse. Perseus continued to make silent faces at her, teasing her, and trying to get her to relax. This led to a non-verbal argument between them and another smack from Danae's wood spoon.

Alexios appeared to take the whole thing in stride and ate his meal.

"Alexios," Perseus began, "did you know that Mehdi loves the sea as much as you?"

He took a small sip and set down his cup. "Are you also a sailor?"

Shaking her head in reply, she saw Perseus gesturing the word *Talk!*

She gulped. "No, I enjoy being in the water, not on it."

He nodded. "I agree. It is quite blissful to submerge yourself and bob in the current."

"Yes!" she replied.

"Do you swim?"

"Of course."

"There is a lovely spot near my house where no one goes. It has an oyster bed, shallows for farming scallops, and is an excellent location for cast fishing."

"That does sound lovely," she replied, trying to

remember the last time she went cast fishing. Her posture slumped when she remembered it was just before the trial.

He stopped eating. “Did I say something?”

Straightening herself, she assured. “No, I just remembered I have not fished in a long time.”

“You are welcome to the place I mentioned. I’m sure Perseus can show you.”

Swallowing his food, he replied, “We were there today. Where you played in the waves, Mehdi.”

Her eyes flared at Perseus, telling him to shut up.

She glanced at Danae and Dictes, who ate, allowing the younger folk to carry the conversation, and she got suspicious of their motives.

“Good,” Alexios stated, either unaware or ignoring underlying machinations. “You are welcome anytime. However, stay clear of the small island on the outer edge. There is a sea monster.”

She looked at him. “A sea monster?”

He nodded. “Don’t worry. Relatively harmless, like most sea monsters.”

She chuckled. “You know many?”

He paused mid-bite. “I do... but most just want to live peaceful lives.”

“But they are monsters.”

“What is a monster?” he asked, still eating.

“A terrifying creature that attacks villages, ships, and people.”

“Why are they terrifying?”

She stammered, “Because they are monsters.”

He gestured. "Or, are they just different?"

His words sank in. "They still attack." She replied.

"Why? Maybe a monster attacks a ship because that ship has sailed into its home. Or, attacks to defend itself. Or, perhaps they attack because a god makes them. Men have done the same, and we do not call ourselves monsters."

Mehdi snorted. "Perhaps we should."

"Mehdi," Danae chided.

"Tell me there are no monstrous men." She fumed.

"I..." Danae began, "I cannot."

"Maybe then it is the wrong word for creatures that don't look like us," Alexios suggested. "Maybe monster is a title and not a thing."

Mehdi mulled over the statement. "I like that."

He turned his head in her direction and smiled. "You're welcome."

Mehdi smiled back and then realized he couldn't see it. She didn't know what to say to relay her thoughts and stuttered out, "Thank you."

He laughed. "It's okay. I could feel your smile...and wince."

She covered her face in nervous shame, but was curious. "How?"

"If you pay attention, you can feel the changes in the surrounding air. Like the way you and Perseus tease each other. It is very amusing."

"It is not," Dictes groused. "It is very annoying."

Everyone laughed, and the rest of the table joined in the conversation. After dinner, the men sang, while Danae played with Mehdi's hair. She leaned into her lap and enjoyed the tender attention. As Danae kissed her on the head, she remembered why she loved this place.

Dictes and Danae settled in for the night, leaving the youth to themselves.

They built a fire on the shore and Mehdi regaled the boys with stories of mock battles, catapults, and smoke machines. The three fell asleep around the fire. When the sun rose, she got up and noticed Alexios was already gone. Thinking little of it, she gave Perseus a kiss on the forehead and stumbled toward the house.

Knowing that Danae was already up, she went inside and before she could ask, there was a pasteli in her hand. Dictes shuffled around, looking for his son.

"Outside," Mehdi said to him.

He grumbled, kissed his wife, and headed out the door.

The two women quietly giggled.

"Can I borrow a net?"

Danae shrugged. "Sure."

"Did you want to fish here?"

She shook her head. "No, I think I will try out the place Alexios mentioned."

"Mmmhmm," Danae teased.

Mehdi bumped her gently. "Just fishing."

Danae smiled coyly. "Have fun."

CHAPTER 8
THE SECLUDED COVE

Collecting a net and slinging a basket to her side, she wound down the hidden path to the secluded cove. Breaking past the rocks and grass, she jumped, startled by the gigantic creature leaping out of the water.

The sea monster. It was massive, long, dark, and terrifying.

She hesitated, unsure whether to fish, but remembered Alexios' words. Mehdi slowly waded into the water, keeping her eyes on the large wake it left, as it swam around the distant island. Gathering up her net, she tossed her first cast. Her muscles remembered. The net flew out smoothly, fluttering to the surface, then sinking below. Using both hands, she jerked and drew it in.

A frown crossed her face when she found little in the net, but it was a new fishing ground. She just needed to find the right location. Wading to another spot, she glanced around for the creature, but did not see it.

Mehdi continued to swing the net and fish. Unfortunately, she was still unsuccessful.

About to give up, she noticed the water a short distance from her stir. The creature returned, and it was swimming back and forth in a pattern.

As Mehdi tried to figure out what it was doing, the surrounding water darkened and rippled, then all forms of sea life rushed towards her. It was herding the fish towards her.

Stumbling back, she quickly gathered up her net. A giggle bubbled out of her as she tossed it high in the air. Swoosh, plunk.

Tugging, Mehdi used all her strength to pull the burgeoning net closed. Laughing with delight, she wrangled and dragged her catch to the shore. There, she frantically worked to get everything sorted and into her basket, but there was too much. All around her fish flopped, crabs scurried and seaweed slowly floated back into the waves.

Trying to decide what to do, she saw the sea monster out of the corner of her eye. Its nose flaps opened and closed, and its eyes blinked. It was close to the shoreline but did not move, only watched.

What if it used the fish as bait, and would eat her? But Mehdi sensed no menace.

A fish flopped and flailed onto her foot. She kicked it up into her hand and the creature followed it. She tossed the fish, and the creature caught it. Finding another, she released it into the water near it. Its neck whipped with lightning speed and snatched the fleeing prey.

She tossed him a few more, but wondered what would happen if she denied it. Picking up another fish, she held the creature's gaze and said, "Not this one. This is for Poseidon."

The creature pulled its head back and let the fish swim past.

Its intelligence surprised her. Mehdi hefted the laden basket onto her shoulder and smiled. "Thank you."

SHE RETURNED the next day and a routine between them began. It would herd the fish. She would catch them, and then they would play.

Initially, she experimented with various ways of tossing fish for it to catch, but then she started frolicking with the enormous creature in the water.

It was the size of two horses and had clawed fore fins that it used for swimming, crawling, or climbing. While faster in the water, it moved quickly on shore, but never left the waves.

Confident the creature would not hurt her; she started swimming with it.

Holding onto his fore fin, the creature would glide her around the cove. They swam deeper and deeper into the water. Mehdi wanted more.

One day, it lowered its neck, and she slipped on its back.

It took off with great speed, leaping into the air and down under. Holding her breath, she opened her eyes to take in the world around them. It was more beautiful than she imagined, and she could have stayed, but the creature brought her back to the surface.

Gulping in more air, she called out. “I can stay under longer.”

Understanding, it dove again, swimming over to the oyster bed. The place was a treasure trove, but she did not have the tools to break the oysters free. The creature turned and violently whipped its tail, breaking a shelf of oysters free.

She wanted to gather them but needed air. After tugging on its neck, it brought her to the top and then down again at her signal. Once at the bottom, she slipped off the creature and collected the shells in her bag. Then they returned to the shore, departing for the day.

Oysters, fishing, swimming, and chases along the beach filled her spare hours away from the temple. Mehdi noted one day that when it climbed the rocks, some part of it remained in the water.

Today, she taunted it with a fish, standing on top of a tall, craggy outcropping. It climbed after her but stopped, leaving its tail to thrash and swish in the water. She grinned, her heart racing, wondering if she could get it to come out. Mehdi held the fish with one hand and crawled a little higher.

Her foot slipped and she fell. Grasping at the rocks, they tore at her hands, making her fingers slippery. Unable to grab hold, she hit another outcropping and cried out in pain.

As her body fell through the air, she knew the rocks at the bottom would kill her. Closing her eyes, she waited.

Her body hit, but the impact was leathery and wet. Opening her eyes, she found the creature cupping her in its fore fin. Clutching her to its breast, it carefully positioned itself on the rocks and then pushed off with substantial force.

Together, they flew and dove into the water below. She barely had time to hold her breath as they went under. The creature kept her close and swam her to the small island, releasing her on the shore.

Gasping and crawling onto the beach, Mehdi cringed in pain, blood running from the various gashes and tears. Staying in the water, the creature nudged her, motioning towards something behind her. Hissing, she wrenched her body and looked upward, spotting a small house hidden on the island. She wondered if this was where Alexios lived. If it was, was he here? Was he always here, listening to her play with the sea creature? Clenching her teeth, she ignored her pain and stood.

Whether or not he was here. Right now, her wounds needed tending. When she attempted to walk, her ankle refused to take any weight. Assessing it, she concluded it was only twisted, nothing broken, but difficult to use.

Hobbling up the stone steps, she saw no life inside. The firepit was in use, but cool. It was a small place with little more than a bed and a place to eat. She worried if the owner would mind her borrowing items to clean her injuries but made a promise to replenish the supplies.

Rummaging through the small pantry shelf, she collected the necessary herbs and something for a salve. The wound on her hand was ragged and deep, making it hard to do anything. Using a knife and her teeth, she sliced her chiton, creating a nick in the fabric. Pulling at the tear, the fabric came off in symmetrical strips.

Gathering the strips up, she fussed over if she should clean the wounds quickly or correctly. Correctly would mean boiling the bandages, which would take time. Her head shot up, hearing something coming towards the house. Mehdi stood, instantly drawing her dagger from its sheath with her good hand and winced when her bad ankle went into a fighting stance.

Alexios stumbled through the door. "Are you all right?"

Mehdi found it odd that his hair was wet, but his chiton was dry. His head frantically twitched about listening.

She sheathed her knife, "I am okay."

He followed her voice, moving in the room with confidence, but seeking her. She dropped back down on the stool. Hearing her, he came to her side, placing his hand on her knee.

When she sucked in through her teeth, he flinched away. "Sorry."

"It is okay. I'm okay. Just a little accident."

Chuckling in disbelief, he lifted his hand covered in blood. "Little?"

"Fine, I'm wounded."

"Anything broken?"

"No," she sighed, "just my common sense."

His head tilted, curious.

She didn't answer and instead asked, "Where did you come from?"

"I," he stuttered, "was in the garden." He moved to start a fire. "What happened?"

"I was being reckless and fell off the rocks."

"You're lucky to be alive."

"I know." She glanced out the door. "The sea creature saved me. You were right." She looked back at him. "It is not a monster."

He didn't respond, only pausing for a moment before picking up a bucket. "I will get some water to boil."

She busied herself with wadding the torn cloth into a pot and setting it next to the fire. Then tended to her disheveled state by brushing away the sand, wringing out her hair, and fanning her chiton dry.

Alexios came back with water and leaned down near the fire. He yelped, when his knee landed in the pot Mehdi had moved.

"Oh!" she cried out. "I'm so sorry. I was trying to help."

Unwedging his knee from the pot, he waved her off. "I'm fine."

He pulled the bandages out of the kettle, poured the water in, then set it over the fire to boil. Task complete, he pulled the second stool from under the table and sat down.

"You live here alone," she asked.

He nodded. "The water will take a minute to boil, then cool."

"That is okay. I need to make a poultice."

She turned back to the table, where she had laid the items and piled them on the stone cutting board. Bringing the scraper down and she rocked it left to right, chopping the herbs. As she scraped the herbs back and forth to create a paste, the board kept moving causing her to huff in frustration.

Alexios quietly assisted by stabilizing the board.

As she grounded down the herbs, the sound of the scraper against the stone was serene and soothing. With his help, she made a fine gooey paste.

Picking up the oil, she added it to the mashed herbs and asked, "Do you have any honeycomb?"

"Honeycomb?" he repeated. "Second shelf"

They both moved to retrieve it. She flinched, thinking he was going to bang into her when he coughed in his throat and deftly stepped out of the way. The sound startled her, causing her to lose balance, roll her ankle and fall back onto the stool with a groan.

"Sorry." He apologized again and set the honey jar on the table.

"No, no, it is my fault." She closed her eyes and pushed away the pain. "I shouldn't be here."

"What? No!" he stammered, "You can be here."

"Clearly not. I am disrupting everything."

"I'm okay. I startled you."

She tried to calm herself down, but the cuts were closing and starting to sting. Her hand throbbed, and she felt like an intruder. Her head started to swim, and her breath to shorten.

Placing his hand on her arm, he soothed, "Everything will be fine. Please allow me to help."

She exhaled, and her vision cleared. "I need the comb inside the jar. Or some of it."

He opened the container with a small knife, then fished out the comb. It dripped and oozed. Alexios did his best to keep the honey in the jar, but honey failed due to its messy nature.

Mehdi tried to break off a piece, but it slipped off the knife and onto the table.

Alexios made that same coughing noise mixed with a chuckle and stabbed the honey. "I have it pinned, go for the kill."

She choked out a laugh and used the scraper to cut off a section with a loud thunk.

Alexios cried out in victory, making Mehdi smile.

She put the chunk of honeycomb in the mixture and returned to pulverize the poultice.

Eyeing the pool of honey on the table, she bemoaned. "All that honey. Such a waste."

"I think we can save it."

"How?" she asked.

"Are your wounds closing?"

"Yes." She sighed with frustration.

Running his finger through the honey, he requested, "Tell me where to put it."

She guided him to the cuts on her hand.

He stroked the honey into the wound, softening it and loosening the debris. "Now when we use the hot water, the dirt will stick to the honey and wash away. Where else?"

Together, the two rubbed honey into her various cuts. The surrounding tension dissipated, and Mehdi found freedom in his lost sight.

He didn't stare, gawk, or gape at her. He was literally blind to her physical beauty. It also allowed her the ability to stare at him. With most men, she averted her gaze, because any sign of reciprocation was dangerous. And if Alexios could see the way she looked at him, it would be very dangerous.

She allowed herself time to study his form. He was fit and strong. Older than her, but she couldn't tell how much older. He didn't keep his hair in tight ringlets, so it softened into deep waves as it dried. The weave on his chiton was temple made, which meant it was a gift or donated. Again, she wondered why his hair was wet, but not his clothes.

Mehdi hissed when he rubbed a cut open.

"Sorry," he said again.

"It's okay. That was the last one." She reached over to the bucket of water and wetted the rag he had handed her. They wiped their hands and the table clean.

"Can I check your ankle?" he asked.

She nodded, noticing he didn't respond, and said, "Yes."

Lifting her leg, he placed it in his lap. "No cuts?" he asked.

"No, just twisted."

"It's already swelling. Can you hand me the bandages you made?"

She handed him one long piece. He slowly wrapped her ankle, then tied off the cloth.

She moved to put it down, but he braced her leg. "Leave it here for now. It should stay elevated."

"I feel awkward."

"I always feel awkward," he offered.

She chuckled. "Fair."

After a moment, he stood, placing her ankle on the stool, and fetched food for them to eat.

Mehdi noticed the water beginning to boil and moved to pull it out of the fire. He placed his hand on her shoulder for her to stay.

Sipping the offered cup of wine, she watched him pour part of the pot into another to cool, then dropped the bandages and more rags into the boiling water.

Her eyes softened as her pain ebbed, and Mehdi relaxed. His ability to move with confidence, yet see nothing, mesmerized her. Using a rod, he lifted the bandages out of the pot and hung them to dry.

Grabbing a cooking tine, she pulled out a rag from the pot, hovering it in the air until it was cool enough to touch, then dipped it into cooler water to wash her wounds.

"Can I help?" he asked.

She started to nod, then replied, "Yes."

He followed her directions and stroked the warm cloth across her body. Mehdi felt strangely vulnerable and safe at the same time. He ladled warm water out of the pot to rinse away the deeper wounds. Needing to guide him, forced her to be patient and trusting. Alexios responded in kind, only touching where directed.

The surrounding air hung sweet and heady. Mehdi's skin flushed with desire, reveling in his touch then a surge of shame flooded in. Recalling the power of her girdle, she grasped it in fear.

She wore it every day to display her virtue. Over the years, she learned how to use it, including sensing danger. Unaware of its powers, Alexios swiped the cloth down her arm, and the snake remained unmoved.

Clearing her throat, she scooped up the poultice, and they applied it on the needed wounds.

He massaged the concoction into her hand and chuckled. "You smell like honey."

She huffed a laugh. "You do too."

His head turned to her face, and they both froze.

Her eyes focused on his lips again, succulent and smooth. If she kissed them, would they taste of honey too?

Alexios stood abruptly. "I'll get the bandages."

Mehdi shook her head clear and together they covered the larger cuts with the bindings. After typing off the last of the strips, he remained, his finger fiddling with the edge of the cloth. She stared at his face and dark lashes, then blushed. Luckily, he did not see that either.

"We're done." She shivered and turned away from him.

"Are you still in pain? Would you like to rest?"

She gazed at his face, full of kindness and concern, patiently awaiting her request. She shook her head. "I should probably get back to the temple."

"I..." he wavered, "don't have a boat."

Baffled, she stammered, "You don't have a boat? How do you get to shore?"

"Swim?"

She was very confused. He lived here all alone with no boat to ferry him to the main island. Why?

He popped to his feet. "I'll go get one."

"Where?"

"Perseus!" He started out the door then came back. "Sleep. You should sleep, until I get back. You can use the bed." He went out the door and out of sight.

MEHDI WOKE up to the touch of Danae's hand on her forehead. She smiled weakly and tried to sit up.

Danae gently pushed her back down, "You should keep resting."

Her mouth was dry. "I." She swallowed a few times, "Do you have the boat? I need to get back to the temple."

"I sent Perseus to tell them where you are, but you are in no condition to climb all the way back up to the temple."

"It's just a sprain," Mehdi asserted.

"Can you walk on it?" Danae asked, an arched brow indicating she knew the answer.

She frowned. "I'm sure I can." She moved to stand.

Danae made a disapproving noise, but let her try.

Mehdi slowly transitioned from sitting to standing.

Once she had her balance, she put weight on the bad ankle. Searing pain shot up her leg and she immediately removed the pressure.

Danae looked at her knowingly.

Mehdi huffed and plopped back down on the bed.

"Alexios has already offered that you can stay and sleep here."

"Where will he sleep?" she asked.

"He has made other arrangements."

Alexios stepped in, laden with supplies. "Yes, but before I leave. I will show you where everything is and how to collect water if you need it."

Danae went over to the dying fire and got it going again. She took a water skin from Alexios and poured it into a pot. "I will make you some tea to help you sleep."

Alexios carefully set everything down and Danae helped him put it up.

"Ankle up, please," Danae chided.

She propped it up. "I've been injured before and worked in the sick quarters. I know how to care for myself."

Danae clucked her tongue, "You are lucky you are not dead."

Alexios nodded in agreement.

Mehdi narrowed her eyes at him. "You know I can see you."

His head jerked up in surprise.

Danae softly snickered.

Mehdi watched them prepare the cottage for her and sighed in frustration.

They ignored her annoyance.

Alexios walked about showing her where everything was stored and located. Fresh herbs in water on the kitchen window. Food in cupboards, buckets for waste, everything had a place and with good reason. She was sure a misplaced pot was the least of his dangers.

Her eyes followed him around the room, unabashedly taking in all of him. His voice, his movement, his mannerisms. He was reserved, but displayed an openness. He didn't swagger or posture like most men. He spoke to her and Danae in the same friendly manner. There was also no need to put up walls or masks to protect herself, because he wasn't studying her every move for a reaction. She did, however, see Danae's broad grin watching her.

Mehdi rolled her eyes and looked away.

Danae softly chortled to herself and handed Mehdi the comfrey tea.

Alexios stopped talking, and looked between them.

Mehdi sipped her tea, then paled when she remembered what he said at supper, that he can sense energy in the air. Did he know she was staring at him and simply being polite. Was she no better than all the men that looked at her? She put down the tea, tucking it under the bed so he didn't kick it, and quietly rolled over to face the wall.

After a few moments, she heard someone lean down next to the bed.

"Are you okay?" Alexios asked.

"Yes," she replied, ashamed of her thoughts.

He cupped her shoulder.

She didn't flinch.

Softly stroking his thumb over the round of her shoulder, he asked, "Truly."

Recalling his hands running along her body earlier, she turned to look at him and found it hard to swallow. There was definitely something in the air between them.

"Danae needs to get back home and you should sleep," Alexios informed her.

"Can you stay?"

He thought for a second then replied, "Yes, for a little longer."

Danae strolled over. "Where is your tea?"

She rolled to lay on her back. "Under the bed."

Alexios shifted his foot and tapped the cup softly. He picked it up and offered it to Mehdi.

She sat up and finished her tea.

Danae took the cup and kissed her head softly. "Stheno or Euryale should be here in the morning."

She hugged Danae's neck and bid her farewell.

Exhausted from the day's adventures and reluctant to ruin the quiet, she watched the sunset through the window.

He sat on the ground beside the bed, propping his arm on the edge.

Slowly but sure their hands mingled and interlaced.

He asked, "Is the sun setting?"

She nodded, then squeezed his hand. "Yes."

"Can you describe it?"

She saw his longing to see it. Turning back to the sky, she focused and described it to him, "The sun is low so it is very orange, almost red. The top is shifting into the dark purple of night, but...the prettiest part are the clouds. They are in long strips with pink bottoms and darkening tops."

"I like long streaky clouds," he mused.

"Have you seen the sky before?"

He nodded. "When I was younger."

"Do you miss it?"

"Yes..."

She felt his sadness and wanted to ask how he lost his sight, but didn't. "Can you sing for me?"

He obliged and sang a song of a sailor sailing back to his love.

Her fingers softly danced with his, as her eyes grew heavy. She squeezed his hand once more before his sweet words sailed her into a land of blissful dreams.

"TWO WEEKS AT LEAST," Stheno said, as she stood back up.

"Two weeks. Stheno, I can see the temple from the doorway?" Mehdi protested.

"Can you climb up that hill?"

She glowered. "Can't I be carried up?"

"Sure, taking the long route, still requiring us to move you over rock croppings and then..." Stheno paused for effect, "through the marketplace."

Mehdi furrowed her brow.

Stheno smirked. "That's what I thought." She propped a crutch against the wall. "Use this only when absolutely necessary. After a week you can try putting a little weight on it, but don't overdo it."

"Can I swim?"

"Not until your wounds heal," she firmly stated. "Let me see your hand?"

Mehdi thrusted her hand upward.

Stheno examined it, looking under the cloth, "I brought fresh bandages and herbs so you can make more poultice. Remember to change them regularly."

"Yes, Head Priestess," she snarked.

Stheno released her hand. "Do I need to send someone daily to check on you?"

"Please no!"

Stheno simmered over the thought.

Mehdi squared her shoulders. "I am a grown woman. You trained me to be a strong, independent warrior. If I can't take care of my own wounds, then you should abandon me in the fields."

Stheno chuckled. "Fair enough. I will send someone with fresh supplies every few days or so. If you need anything," she pointed a finger at Mehdi, "or start running a fever then you send Alexios immediately."

"Will he still be here?" Mehdi asked.

Stheno nodded. "He can't be here all day, but he has agreed to check on you regularly."

Mehdi grinned softly, looking forward to it, then touched her girdle, "You trust us here alone?"

"You are a priestess of Athena. I trust your choices and your ability to take care of yourself." She grinned. "Even when wounded."

Stheno fussed about a little longer and then left her to rest.

Mehdi was not tired. She sat up and reached for the crutch. It was then she realized the hand she needed to use was the one wrapped in bandages.

She threw the crutch across the room. "You've got to be joking."

Alexios halted at the doorway. "What was that? Are you okay?"

She sighed, "I'm fine."

"I'm going to prepare some food." He cleared his throat, walking over to the kitchen area, and stepping right over the discarded crutch.

Mehdi watched in disbelief. "How did you do that?"

"What?"

"Walk over the crutch."

He hesitated then said, "I heard you drop it. Well, throw it."

She was not convinced.

He moved about preparing the table.

She tried to stand again and got angry, when she could put even less pressure on it today versus the day before. Grumbling in frustration, she proceeded to hop over to the table on one foot. It wasn't graceful, but it worked. "Ha! All those balance drills at work."

"Your balance is very good. I was shocked when you slipped."

She looked at him funny and blurted, "So you were watching!"

He stopped chopping and stood still, then said, "What do you mean? I can't see."

"Then how do you know my balance is good and why were you shocked when I slipped?"

He put down the knife and scratched his brow. His back was to her, but she watched his movements and they indicated he was lying or hiding something.

"And the crutch. You stepped right over that. Like you could see it!"

"That...that is totally different," he replied and tried to go back to cutting.

"Are you even blind!" she shouted.

"Yes!" he snapped back. "I am blind!"

"Then how?"

He put the knife down again, turning around. His hand rubbed across his forehead, then he exhaled. "I can sense things. I can't see them, but I can make a picture in my head."

"You are not making any sense."

He sighed, picked up the knife, and made that strange noise in his throat. This time he didn't hide it under another sound. "The window ledge. Across the room." He stated, then threw the knife.

It sank into the ledge.

Her mouth dropped. "How?"

He tapped his brow. "I told you. I can see a picture in my head. Not with colors or textures, but shape and depth."

"So...technically. You can see me?"

He smiled and his cheeks reddened. "Yes."

She blushed.

"But only when I make that click...cluck. That noise..."

Her own brow furrowed, as she contemplated his explanation.

He sat down. "Most of the time it's just sound, smells..." He reached for her fingers. "And touch."

She stretched out her fingers and touched him. Her heart started to race, but she still had questions.

"But you said you saw me fall. How? You're telling me you saw... sensed me fall way over there, while on the island."

He pulled his hand away and slumped. "No."

"Then how?" she insisted.

He put his hands over his face and fretted.

She pushed, "How?"

Alexios exhaled in frustration, "I had everything worked out. Two hours, three times a day and you wouldn't know."

"Wouldn't know what?"

He pinched his nose and admitted, "That I'm the monster."

Her eyes narrowed. "You're a monster?"

"No," he gestured outside, "I am the sea monster."

She stared at him incredulously.

"Grah." He thumped the table in exasperation. "Fine,

you don't believe me. I guess we are doing this." He popped off of the stool and marched out the door.

"Doing what?" she called after him.

He kept walking.

She hopped to the door and watched him stride down the path to the shoreline. When he got to the edge, he took off his tunic and sandals.

She gawked.

Naked, he waded into the water.

Though a good distance away, she covered her mouth in shock, when he dove into a wave and his body changed into the long, dark, sea creature.

He swam out a little deeper, then came back to the beach.

She stared in awe.

As the creature, he crawled back to the rock where he left his chiton and waited. No longer touching the water, his body returned to a man.

Alexios stood, brushed off the sand, put back on his clothes and hiked back to the hut.

Mehdi stood on one leg, utterly shocked. "You were it the whole time."

"Yes," he said and stepped past her.

She hopped back to the stool and sat. "Why didn't you just tell me?"

He yanked the knife out of the window ledge. "How, Mehdi? How was I supposed to tell you?"

"I don't know, but why keep it secret?"

His voice wavered, "Because monsters are monsters." He clicked his throat again, then walked across the room.

"But I told you that I didn't think of it as a monster."

He nodded, holding the knife over the veggies, but not chopping.

She got up, jumped around the table and stood behind him. "You are not a monster."

His head dropped slightly.

She balanced against the table and turned him around. "You saved me."

Blinking back tears, he confessed, "It was my fault. I tried...I wanted to tell you, but you seemed so happy."

She smiled. "I was! That's why I was careless. I was having fun!"

He caressed the back of her arm, "Me too."

Her arm naturally drew up and reciprocated the motion. "And I wanted to know why you wouldn't leave the water."

He choked. "You noticed."

She bit her lip and nodded, "Now I know."

"Again. I'm sorry. I just didn't know how to explain it."

She brushed away his tears. "This actually explains a lot."

He pressed her hand to his cheek. "What do you mean?"

"How I felt like I already knew you." Gazing at him, she sighed. "It's all blending together." Her hand glided down his neck to his chest. It was still damp from the sea. "You, the creature, all that time." Her heart started racing and her breath quickened.

He pressed her hand into him and stepped closer. "I thought I'd have to start all over and didn't know if you'd..."

She started to softly tremble. “You told me you could feel things change in the air? What do you sense now?”

“I...” He huffed, his own breath, short and fast. “I think you want to kiss me.”

She brushed her lips against his as her answer.

He inhaled sharply, clasped her face and kissed her.

Her other knee weakened, and all her weight hit the table. She let out a soft moan and kissed him back.

The two lingered there, intertwined, fervently embraced.

Mehdi did her best not to hurt her hand or leg, as she grabbed him, pulling him close and tight.

It was different from Cassia, definitely different from Alcibiades. Certainly, more feral in nature, but she wasn’t afraid of his strength. In fact, she craved it.

She shivered, feeling his strong arms wrap around her and his flat stomach press against her. Her bad arm hooked around his neck for support, allowing her free hand to explore and dig into his flesh.

There was only one thing that frightened her. She flinched violently, when he rubbed against her leg.

He pulled away and asked breathlessly, “What?”

Pressing her hand to her chest, she tried to push away the fear.

He took a step back, and gently held her steady. “What is it?”

Completely shaken, she could not find the words. “I... how do I say this?”

“You’ve never been with a man,” he blurted. Immediately wincing and covering his face, at his own tactlessness.

Shocked at his boldness, she pointed a finger at him. "Yes...and...a little worse than that."

He pulled the stool out and sat. "A man has hurt you."

She looked at the floor nodding. "Yes."

He leaned on his elbow, sitting his face in his hand. "Now I don't know what to say."

They sat there a long time, not moving, not talking.

Mehdi felt the fear start to subside but worried it would come back. It was a little hard with Cassia, but they took their time and Cassia showed her that it didn't have to be pushy or scary. That it could feel good, and she was safe.

Alcibiades forced her hand to rub him through his clothes. She never knew what she was touching, only that it had a mind of its own, jumping and writhing under her palm, and it made Alcibiades groan and grope her more. There were no pleasurable memories tied to it.

She looked at Alexios and wondered could it feel good with a man? Could she feel safe? She closed her eyes and still felt his lips on hers. She liked touching him, feeling him touch her. She just had to separate that, from the bad memories etched in her flesh.

"Slowly," she finally said and took his hand. "Slowly."

He was nervous, but softly shivered when she kissed his fingers.

"Slowly," he replied.

They continued to sit there.

Mehdi trailed her fingers across his palm and up his arm.

Alexios responded in kind and their arms mingled, caressing each other. "Touching me doesn't scare you?"

Her nails glided along his forearm. “No.”

He swallowed hard. “And you liked the kiss. I mean you kissed me.”

“I did. I want to.”

“Just...” He left the word hanging in the air.

Mehdi nodded and then forced herself to say, “Yes.”

“Can I ask? I...mean you said...you hadn’t...”

Mehdi pulled her hands away and dug her nails into her good palm. “No...but. I have been attacked. I just fought him off.”

“I don’t doubt it.”

She grinned at the compliment, then exhaled. “I have had zero pleasant experience with...” Gazing at the roof, she swallowed. “Men grab themselves and waggle them at me. Alcibiades... he made me touch him.”

Alexios remained silent.

She huffed, “I shouldn’t have said anything.”

He touched her hand. “No, I want to know, so I don’t hurt you.”

His words lessened the pain and fear.

Clearing his throat, he stated, “Let’s eat and talk.” Standing he finished prepping the food and smiled, when he heard her drag the other stool to the same side of the table.

They ate and spoke on various subjects including their time chasing each other on the beach. She thanked him for herding the fish and he thanked her for reminding him how to have fun.

“How many times did you want to change and just tell me?” she asked.

“So many times, and each time I envisioned you screaming and running away.”

She laughed. “I would have come back.”

He sheepishly grinned and quietly chewed his food.

“Can you see, as the sea monster?”

He scratched his cheek. “Kind of. It’s black and white and blurry in the sun.”

“So...you really don’t know what I look like?”

“Just your shape.”

“That is enough for most men,” she retorted.

He chuckled, then gently touched her arm. “You feel beautiful.”

She blushed and looked away.

He pulled his hand away.

“No,” she softly replied and gripped his arm. “I’m sorry I don’t take compliments well. Never have.”

“I understand.”

She scooted to the edge of her stool and touched his face.

His cheek caressed her hand, as he leaned forward.

Her lips pressed against his and he softly sighed.

Earlier passion ignited again, mouths groping, hands wandering, then Mehdi flinched again hissing loudly.

Alexios’s hands flew back. “Are you okay? Did I do something?”

“No.” She groaned. “My stupid ankle.”

She watched his face contort in thought, clearly running through options.

“I have an idea. Can I pick you up?”

She put her face in his hand and nodded.

Alexios spent a moment stroking her face then stood. Stepping in front of her, he picked her up, and clicked in his throat.

The sound thrilled her and she held on as he crossed the room to the bed. "I thought we said slowly."

"Trust me," he whispered gently in her ear.

Her eyes closed in delight.

He gently laid her down on one side of the bed, propping her leg the best he could.

She watched him curiously, as he laid next to her.

He placed the pillow between them. "You lead. I will follow."

She leaned in and kissed him. They lingered in the kiss as he moved closer. Her body followed suit. Hand ran across ridged and curves grasping each other pulling closer, tighter.

Grimacing in frustration while struggling to maneuver with her foot, Alexios pulled her half on him tucking the pillow firmly between them. Understanding his considerate action of using the pillow as a buffer she pressed up against him, and reveled in the thrill of her body against his without an unexpected guest.

Alexios seemed to like it as well, as he rubbed her up and down his body in slow waves.

The motion was exhilarating, and she wanted more. Moving on top of him, she drove her hips down as he clutched her sides and moaned.

Her relationship with this particular pleasure was convoluted. One that haunted her and made no sense when it came in waves, and she had to rub it out. Something a child should not have known, but as a woman she wanted more. She arched her back and used him and the pillow to bring on the sensation.

Alexios' head slammed against the bed, and he groaned loudly, guiding her, helping her push down him.

She leaned down and kissed him, the whole length of her body gliding along his.

He trembled and moaned into the kiss.

She groaned back, feeling herself getting close. Sitting half up, she straddled him grinding hard into the spot that begged release. She cried out with delight as the damn inside her broke and waves of pleasure rippled through her followed by guilt and shame.

Collapsing against him, she peppered him with penitent kisses. "I'm sorry. I'm sorry"

He embraced her and chuckled softly. "Why are you sorry?"

She buried her face into his chest. "I just used you to feel good. And I said slowly."

He stroked her hair and squeezed the back of her neck softly. "You didn't do anything wrong. That was amazing."

"Is that it then? Isn't there more?"

He kissed her gently. "There is definitely more, but that can wait."

She kissed back and licked her lips, "I want more."

He stammered, "Right now?"

She ran her fingers through his hair. "Right now."

He traced her face. Stroking along her chin, across her lips and down her throat. "Do you trust me?"

She shivered and smiled. "I do. I really do."

He rolled her back onto the bed and tossed away the pillow. Taking in a slow breath, he asked, "Do you know the story of man. We once had 4 arms, 4 legs, and two heads?"

She nodded. "I always thought it was strange. How did they walk around?"

He blinked in thought then chuckled. "Good point. But more importantly how did they fit together?"

She tried to think about it but was not grasping the concept.

"When a man gets... aroused he becomes a key."

"A key," she said, confused.

He nodded. "A key. What do keys do?"

"They unlock things."

He nodded again. "More importantly they go in a lock to unlock it."

Mehdi's eyes grew wide with understanding. "I'm the lock."

He smiled and swallowed. "A lock I want to very much pick." He paused and sincerely said, "And make you feel the way you did a moment ago, but while I'm inside you."

"So...no hands?"

He grinned in surprise. "No, hands can work, but a man has a...special hand."

A lot of things started to make sense to her. "So you go inside me."

He trembled slightly. "Only if you want me to."

"You can make me feel like that?"

He moved closer. "We can feel that together and more."

"Okay," she announced, with the same eagerness when learning a new combat style, "Where do we start?"

He ran a hand over her hip. "Clothes on or off?"

"Clothes can come off?"

He shook his head and smiled. "Oh Mehdi, we are about to have a lot of fun."

CHAPTER 9
LOCK AND KEY

SPICY, BUT SOME GREAT DIALOG AND INSIGHT. SKIP THIS CHAPTER IF DESIRED.

He sat up and pulled off his tunic.

She reached to unlatch her girdle and noticed despite their interactions the snake remained undisturbed. Alexios was no threat. She let the girdle slither off the bed and raised her arms, so he could pull off her chiton.

As he kissed her, his hand ran down the length of her body. Never completely leaving her flesh, delicately moving from one spot to another.

She shivered with delight.

Like with Cassia, she mimicked his actions and measured his response. The reactions were good.

He slipped her hand into his, "Same rules, your pace."

He inhaled and asked, “Now that you can see all of me...Do you want to touch me?”

“Okay,” she said a little apprehensive. Alcibiades would grab her hand and shove it on him. She never willfully did it.

Alexios patiently waited.

No illusions of control this time. She was in charge.

She studied him, never seeing one before. It was bizarre and strange, and certainly not as attractive as the rest of him.

Finally, she reached out and ran her fingers along his length.

Alexios inhaled sharply with pleasure.

She was shocked at how his body shook and shuddered. She touched him again the same way and he fell against the bed trying to reign in his reaction.

“It’s that sensitive,” she declared.

He bit his lower lip and nodded.

“How do you walk around? How do you function?”

He put his hand to his head and laughed. “Very carefully.”

She shook her head. “No wonder men are mad beasts.”

“It’s not an excuse, but yes, it requires willpower.”

Mehdi looked at it with the eyes of a crafter. It was a tool, and this tool clearly had a purpose. The lock and key analogy made perfect sense. “That’s pretty ingenious.”

“What?” he asked desperately, trying to remain sane.

“It’s a tool that likes to be used. Still stupid to put it permanently on the outside.”

He chuckled. “Well, it does retract a bit when not in use. Or should I say when it doesn’t desire to be used.”

Shocked she asked, “You mean it just comes out.”

He nodded, still pinching his nose.

She touched it again, admiring its construction.

He inhaled sharply and gently grabbed her hand. “That is very nice, but…”

“Oh!” she replied softly and pulled away. “Do you want me to stop?”

He tried to soothe her, “No, what I mean is once it comes out it wants to be used. It doesn’t mean it has to be, but it…” He sighed. “This is going badly.”

“No, No,” she replied and pulled him closer. “You liked this.” She rubbed her stomach against his, pressing him between them.

He sighed. “Yes.”

Now that she knew what was attacking her under all those clothes the sensation was nice. Warm and firm against her flesh.

He drew her up higher and rubbed himself into her pelvis hitting that spot that made her gasp. “See.” He groaned. “Mutual pleasure.”

Mehdi trembled, intoxicated by the sensations. She rocked against him.

He gripped her hips, keeping enough distance that they could move and slide.

Her head started to swim, and she wanted more. She draped her leg over his hip and pressed their bodies together. It felt wonderful but seemed to lack full satisfaction.

He grabbed her thigh and dug in his fingers.

Mehdi cried out softly, breaking their kiss as her back arched.

He dove into her breasts and suckled her nipple.

She moaned, the sensations driving her mad. She grabbed his hand and pulled it down.

He obliged.

She moaned and pressed his hand in deeper. This she knew, and like a good general, she helped him stroke and caress just so, making her body shudder. She clutched his hand, increasing the pressure.

Kissing her neck, he asked, "More?"

She groaned, as her reply.

He rolled her flat on the bed again and this time hovered over her. "Lock and key?" he asked, waiting for consent.

She huffed, when he spread her legs. "Special hand?"

He kissed her, then pushed, "Special hand."

She trembled. "Yes!" Then her ankle twisted and she winced.

He caressingly picked up her leg and slipped fully inside. They both groaned as he slid in and out.

She grabbed the back of his neck with her good hand and cried out. A new kind of pleasure bloomed inside her as he picked the lock.

He laid his body close against her, driving harder and rocking into that special spot.

Two flowers bloomed, and she could not stop her moaning. He joined her with soft groans and then he clicked his throat. The sound rushed through Mehdi, causing her to gasp.

He started to rhythmically click with each thrust. Hit with wave after wave, all she could do was cling to him and swim in a sea of ecstasy. Her body shook and trembled, unable to take much more. She pushed him harder inside her and tightened around him. Her legs curled around him. Pushing. Tightening.

He groaned, clicking so loudly the room shook.

Mehdi cried out, "More!"

He did it again and again.

Mehdi contracted around him, screaming out as she climaxed, and he exploded inside her.

The walls shook.

CHAPTER 10
BEHOLDEN

"That was..." he said gently, slipping off her and melting into the bed.

"Magical." Mehdi sighed with delight.

He nodded, his face buried in the mattress.

She rolled over and draped across his back. Kissing him softly, she stated, "I'm officially all about the lock and key."

He gave her a thumbs up and then let his arm thunk on the floor.

She laughed. "I didn't know your throat could shake the walls."

He turned his face toward her. "Me either." Smiling, he said, "Want to know the best part?'

"What?" she asked gleefully, feeling his excitement.

His smile widened. "I could see you and you are more beautiful than I imagined."

Normally, mention of her beauty would have made her

sad, but the sincerity and pureness of his voice made her feel divine.

They spent most of the day in bed, talking, touching, and sleeping in each other's arms. As the day grew longer, she noticed he was restless.

"Is something wrong?" she asked her arm hooked under his neck and crooked so her fingers could play in his hair.

"I can't stay," he replied mournfully.

She sat up concerned. "Where are you going?"

"I..." He exhaled hard. "I only get a certain amount of time as a man."

She touched his face, struck by sadness. "Why?"

"It's just the way it is. That's all I was given."

"I don't understand."

He sat up and pulled on a chiton.

She stopped him, giggling, while his arms were still up in the air. "That one is mine. Here." And moved his hand to his clothes.

He slipped his arms through his chiton, "When..." he tried to say, but his voice tightened. "I asked Poseidon if I could be a man again. He granted my wish, but I can't see and I can't be out of the water long. Around six hours is the longest I've been out. I think he did it so I could never leave the sea or him."

"Poseidon. God of the Sea," Mehdi stated flatly.

He grimly nodded.

"You said man again. You were not always a creature?"

He shook his head and rubbed his knees, fretting, "Just a

young sailor who got trapped at sea. I was dying and I called to him. I...I said I would serve him eternally if he saved me."

She pulled herself up, wrapping her arms around him, and laying her head against his shoulder.

He swallowed hard and continued, "He granted my request and turned me into the sea monster. I served him as promised. Doing his bidding and living in the deep fathoms of the sea, but..."

"But?"

"I missed the sky. I missed being on land. Eating cooked food. The heat of the sun. So, I asked him if I could be released. He was not pleased."

"What did he do?" Mehdi asked, knowing most gods were selfish and cruel.

"He granted my wish on the caveat that I never deny or refuse anything he asks."

"You sound very sad when you say that."

"I've done terrible things." His voice quivered.

"Of your own will or because he demands it?"

He shrugged. "Does it matter? I swore fealty to a god. My will is not my own."

"You can choose your own path."

"At what cost? I've seen his vengefulness...I've been his vengeance." He trembled. "Even now I worry..."

Mehdi shifted in concern. "What?"

Alexios swallowed hard. "Nothing." He tilted his head softly and searched for her lips.

Mehdi caressed his face and guided him to her mouth.

They softly kissed in silence, letting the moment wash away any thoughts or fears.

Mehdi broke the embrace and stroked his face. "I am sorry you are beholden to a god against your will."

He squeezed her arms and sighed. "It is a decision I made. I am reminded of that every day."

SHE WOKE to a soft hand on her shoulder and opened her eyes to his smile. Mehdi flinched sputtering as she sat up, wiping water from her face.

"Sorry!" he cried out and grabbed a cloth to dry his hair.

"It's fine, just surprising." She chuckled and watched him dry his hair and legs.

"Did you sleep well?" he asked, sliding a stool near the bed.

She nodded. "Drug induced, but yes."

He started to sit but stood back up. "Food. I should make you food."

Grabbing his wrist, she asked, "Can I have a kiss first?"

He nodded, excitedly.

She drew him down and guided his lips to hers, then tasted her own mouth and stopped.

"What?" he asked, confused.

Grimacing, she stated, "I need to drink something first."

He grinned and licked his lips. "I eat raw fish. I can handle it."

Her eyes narrowed and her lips curled into a smirk, "But do you want to?"

He nodded eagerly, closing the space between their mouths.

She put up her hand and queried, "Did you say raw fish?"

Pausing, he leaned back and released a defeated sigh. "I will get us something to eat."

As Alexios prepared a light breakfast of grapes, bread, and honey, she hopped over and sat at the table.

Her hands lightly tapped the wooden surface. "I'm not used to being waited on."

He poured wine and water into a pitcher then set out cups. "I told myself if I am going to be a man again, then I should learn how to take care of myself." He put down the platter, smiling in her direction. "I'm happy to take care of you too."

She smiled back and softly brushed his arms when he passed by to fetch the other stool and bring it back to the table. "It's impressive how you move around," Mehdi remarked.

Alexios set the stool next to her and teased, "Easier when someone doesn't move things."

Mehdi touched his arm. "I'm learning. I promise."

He grinned, clicked in his throat, then reached for the food.

"Wait!" She offered, "Let me help a little." Mehdi drizzled honey onto a piece of bread and handed it to him.

He located the cups and slowly poured the weakened

wine. She noted his finger on the inside of the cup and how he used it to know when to stop pouring.

They exchanged bread for wine and quietly ate. A cool breeze flowed through the small house, and waves softly crashed in the distance.

Mehdi shuffled in her seat trying to ignore her ankle.

Alexios patted his lap and put out his hand.

She scooted and laid her thigh on him. His soft hairs tickled the back of her thigh and made her shiver.

Alexios rubbed her leg subconsciously. Moving his hand in soft swirls over her knee and up her thigh.

She reveled in his touch and found herself watching him. The sun glinting off his skin, the stubble on his chin. She twirled her fingers along the hand on her leg and inhaled the bliss of the moment.

The smell of honey and wine filled the room, beckoning memories of him softly bathing her in warm water and gentle strokes.

Mehdi ate a few grapes and noticed honey dribbling down Alexios' palm. She drew his hand to her mouth, sucking the honey off and kissing his knuckles.

Alexios leaned in and swallowed softly. "Now can I kiss you?"

She nodded and closed the gap between their lips. His mouth was sweet and intoxicating. Mehdi inhaled intensely, images of yesterday playing in her head.

Alexios put down his cup and used his foot to pull her stool closer.

She let the grapes in her hand drop to the floor and

cupped the back of his neck. Her fingers splaying and tangling in his hair.

He pulled her on top of him and continued to kiss her passionately.

They lingered in this embrace, enjoying the sweet kisses and hot bodies.

A sharp moan escaped her lips, when Alexios dug his fingers into her hips and started rocking her. She was ready for him. Ready for more when she heard...

"You two could not even make it one day!"

She broke the kiss and looked up to find a frowning Euryale.

Alexios froze, unable to do anything with Mehdi on his lap.

Mehdi gripped the table with her forearm and pushed back in her stool. Hanging her head low, she replied, "Sorry."

"No, it is fine. We expected it, but," she shook her head and dropped a bag on the bed, "I brought your fresh clothes, since Stehno said you were wearing your torn up chiton."

Mehdi tugged at her short, ragged dress and looked away.

Euryale shook her head again. "Stop." She sighed and looked at them both.

Mehdi kept her eyes down and fidgeted with her nails in shame.

"You are a Priestess of Athena. Lift your gaze," Euryale commanded.

Mehdi came to attention, straightening her spine and resolve.

"Is it consensual?" she asked.

"Yes," Mehdi replied, grabbing Alexios' hand.

"When was your last flow?" Euryale inquired.

"Uh." Mehdi stuttered, "A week ago?"

Alexios stood and moved to leave.

"Sit down," Euryale ordered. "It takes two, so you will both take equal responsibility."

Alexios plopped back in his seat.

Euryale walked over and sighed at the couple. "I'm not going to ruin your fun, but before you next flow you need to go to the infirmary and get silphium juice."

"Lover's Heart," Mehdi confirmed. "Got it."

She looked at them both and emphasized, "Once a month before your flow."

Alexios squeezed Mehdi's hand and firmly replied, "Yes, Euryale."

Euryale let out another long sigh, then gave her a soft smile. "Don't feel guilty. Just be careful."

CHAPTER 11
MAKING WAVES

"A few more steps. You are almost there," Alexios said, holding her arm as Mehdi hopped down the hill.

"I never noticed how hilly this land is." She grunted and dug her fingers into his arm.

He chuckled. "I can attest the same thought plus the random outcropping of rocks."

She snorted. "Or the roots of trees."

Laughing, he caught her when she wobbled.

She was using the crutch, but only after modification to create a brace for her arm and wrist. It was inconvenient, but after a week trapped in the small house, she was determined to be more mobile.

When he was there, it was blissful. When he returned to the water without her, it was intolerable. She no longer craved solitude. They made it to the shoreline, and she sat down.

Mehdi fussed with the strapping and took off the crutch. "That needs work."

He crouched down next to her. "Are you sure you just want to sit here?"

She stretched her toes out toward the lapping waves. "For a little while, at least. I'd prefer to go in the water with you."

"Not for another week," he replied, repeating himself.

She frowned. "Then let me soak in the sun and watch you swim."

He reached out for her face.

Mehdi softly guided his hand and sighed when he kissed her.

"I'll be back," he promised. His lips brushed her neck once more before he stood and slipped into the rolling waves.

Mehdi tilted her face towards the sun, soaking in the rays. Stretching out, she listened to the waves and wind. As her breath softened, and sleep beckoned. She heard him leaping out of the water and grinned, then felt something wet thwack her leg.

Sitting upright, she glanced down at her leg and found a seaweed pod.

Out in the water, large black eyes stared back, anxiously waiting.

She giggled and smiled, then threw the pod as far as she could.

He bounded after it, his pectoral fins pushing him across the sand as his tail whipped water into the air.

Mehdi cried out in playful protest at the unexpected shower.

He retrieved the pod and galloped back to her. Staying in the water, he flicked the pod at her feet.

She arched a brow at him. "This is how we got in trouble last time."

His tail thrashed in the water and his nose flaps huffed loudly.

Laughing, she threw the pod again and their game continued.

A NEW ROUTINE BEGAN.

As planned Alexios, broke up his time between land and sea, so that they were not apart for long. Normally, injuries like Mehdi's would take months to heal, but she was up and hobbling around by week two and her hand was scarring. When Alexios was in the water, they played, and she wandered the island or helped tend the garden.

They received visitors, who would bring them supplies they could not produce on the island and provided company. No one objected to their union. Perseus seemed to revel in it.

By the end of the second week, she was in the water with Alexios collecting sea life to eat.

While harvesting oysters one day, Alexios transformed back to human form and bobbed in the water.

She smiled. "I wasn't sure you could do that."

He grinned playfully and pulled her into a kiss.

Treading water, she returned his embrace. "How long have you wanted to kiss me in the water?"

"A long while," he admitted.

She laughed, tightening her arms around his waist.

Rolling his hand down her arm, he touched her wrist. "Follow me."

They swam over to the sandy shoals. Mehdi put her feet down gently and stood. Her ankle was still weak, but the water allowed her to not rely on it too much.

"Look down," Alexios said, excitedly.

The translucent water exposed the sand bed and sea life below.

He flicked his toe and a sea scallop fluttered, trying to escape.

She listened to him click in his throat and snatch the scallop mid flight.

Mehdi giggled. "This will be fun."

Together they skimmed the shallows, chasing scallops and each other. Their laughter and joy filled the space around them.

"I think you are faster in your other form," Mehdi teased, dodging his grasp.

"I could see you!" he jibed and snatched at her.

She laughed. "Ah, the sound thing doesn't work as well with a moving target."

Clicking, "Not perfectly, but," he panted, nabbing her

wrist, "works well enough." Pulling her down into the shallowest end, they sat and intertwined.

She straddled him, exhilarated by the feel of the water and him. "Can you see me now?"

He clicked and grinned. She pulled off her tunic and dropped it into the water.

"What if we lose it?" he asked.

"I know a sea monster that can find anything."

Clutching to each other, they rocked with the soft waves. Their passion grew, as he clicked rhythmically in his throat. Mehdi sighed into his embrace, hearing the water crash away from them.

Entwined, enraptured, and encapsulated in each other, the world fell away. The water rippled and the earth quaked around them, as Mehdi threw her head back, clasping him to her chest. Alexios clicked once more, and they cried out in ecstasy.

Draping her arms over his shoulders and curling them around his head, she released a pleased sigh. "Is it crazy, that I want more?"

Alexios languidly ran his hands over her thighs to her hips, and up her torso, replying, "No."

ALEXIOS LEFT to hunt for her clothes, as she returned to finding scallops. A pink shell peeked out of a patch of seaweed, glistening in the water and light. Holding her breath, she dove under to grab it, when a large eel slithered from under a rock and locked eyes with her. Fear rose inside Mehdi, freezing her mid action. She could not move.

The eel's black eyes remained unblinking, as it slithered around her arm, across her torso and down her leg. The sensation was alarming, and she feared it would attack. It did not. Instead, it continued to linger, as if it was examining her, hunting her.

As her lungs burned for air, she carefully placed her good foot on the ground and lifted her head above the water, watching the eel the whole time. He stared back. She stood, breathing in the fresh air, but kept her gaze on the eel.

It moved towards her again, rubbing against her, but not biting. The sensation of its skin sliding across hers was both frightening and strangely elating. She glanced around for Alexios. He was far off, collecting her clothes.

Her breath quickened, not from fear, but from a strange fuzziness. Her head felt foggy, as if she were intoxicated. She shuddered as the eel slowly slunk between her thighs and up her back.

Her thoughts grew fuzzy, and her body leaned into the creature's pleasant tough. As her knees grew weak, the idea of closing her eyes and going to sleep took prominence. Images of dancing among the seaweed, forever happy and free of mortality. She fought the allure and looked around again. A large black tail flipped out of the water.

"Alexios!" she cried out.

The eel tightened around her, shocking her lightly. The water lapped promises of protection from the cruelties of land. All she needed to do was sink into its eternal embrace. Deep within the intoxication Mehdi grew angry.

"No!" She shouted and deftly grabbed the eel by the head.

It thrashed and whipped violently. Shocking her again. She yelled and chucked the eel as far as she could.

Alexios transformed and came up to the surface. Unsure of her location he called out, "Mehdi? Are you okay?"

"Yes and no," she said, watching the eel swim back toward her. "I seemed to have made a friend."

"What?"

"An eel," she said, a little breathless. "I have an eel swimming around me, and he won't leave."

"Can you catch him?" he asked, working his way towards her.

"That isn't the problem." She tried to dodge the eel, but he quickly slipped around her again.

"Mehdi?" he asked in the long pause.

"He's on me." she stammered.

His eyes widened in alarm, as he clicked his throat. The eel squeezed and shocked her.

She yelped, pawing at it, but it didn't move.

"Okay," he replied and moved towards her.

"He's around my waist." The intoxication returned. Its head slipped between her breasts and stared up at her. She stared back and her long desire to slip under the water forever intensified.

"I have your chiton, maybe."

She shook her head. "I. Can't...think...clearly. Something...is...wrong."

Alexios stopped moving and softly muttered something, but Mehdi could not comprehend what he said. The eel let go and swam away.

Mehdi came out of the trance. Her eyes followed the eel, fighting the allure to follow. Images of living forever underwater were unusually compelling. As it swam out of sight, her head began to clear and she looked up at Alexios. "He's gone."

"I think that is enough for today." Offering her the chiton, they swam back to the island.

Alexios was unnerved. He appeared worried and lost in thought.

Mehdi was disturbed by the encounter but pushed the incident out of her mind. Back on solid ground, she wrapped her arms around him. "I'm okay."

He sighed in relief and returned her embrace.

"The boat is here," she remarked. "We have company."

They walked up the small incline and approached the door.

Alexios stopped.

Mehdi thought he wanted her to open the door, so she did.

When he heard the door creaking open, he squeezed her hand and blurted, "Wait!"

She was already peering through the fabric covering the door and saw Stheno and Euryale passionately entwined.

"Oh!" she uttered in surprise, stepped back from the door and crashed into Alexios arms nervously giggling.

The noises on the other side abruptly stopped and Euryale peered through the curtained doorway. "Yes?" she asked, her skin flushed and breath short.

"Nothing." Alexios mirthfully replied, "We can come back later."

Mehdi stepped away from Alexios and turned to leave.

"No, please," Euryale said, putting out a hand, "Stheno and I were just discussing you two."

"You were?" Mehdi asked, surprised. "Just now?"

"Well...not just now," she replied with a soft chuckle. "A moment ago."

They stepped in.

Stheno straightened her chiton and leaned up against the small table. "Mehdi."

"Head Priestess Stheno," she choked out. She had known both these women for many years and knew they basically ran the temple. To think they were more...to not know till now. Mehdi chided her own self-absorption.

Alexios moved to a stool. "Hello Stheno, how is the temple?" He set the bag of scallops and oysters on the ground and reached for a pre-positioned knife.

"It is well."

There was a rap on the door frame. "Hello." Perseus peaked his head in. "I'm not late, am I?"

"No, I haven't even started. Please come in. There are a lot of people, can you grab the benches from the garden?"

"Certainly," Perseus replied.

Mehdi watched the familial interactions and felt her stomach knot. “Excuse me,” she said and rushed out the door.

Outside she bent over and tried to slow her panicked breathing. That did not work so she straightened and stared upward exhaling long deep breaths. She felt a light touch on her shoulder.

It was Stheno. “Mehdi, are you okay?”

“Me?” Her eyes darted around. “I’m...fine.”

“Clearly not.”

“This is all just...I’m...” She gasped for air.

Stheno pulled her into a hug. “Breathe, Breathe. What is wrong?”

Large fat tears rolled down her face as she choked out. “I’m...happy.”

Stheno held her and let her sob, before saying, “It’s okay to be happy.”

She sniffled. “I just...I feel at home here.”

“Then don’t leave.”

Mehdi looked up at her. “I don’t have to leave?”

“Not unless you want to.”

“But my duties.”

“I am certain you can fulfill your duties to Athena and be happy.”

Mehdi swallowed and replying with relief. “Thank you.”

They leaned against each other watching the sun dip into the horizon. “How was fishing today?”

Mehdi blushed, recalling Alexios intertwined with her in

the shallows. "We went scallop hunting." She felt it best, not to mention the eel. She wanted to forget the eel.

Stheno paused, as her eyes drifted down the path. Mehdi turned to see a man approaching. He was tall and golden tan. His hair was thick and long. He wore a bright blue chiton crested with a border of white waves fastened only to one shoulder.

Stheno tensed and stepped in front of her.

The man smiled, baring bright white teeth. He spoke to Stheno, but stared at Mehdi. "Hello. Is Alexios home?"

"Yes," she replied with one hand guarding Mehdi.

Mehdi found Stheno's reaction strange but comforting.

The man inhaled deeply, "Is he making his stew? I'm famished." He did not wait for an answer and casually strode inside.

The women followed. Stheno appeared alarmed and kept Mehdi behind her. Mehdi did not like being protected, so she moved to Stheno's side keeping herself alert.

"Alexios," H=he boomed.

Alexios stood. Alarm ran across his face, but he quickly recovered his composure. "P....uh..T...Tavros. Is that you? What brings you here?"

"I saw you in the scallop beds today and thought it had been some time since I visited."

Saw? Mehdi thought. She never noticed anyone watching them, ever.

Alexios fiddled with the knife in his hand, "And you were compelled by the thought of my stew."

"Why yes... among other things." He beamed. "Perseus, you are here too? How are you?"

"Well," Perseus replied, sidling up next to Mehdi and exchanging silent glances with Stheno and Euryale.

"Please," Alexios said, fighting the clipped tone in his voice, "come and sit at my table," he offered. "Have you met Mehdi?"

"Not personally," Tavros replied and quickly shortened the distance between them.

Mehdi knew his gaze too well. He stared at her as most men do. Eyes ablaze with excitement, as they darted up and down her form. Her response was always the same, a mixture of confusion and alertness.

When she was younger, she often translated this intense stare, as something being wrong with her. Her mind would race to fears of knotted hair, a sooty face, or a torn garment. People looked at her differently but would never say why.

That is until she was older, then they would tell her she was beautiful, that they wanted her, needed her. Each time a new person stared at her in this manner, she felt an urgent need to flee. Yet, politeness cemented her feet.

"Alexios, who is this creature?" Tavros asked, grabbing her hands and forcing her into a displaying pose.

"This is Mehdi, a priestess of Athena," Stheno replied coldly.

Tavros' mouth turned downward in disapproval and let go of her hands, "That's a shame."

"How so?" Stheno spat.

"A creature such as this should be on the arm of a god, not on her knees in prayer."

Mehdi did not know whether to be flattered or insulted. She chose to be insulted. "I choose my own path. I choose to serve Athena and not any form of man."

He sniffed indignantly. "And what have you received in return for such devotion."

Mehdi reached out her hand. Her silver snake girdle whipped from the bed and around her waist. "Protection."

His eyes narrow. "From who?"

"Those like you!" Euryale said, stepping to the other side of Mehdi.

"Please," Alexios spoke trying to disarm the rising tension, "is there a misunderstanding I am failing to see?"

"It is my fault," Tavros cajoled. "Apparently, something I said was misconstrued. Please forgive me, Mehdi. I meant no ill intent."

His remorse sounded sincere and disarmed Mehdi, who replied, "The fault is mine. I... I do not handle flattery well."

"Oh, but if Alexios could see your beauty, he would surely keep you to himself and never invite me back."

Mehdi wasn't sure that was a compliment and glanced at Alexios. He was unnerved but said nothing. Everyone in the room seemed on edge, but afraid to act.

Tavros continued to look at her with a punitive face, begging for kindness.

For the sake of peace, she reluctantly conceded. "Your comments are forgotten. We are both guests here. Let us not insult our host." She looked away from his intense stare and sat at the table.

Stheno and Tavros remained standing.

Alexios attempted a chuckle, "I've never had so many guests. I've run out of seats."

Euryale and Perseus helped set the table and ladled the stew to the guests.

They crowded around the tiny table on benches and stools and ate mostly in silence except for a few polite words.

Tavros' vocal brashness temporarily abided and was replaced with an attempt at congenial banter. "Tell me Mehdi, do you enjoy the sea?"

Cupping her mouth as she swallowed a bite of bread, she replied, "I do."

His fingers swirled along the lines in the wooden table. "What do you like most?"

"Being under the water. Sometimes I wish I could go down and never come up." She stopped mid-bite, perplexed as the words came out of her mouth of their own volition.

Tavros grinned broadly, finished eating his food, and presented her his closed fist.

She glanced at him, curious.

"Open it."

Prying his fingers open, she gasped at the giant pearl cradled in his palm.

He rolled the pearl to the tips of his fingers. "Place it in your mouth before you swim, with it you can breathe underwater."

She gaped at him, astounded by the magic and offer.

"It is yours."

Glancing around the table for guidance, uncomfortable with his presence, their unease radiated back. Stheno's eyes darted to the pearl and back to her with a warning glance.

That was all Mehdi needed to know. Shaking her head, she refused. "I cannot."

"I insist," he persisted.

"Your offer is appreciated, but I am careful about accepting gifts from strangers."

"But I am not a stranger." He motioned to the room. "Known by all here."

She looked around. Known but not liked.

"Again, thank you, but I must say no."

He squeezed the pearl in his fist. "I'm not used to hearing the word no."

Her gaze hardened as her tone solidified. "You may not be used to it, but I am allowed to say it. Again, thank you, but no."

The earth rumbled.

Alexios bound to his feet. "Perhaps, you can leave it here. Then if she chooses to take it, she can."

Mehdi glared at him, fuming. "I don't want it."

"He is my guest and to refuse a gift would be...unthinkable. I will keep the item for her." He put out his hand.

Tavros glowered at Alexios with disapproval. The muscles in his neck tightened and twitched as his jaw sawed back and forth.

Alexios remained stalwart, hand outstretched for the gift and head dipped in reverence.

Accepting his act of prostration, Tavros dropped the pearl into his hand.

"Thank you. I am honored," Alexios replied, dropping to one knee.

"You and I will speak later," Tavros ordered and rose.

Stheno stood and cupped her hand. "Mehdi, I see you are able to walk. You should come back to the temple. Tonight."

Mehdi drew back her hand, upset and confused. The last thing she wanted to do was leave Alexios. 'I don't think I can walk that path in the dark."

His mouth curling in a churlish smile, Tavros crooned, "Stheno, let the lovers have one more night together. I am sure Athena can wait." Standing his full height, he commanded a presence over the other guests. "Come. I feel we have all overstayed our welcome."

Under his watchful eye, the others stood and departed without hugging her or offering parting words. Mehdi could only glean their worry from furtive glances and Perseus faltering steps. Annoyed at his authority Mehdi elbowed past him. "Allow me to walk you down to the shore."

Tavros objected, "Nonsense, you two should enjoy your evening. I will ensure they are set off safely." Not waiting for objection, he leaned over whispering something into Alexios's ear, then patted his shoulder before exiting.

Arms crossed, she stood in the doorway watching her friends depart. As they disappeared into the darkness she snapped at Alexios "Who is that?!"

Alexios placed the pearl in a box and set it on the kitchen windowsill. "Someone you do not cross."

Mehdi scoffed. "Clearly, everyone was afraid of him. I don't think I've ever seen Stheno or Euryale afraid of anyone."

He covered his brow, fighting his body as it trembled, "Mehdi, please."

"Please, what?"

"Let's not talk about it. He is gone."

"Is he dangerous? What if he comes back?"

Horror etched into his face as his head shot up and he reached out for her. With assurance, she placed her hand in his. He gripped it tightly, pleading. "If he comes back, get as far from him as possible, okay?"

All her anger vanished, seeing his fear. Touching his face, she agreed, "Okay."

When they came together that night, he seemed particularly impassioned and held her tightly. Lingering on every kiss, sighing with each embrace. She could feel him clinging to each moment. Before rising from the bed to return to the water for the night, he gave her one last long, gentle kiss.

Hovering at the door, shadowed in darkness, he swore, "I love you."

CHAPTER 12
GONE

When she woke the next morning, he was not there. Ignoring the foreboding, Mehdi went about her morning routine. She noticed the boat was moored on the island, though it should be docked on the shoreline. After hours of searching the water around the island for a flip of his tail or an unnatural wave realization started sinking into her skin.

By midafternoon, she loaded into the boat and rowed to shore. Her ankle ached from bracing against the bow she rowed the oars and drew the boat onto the beach. Two paths lay before her. Danae's or The Temple. Neither would be easy, but something was wrong. Inhaling deeply, she trekked up the steep path to the temple.

She chuckled to herself as she struggled up the path, recalling less than a month ago bounding down these rocks with ease. Injury or not, her mind was determined. By the time she located Stheno, her ankle throbbed and barely supported her weight.

"Mehdi!" Stheno cried out, coming to her aid. She pulled out a stool and beckoned her to sit.

Mehdi took a seat and tried to catch her breath. The climb was a challenge, and the exertion made her heart pound, but too many questions burned in her brain and they needed answers.

"Is everything okay?" Euryale asked, rushing from the other room. She tossed the scroll in her hand on the table, crossing the room to kneel at her side.

Mehdi sipped from the offered cup and worked to catch her breath,."Alexios. He's gone."

Stheno and Euryale exchanged glances but said nothing.

She stared at them both in shock. "You know?"

They shook their heads. Euryale clutched Stheno's hand. Mehdi watched their fingers intertwine and fret.

"No, no, we didn't know," Euryale replied. "But..."

Mehdi waited for her to finish. "After last night," Stheno replied, "we feared it."

Hesitation and fear ran across both their faces. A sight Mehdi had never seen. These were her mentors, the women who took her in and taught her how to be strong and sure. What did they fear?

"Where did he go?" Mehdi pleaded, if they knew they needed to tell her. She didn't care if they were afraid.

Euryale touched Mehdi's shoulder. "We don't know."

"Will he be coming back?" she asked, her voice cracking, because she already knew the answer.

Stheno let out a long heart wrenching sigh. “We don’t know that either.”

“Then what do we do?” she implored. It was not like them to not fight, or at least come up with a battle plan.

They said nothing and averted their eyes.

She thrust herself out of the chair. “What are you not telling me?”

Euryale gave her a sorrowful gaze. “We are telling you what we can, Mehdi.”

“It’s that Tavros, isn’t it.” Mehdi seethed, “He sent him away. Why? How?”

Stheno nodded weakly. “Yes, we are sure that is who sent him away.”

“Where could he go? He can’t be out of the water for long. He said Poseidon wouldn’t allow it.” Mehdi stopped pacing and gaped at the unthinkable truth.

They stared back with great sadness. Her teachers now cowered before a power greater than them. What could make two priestesses of Athena relent?

“No...why would he care? Why would he bother? It couldn’t be. Why would a god...No!” She shook her head, “He’s just some arrogant man.”

Stheno tried to imbue a tone of wisdom, but dread still laced her words, “Man or God. He is likely the reason Alexios is gone.”

Mehdi felt her heart breaking. Her happiness stolen again. She swallowed back hard tears. “I refuse.”

“Mehdi,” Stheno implored, “you can’t defy the will of the gods.”

Mehdi stood to her full height, preparing her mind and body for a fight. "Watch me."

Disgusted by their lack of action, Mehdi left the temple and went back to the cove. Adrenaline masked her exhaustion. She got back to the island and dumped the pearl out of the box. If he was going to take Alexios away, then she was going to use his gift to find him.

Strapping on her vambraces and shin guards, she then fetched a spear. Mehdi ignored her own pain and tightened the straps of her sandals. Spear in one hand and pearl in the other, she entered the water.

Under water, she inhaled the pearl as instructed. Her body jerked a few times as it expelled air out her nose and drew in water, but she did not drown. Finally, she could breathe! The sea was hers to explore.

Mehdi swam around the cove, hoping to find him or some clue where he went. She searched the oyster beds, the shallows, and all around, but he was nowhere.

Her body ached from exertion. She didn't need air, but she did need rest. *When was the last time I ate?* Angry at her own frailty, she resigned herself to look more later and swam back to the island.

Passing the jutting rocks that capped the cove on one side, something out of the corner of her eye. She glimpsed a black tail slithering around a rock. *Was that him?* Was he hiding from her this whole time? Changing direction, she followed it into the deep.

In her peripheral, the swish of black lured her into an underwater cave. The cave looked too small for Alexios, as the sea creature, but perhaps he had transformed.

The water was dark and murky, making it hard to see. She couldn't speak or call out. Swimming a little further, she found the back of the cave. Her hand ran over the rough edge confirming a dead end. Defeated, she shook her head, and turned around.

Twisting to go back out the way she came, she jerked in fright when the eel blocked her exit. Her sense of danger screamed in her head. She tried to move past it, but the creature watched her every move and maneuvered to keep her trapped.

She jabbed her spear at it, but with no footing, there was little force to her attack. Her muscles burned from exhaustion, but she would not relent. Frantic, her eyes darted around for any escape or advantage, when she looked back, the eel was charging.

Mehdi lifted her arm to block, hoping her vambrace would protect her flesh. As something shifted and moved around her waist, her other hand moved to grab it, worried there was a second eel.

No, it was her girdle. Slithering to life, it flew off her waist and attacked her opponent. They became entangled, each trying to bite and strangle the other.

Sunlight glinted off metal snake as the path to the mouth of the cave cleared. Mehdi did not linger to watch the fight, swimming with the little strength she had and escaped. Not stopping, she climbed back on shore and spat the pearl to the ground. Gasping and wheezing for air, her body collapsed into the sand, unconscious.

She inhaled sharply, as she woke and sat up choking on her own spit. Exhausted and confused, her heart pounded as she looked around. The last bit of the sun sunk beneath the horizon as deafening silence shrouded her. Her body quivered and shook as she tried to stand. Legs jiggling and wobbling, she successfully got to her feet. Gazing out at the water, she hoped that when she walked back to the house, he would be there.

He was not.

Two emotions filled Mehdi's thoughts, anger and sadness. Anger that Poseidon made Alexios leave and that Alexios obeyed. Sadness that she would sleep alone tonight. His absence surrounded her. Was he a prisoner? Is that why he didn't come back? *Did he want to?* Were men as helpless to rulers as women were to men? Even Stheno and Euryale refused to defy a god.

Mehdi shook her head. She would not be so weak.

As soon as dawn broke, Mehdi dressed and prepared to reenter the water. Her muscles ached, and her ankle throbbed, but she ignored it all. Determined to last longer in the water, she ate what she could, but her patience wore thin, and each bite took too long to chew. Another large gulp of honeyed water and she traipsed back down to the shore.

The waves were hitting her knees, before she froze in

fear. In front of her, the eel stared directly at her, watching, waiting, beckoning. With the reflexes of a warrior, she threw her spear at it and stabbed it in the middle.

"Ha!" she cried out and drew her knife to finish the job. As she approached, the eel thrashed and screeched.

Mehdi had to cover her ears, and involuntarily shut her eyes. The sound was excruciating. Forcing them back open, she saw the eel rip itself in half, freeing it from the spear. The two halves quickly formed into new eels. Horrified, she tore her spear free from the sand and backed away.

Two sets of eyes hunted her and the sensation to follow them into the deep returned. She shook the thought away and ran for the shore.

The eels gave chase. One snapped at her ankle. She swiped at it with her spear, flinging it away from her. The other bit deep into her leg.

Crying out, she grabbed it by the body. Spiky fins stung her hand, but she did not let go. Neither did the eel. Instinctually using her knife to chop off the head, she flung the body and unhinged the head from her leg.

Both pieces started to grow, as the first one headed straight for her.

Mehdi launched herself off the ground and up the beach. Free of the water, she turned back to three sets of eyes staring back. Swimming was no longer an option.

She limped over to the boat and the eels followed her. Shaking her head, she knew they could easily tip the boat and send her back into the water. Why did they want her?

Hobbling back up to the hut, she sat and dressed her

wounds. As memories with Alexios flooded her head, she failed to notice the shadow coming up the path.

"Hello?" Perseus called.

She stood, exclaiming. "Perseus!" Nausea swept over her body forcing her to plop back into the seat.

He rushed to her side. "Mehdi, what happened?"

Furious at her own weakness and misery, she returned to wrapping her wound and sputtered, "Alexios...he's gone."

Perseus nodded sadly. "The sisters told me. They were worried you did not return last night, and that the boat was not on the shoreline."

Heart aching, she sighed. "I tried to find him."

His eyes bulged, seeing her wound. "Were you attacked?"

She nodded, tying off the bandage. "Twice."

He shook his head and poured her something to drink. "You can't go back into the water."

She gulped from the cup. "I know...there is something strange about that...those eels. But Alexios..."

Sitting down on the other stool, he took her hand, "I know, he is my friend, too. But he is..."

Her eyes narrowed and anger welled. "Why didn't you tell me that Tavros was Poseidon?"

He held her gaze, but did not speak, then his shoulders slumped in resignation. "For the same reason I don't tell people Zeus is my father."

Mouth agape, she stammered, "Zeus is your father? Danae never said..."

"Why would she? It's dangerous to be associated with gods. Not just from the gods themselves, but from people knowing and acting out. Some people will fear you; others will try to destroy you. If my uncle, the King, knew... He is already jealous of my father because my mother is the daughter of a king."

Mehdi put her hand on Perseus and smirked. "You are telling me you are the son of a God and the grandchild of a King. You're royalty."

He shrugged. "I mean even if Dictes was my father, wouldn't I still be?"

"I suppose, but he chose the life of a fisherman." She took another big gulp. "How long have you known?"

He sighed and poured himself a glass, "For a little while now, but I try not to think about it."

"So, Danae just told you?"

He chuckled and rubbed his unruly hair. "In a way. I started noticing I was stronger and more agile than others." He nudged her slightly. "Well except you."

She brushed off his compliment and listened.

"My mother says, when my grandfather discovered I was born he put both of us in a box and banished us into the sea. Zeus asked Poseidon to insure we lived, so we ended up being found by my...father. He took us in, and they fell in love."

"And your mother told you this."

He nodded. "And Poseidon."

She poured more wine and drank.

He exhaled, "I knew Tavros was Poseidon, but I wasn't

allowed to speak of it. Mehdi...don't go near him, or the water."

She batted away his hand. "If he has Alexios, I will demand his release!"

His brow furrowed, "At what cost?" Perseus stared intensely at her. "He is a god."

"Just another man," she spat.

Perseus shook his head hard and grabbed her wrist. "Mehdi, I know that look."

"Good," she replied. "Then you know you can't stop me."

"Mehdi, he wants you!"

She recoiled and her anger grew.

Perseus nodded. "Why do you think he sent Alexios away? You've been chosen."

As old fears of becoming a sacrificial goat flashed in her mind, Mehdi's fist slammed down on the table. "No one, not even a god gets to choose who I am with. My choice!"

CHAPTER 13
WITH GREAT POWER

"We need to get you out of here," Perseus decided.

"You think Tav...Poseidon will come back?"

He affirmed, "He made it very clear that he has chosen you."

She glanced outside, "The eels."

"Likely, meant to keep you here or worse draw you out."

She nodded, recalling the intoxication and desire. "There are three of them now. If we get in the boat, they may knock us over."

"Perhaps, between the two of us?" he suggested.

Her mind mulled over the best tactics. "This is not the most advantageous ground to fight from. I'll leave, but I am done hiding in the temple from any man."

Perseus exhaled. "Mehdi, I understand wanting to fight, but remember to fall back, when you are overpowered."

"Why does everyone keep telling me to retreat?" She retrieved her crutch and a few supplies, including the pearl.

"Because this is not a battle you want to fight?"

"I'd rather fight than relent and still lose."

They made their way to the boat. The eels were not within sight, but Mehdi could sense them lying in wait. They clamored into the small boat and made it a third of the way across, before there was a crash against the hull.

Mehdi saw the eel's tail flick out of the water, as it twisted around for another attack. The other two were charging. "From the left. Brace!" she shouted.

Perseus gripped the sides of the boat, allowing Mehdi to raise an oar and slam it down on the other two before they hit the side.

It stopped the eels short of their target, but they needed to get across, and fast.

"Together!" she shouted as they each took an oar and rowed.

The bite on her leg throbbed and her weakening ankle trembled but kept paddling.

"Here they come again," Perseus called.

"Hit them before they hit us." She grunted, pulling her oar up and readying her strike.

They struck down and Mehdi was able to flip one eel into the air. It thrashed violently and screeched, as it came down. Mehdi braced against the noise and smacked it again, sending it flying.

"Perhaps we should use the spear?" Perseus declared.

"Do not cut them in half!" Mehdi exclaimed.

The boat rocked from another strike.

"Row!" she shouted.

The oars went back in the water, but they made little progress, fighting against the eels.

"What do we do?" Perseus exclaimed, bracing the boat against another blow.

"The net!" Mehdi exclaimed.

"They will tear through it."

"It will buy us time," she replied, already pulling it from the bow of the ship.

Mehdi gathered the net to cast and waited for the three to ram. She steadied her feet swaying with the boat. As the eels turned, she dropped one half off the side of the boat and held the other. Just before they hit again, she flung the net over them.

Her leg buckled, unable to hold her. Perseus grabbed Mehdi before she fell over from the strike.

The eels' snouts caught in the holes of the weave and their tails thrashed at the dropped half, causing them to tangle each other in the net.

"Go!" she yelled.

They rowed hard and fast, forcing the boat over the capping waves and to run aground. Together they drew the boat up high and secured it to a rock.

"That was different," Perseus replied. "The fish don't usually fight back."

"I don't know what that was, but it was not normal." She laughed, releasing the stressful moment.

Perseus laughed with her. “It was an honor to fight by your side.”

She shook her head, “Nothing like having a Demi-god have your back.”

“Oh...well...” he replied with humility.

“What will you do?” she asked, plopping on the ground to catch her breath.

“With what?” he asked, taking his place by her side.

Blowing her hair out of her face, she replied, “Your gifts.”

He glanced at her puzzled.

“You just told me you are part god and likely heir to a throne.”

“And?” he asked, while checking her bite. Blood soaked the bandage, and the flesh was swollen.

She batted at ministrations and shook her head in exasperation, “You could do so much.”

“Such as?”

Throwing her hands in the air, she extolled, “Rule a Kingdom, right injustices?”

“Injustices?”

She touched his arm. “Do you remember my trial?”

He tensed, but nodded.

“Your uncle sat right behind those men, including your father as they put me on trial. I was the victim and yet I was on trial. At any point your uncle could have stopped it, but he didn’t. If you were king would you have let them treat me like they did?”

He stared at her, shocked. “Of course not.”

She exhaled and smiled. "See?"

They fell into another silence as he thought, "What would you do?"

She tilted her head. "Me?" She stared out into the crashing waves, "I wouldn't get that choice."

"If you were the daughter of a king and/or a god. You are saying you wouldn't have the same choices."

"Nope. Daughters marry. Sons rule. Your mother is proof of that. Even the daughter of a King, she had no say over her life. And to be godly...That may have some merit. There are female gods, but they are still daughters and subjects.

"In the end, even Athena would be required to obey Zeus. Aphrodite was forced to marry Hephaestus. Hera must suffer Zeus' infidelity, as you are proof of that. Perhaps Artemis is the luckiest of the goddesses and they even threaten to take away her powers if she lays with a man. Jokes on them if they think she remains 'virtuous'."

Her eyes focused away from him and on the ground. Digging her toes into the sand, she unearthed hidden shells and twigs. "Yet, male Gods, like male men, can lie, cheat, rape, kill. Paying little for their actions."

He took her hands into his and said, "I think if you had that power, you would be different."

Mehdi returned to the temple and headed for the bathhouse to clean up. She was met with joyous cheers and glad tidings for her return.

"Welcome back!" Myra called, bringing over a tray of

salts and oils. "You look awful. I thought you would be healed by now."

Mehdi snorted. "I was, but then I had a run in with a very persistent eel."

"Oh my!" Tana replied, moving across the large sunken bath to assist.

Mehdi removed her vambraces and shin plates.

Myra offered to help with removing the bandages, which were already soaked in fresh blood, sand and brine.

Tana winced at the vicious bite, "That's awful. How are you walking on it?" She hopped out of the bath and fetched the salve from the apothecary cabinet.

Myra studied the wound. "I'm not sure if soaking will help or not?"

"It definitely needs to soak. I did not have time to clean it properly. Then we will cake it in salt and salve."

The other priestess nodded.

Tana helped her remove her chiton and slip into the waters.

Mehdi sighed, feeling the heat soak into her bones. Staying with Alexios was wonderful, but he had no place to bathe and water only boiled in a small pot. As she sat in the large bath heated by an ever-present fire roiling beneath the stone floor, she realized she missed it.

Closing her eyes, she laid head rest on the edge as her body relaxed. Her sour mood at losing Alexios, learning about Poseidon, and fighting off monsters faded.

"Sooooo," Myra began, sliding next to her, "tell us about the blindman."

Mehdi's head popped up, "What? I..." She exhaled, all the sorrow returning. "There is no blindman."

Tana lightly tapped her arm. "Liar. It's the talk of the temple. You getting hurt and literally shacking up with the blind man on the little island."

Mehdi rubbed her face. "I am sure you all can talk about something else?"

"Town talked about it, too," Myra added.

Mehdi groaned and sunk her head under the water. She stayed there as long as her breath would hold, wishing she had the pearl.

Tana's hand dipped into the water and tapped her shoulder again.

Mehdi came up and reluctantly inhaled.

"You can't stay under there forever."

Mehdi laughed. "Wanna bet?"

"Mehdi," Myra chided, "what happened? Did you have a fight?"

She scoffed. "I wish it was that simple. No...let's just say he was taken away." She really didn't want to divulge the whole truth.

"Oh no!" Tana exclaimed. "What are you going to do?"

Mehdi glowered. "Nothing, apparently. Stheno and Euryale refuse to help, and everyone is telling me to not fight."

"Ha!" Myra snorted, "Good luck, telling you to back down."

A small grin appeared on Mehdi's face. "Thank you."

She sighed. "I can't take P... the man who took him on directly, so I need to think of a better plan of attack."

"I would ask Athena for help."

Mehdi pushed herself back into a sitting position. "That isn't a bad idea. Do you think she will listen?" She wondered if Athena could intervene between her and Poseidon's desires. *Would she?* Mehdi lost the girdle; would Athena consider her worthy enough to defend against another god?

"Can't hurt to ask? I would bring her a special offer though. I suggest something that is special to you both and share that with her."

Mehdi thought of their time in the shallows chasing the scallops. Her shoulders relaxed and frustration eased with the counsel of her peers. "Thank you. I will do that."

Myra bumped her hip. "Can we hear a little about him? If it doesn't hurt too much?"

Mehdi grinned. It would hurt, but also feel good to keep him fresh in her thoughts. Reminiscing over the good and not letting her mind continue to spiral into darker thoughts.

"His name is Alexios..."

CHAPTER 14
PATIENCE AND FUTILITY

TW: SA.

Mehdi struggled with the journey back down to the cove, both mentally and physically. Her heart ached, knowing he was not swimming in the water, or waiting for her in his tiny hut. She cursed Poseidon for taking him away and swore not to even speak to him, if he dared show his face. Huffing from exertion and anger, she stepped off the path and gazed at the waves crashing on the beach. As each crest endlessly rose and fell, she resolved to beseech her goddess a way to fight the King of the Ocean.

As the tide receded she scoured for scallops. In the shallows they laid on the ocean floor, their pink shells softly glistening and their mouths half open waiting to gather food. Here they had to sink deeper, remaining in wait, safe from danger. Walking along the water's edge she sought the tell-

tell sign of bubbles burping from the sand. Digging her toes deep into the earth she flicked the shell free. Exposed to light and air, it fluttered and clamored to bury itself again. Faster than the scallop, she scooped it and the surrounding sand up and clutched it in her palm. The scallop snapped shut, as she rinsed it and put it in her bag.

Her braid worked its way loose, as her hair danced in the wind snapping her in the face. The netted bag slung over her shoulder was laden, but she wanted one last shell. It almost got away when her toe flicked it into the edge of a wave. It flicked and spit at her, but failed to escape. Smiling, she lifted her prize toward the heavens and shouted victorious. "Ha!"

Streaks of pinks and blues scrawled across the sky, reminding her of Alexios song about the sailor and his love. Her joyful victory disappeared, enveloped by the sadness of loss. She slumped into the beachy shore, wallowing in the memory and sorrow. Hot tears stung her eyes, and plopped into the sand below. The water rushed inland swooping them away.

After a few deep breaths, she exhaled and said, "Pink with long orange streaks. The top of the clouds are brilliant white and deep purple on the bottom." Her heart lifted a little. and she smiled.

Her smile faded as she saw the silhouette of a man approach. Wet, covered in mud and falling into a sour mood, Mehdi stood to leave. She ignored him, as she cleaned off her hands.

He tsked. "You are dirty. Perhaps you can take a swim, wash away the sand?"

She grimaced but did not make eye contact. "No, thank you. I am avoiding the water presently."

"Shame, it is quite beautiful today."

"I will be fine. It is just sand." Mehdi turned and walked away.

He followed, catching up to walk beside her and asked, "Where are you off to?"

"The temple," she replied.

"For?"

"What else? To make an offer."

"To Poseidon?" he asked with glee.

She looked at him, stunned at his audacity. "No...Athena."

"And what do you ask of her?"

"Patience."

"Patience?"

"Yes," she said through gritted teeth.

"Patience for what?"

She stopped, her hand curling tight around the bag. "Against men like you?"

"Men like me?" he stammered. "What have I done?"

"Done?!" She gawked at him incredulously. "You ask me that?"

"Why? Because I would like to know you better?"

"Did you even ask if I wish to know you?"

"No, but..."

"Did you introduce yourself?"

"No."

"Did you ask if I needed help? Or merely start helping?"

"You were muddy, and the water was right there."

"You were inserting yourself into my life, because what? You found me pretty?"

"Well, yes," he replied with obvious admiration.

She scoffed and quickened her pace.

Matching her step, he kept the distance between them small. "I came to see you."

Recollecting Perseus's warnings her anger faded, as fear knotted her stomach. She could not stop the waiver in her voice. "Perhaps you can meet me later."

"But we are both here."

Mehdi looked over her shoulder. Just over the hill, the lights of the temple shimmered. Trying to widen the gap between them, she asked, "Why me?"

"Your beauty," he cooed.

Mehdi rolled her eyes.

"The legend of your beauty has crossed mountains and seas. Skin smooth as a pearl, hair long and so dark you could get lost in it and eyes..." He moved closer, his voice dropping low, "that pierce the soul."

Sensing imminent danger, she cautiously nodded and stepped back. Her foot slipped causing her to stumble and fall against a tree.

Seizing the opportunity, he pressed up against her, pinning her between him and the trunk. His breath quickened with anticipation, as licked his lips and drew his hand toward her face.

"I am a Daughter of Athena," she beseeched. "My duty is to her and no other gods."

His hand entwined in her hair. "That is fine." She cringed as his lips ran across her neck. "She isn't here."

Grabbing her face, his mouth groping for hers. She fought his kiss, smelling his sweet sticky breath and spat at him.

He growled at her, furious, and again tried to kiss her.

Mehdi struggled under his great strength, but her hand, still clutching the bag of scallops swung at his head with all her strength. When his hold loosened, she ran.

The path became dangerous under the darkening sky. Tears streaked her face, and rocks tore open wounds on her hands and legs, as she stumbled and pushed her way towards the temple. Without looking over her shoulder, she knew he was behind her.

Her body slammed against the temple doors, but she fell back to pull it open. Scrambling with the latching, she barreled inside and shut it behind her. Reaching up, she dropped down the heavy board, locking him out.

Sliding to the ground, she took safety within the sacred walls. If the door did not keep him back, the wrath of Athena would. He would not dare desecrate Athena's temple.

Her body shook as she let go of the bag and walked over to the altar to give thanks. The serene silence of the chapel stilled her heart and her breath steadied until a great explosion hit her in the back. Her body flew toward the feet of Athena, throwing her into the raised stone.

A sickening crack echoed off the walls as searing pain shot through her body. The explosion forced shards of wood to rain down around her and embedded in her skin. Trembling from pain she turned back toward the entrance and saw a massive horse standing in the doorframe.

Light sparked from its hooves and the earth shook with each clop as he walked towards her.

Frozen in fear and breathing heavily from intense pain, she scampered backward, but the statue stopped her escape.

The horse's head lowered and exhaled hotly onto her face. All around her a voice bellowed. "You cannot deny me and what I want."

As the horse transformed back into human form, Mehdi croaked, "Please, don't. This is the House of Athena. I am a daughter of Athena. Would you anger the Goddess of War?"

He grinned, grabbing her legs and pulling her closer. "She'll forgive me. She always does."

The ground scraped her flesh as her chiton to rode up to her waist. She could see his unbridled lust and understood why everyone told her to run.

Refusing to give up without a fight, Mehdi kicked herself free and pushed off the ground. Coughing blood, she stumbled toward the spears hanging on the wall.

Rushing with godly speed, he slammed her hard against the stones. Her hand clenched a spear but couldn't break free of his grasp. Assuming his reason to be in male form was to enjoy pleasure, he could also suffer pain, she kneed him in the groin.

He roared out and the walls shook.

Sweeping to the left, she twisted the spear in her hand and thrust it into his side.

He growled, wrenching and snapping the spear in half, and then lunged at her.

She blocked his first strike with the broken half of the spear, but he was too fast.

His second blow knocked her into the wall, cracking her head against the stone again, blurring her vision.

His hands grabbed her and slowly slid her up the wall. "I tried wooing you, but you refused me," he said, pinning her hands, as she fought to hit him. "I tried being nice, but you ignored me."

Mehdi heard fabric ripping and his body pushing into her, but injuries muddled any clarity of what he was doing.

"I watched you day after day diving into my waters giving me no thanks for the gifts I gave you."

Her body lurched up and down as sharp spikes of pain shot through her body.

"Then you chose someone else! A mortal. The audacity to fuck him in my sea, when you could have had a God."

Mehdi screamed and whimpered, her flesh tearing and her legs going numb from the unbearable pain. "Please stop," she begged.

He shut her mouth with his and growled when she bit his lip. Poseidon thrashed her body against the wall again and grunted, "Not until I am finished with you. This could have been enjoyable, but you made your choice."

"Athena, please..." Mehdi whimpered.

Laughing at her prayer, he moaned with completion.

His pleasure sickened her.

Lust slaked; he stepped away letting her body crash to the floor.

Broken, unable to move, and vision still blurred, she watched his hazy figure walk to the altar and take a bottle left as an offering. Drinking deeply from wine not meant for him, he expelled another satisfying sigh.

Glancing toward the entrance, he chuckled.

Craning her head in the same direction, blurry priestesses bearing spears and bows rushed into the temple. They charged the invader but lost their footing when the earth shook and rumbled beneath their feet.

Laughing at their angry faces, his amusement ended when two of the priestesses transformed into giant snake women and slithered towards him.

Too foggy to comprehend who just transformed, Mehdi gaped at their terrifying visages in awe.

"Sisters!" he boomed. "Is this where you've been hiding? I should have known." He blocked their blows with ease. Summoning a trident from the weapons on the wall, he fought back. "What brings you to this pithy island? Are you here to protect her? She is special, but as you can see, I've decided I want her." He glanced at Mehdi with malevolent glee. "And I will have her again."

This infuriated the sisters, spurring them to attack. They violently thrashed at him working around the room until they were between him and Mehdi.

"You failed long ago to defeat me," Poseidon taunted them. "What makes you think you can now?"

"Perhaps I can help," boomed a female voice.

A giant hand struck Poseidon and knocked him into a pillar.

Athena's statue stepped off the altar and picked him up.

The mortals stood in astonishment at the feet of the giant, golden Athena gripping an amused Poseidon in her grasp. Her ceremonial pala fell away and her eyes glowed, exuding the fury that rumbled in her voice, "You dare desecrate my temple. My daughter!"

"Niece," he cooed, underwhelmed by the goddess shaking him like a ragdoll. "We should talk."

His body grew in size and stature, but before anyone could react to two deities fighting, the golden Athena vanished with the Poseidon still in her clutches.

CHAPTER 15
BLOOD TO STONE

Once the earth no longer shook, the priestesses rushed to Mehdi's crumpled form, sobbing and barely able to move.

Stheno and Euryale returned to their natural forms and with few words, picked her up and carried her to a bed.

Mehdi remained silent as they picked wood and rock out of her flesh. Only a whimper passed her lips, when they wrapped gauze around her broken ribs.

Basin after basin was taken away with blood-soaked rags.

She stared off into space barely aware of anything.

At some point both Stheno and Euryale tried speaking to her, but she did not respond. They brought a bowl to her lips and helped her drink. It was bitter and she coughed it up.

"Drink, Mehdi," Stheno encouraged, "It's Lover's Heart."

Mehdi choked down the liquid wondering if it could stop the lust of a god.

Myra and Tana washed her hair and dressed her in new robes, then laid her gently down into a clean bed.

She lay there in the cold dark, as the events involuntarily replayed over and over in her head. Time passed, but she did not notice.

Around her, the infirmary filled with people. Her mind was too addled to understand why, but as the beds filled, she needed to be elsewhere. Her legs barely held her up as she rose, tripping and stumbling back to the temple. Back to the altar.

The room showed no signs of disruption except for the missing door. Priestesses had come and gone, cleaning and cleansing the room and new offerings lay at the vacant stone where Athena's statue had once stood.

Seeing the empty space, where the effigy of her goddess once was, Mehdi collapsed to her knees and wept. Her weeping turned to sobs, and her sobs turned to unabated wails.

The grief was too much. She thought of Alexios and their last moments, his gentle, exhilarating touch, tarnished and marred by Poseidon's violent grip and bone chilling grunts.

How could anyone touch me again, without the violent memories of Poseidon's attack plaguing my mind? When will I have to stop fighting off men? Is there somewhere I go anywhere without some man wanting me? She thought about Alcibiades and all the suitors that tried to gain her favor, and the last man. No, not a man. *Now, I have to fight off gods*? He was so powerful. How could she fight against him? *When will it stop*?

Guttural moans of anguish gushed from her mouth, as she curled into a ball confident her sorrow would have no end.

A warm gentle hand fell upon her head and stroked her hair. She flinched and turned, expecting Stheno, but found the face of her goddess smiling down at her. "I am sorry, my child," the goddess spoke. "That should have never happened."

"Why not?" Mehdi sobbed. "I have known nothing but men like him my whole life. I'm sorry I couldn't fight him off. I even lost the girdle. Is that why you didn't protect me?"

Athena drew Mehdi into her arms, "No, no, no. I was shielded from his actions. You were brave and fought honorably in an unfair battle. You were wise to seek solace here. I could then see what was happening. I am sorry I was too late."

Mehdi bawled, overwhelmed by Athena's comfort. She tried to sit up, but stabbing pain shot across her stomach causing her to double over.

Athena pressed her hand to Mehdi's stomach and the pain stopped.

"I still lost the girdle." Mehdi choked.

"Was it lost or stolen?"

Mehdi thought for a moment. "The eel..."

"Sent to watch and lure you to him. The girdle saved your life."

She nodded.

Athena stroked her hair again. “He’s been obsessed with you for some time. I’m sorry I didn’t notice or calculate the level of his desire.”

“Why me?”

“Your beauty?” she mused. “Perhaps something more.”

“My beauty,” she spat, anger replacing anguish. “I wish I was rid of it. It has never served me well.” She clenched her fists. “All it does is draw lust and hate.”

Athena carefully soothed the young battered woman. “Do you still wish to serve me?”

Mehdi nodded. “I do wish to serve you, but I don’t know if I can endure it.”

“Endure what?”

“My beauty.”

“Beauty is a gift,” Athena replied.

“It is a curse.” She fumed, “To never know if I am loved for my body. My lips, my skin, my hair... I am more. It is why I chose to worship you. You are strong and wise. You stand an equal among the other gods, as I wish I could stand among men but no,” she sniffled, “the only man that saw me and not my beauty is likely dead. No...” she mournfully sighed, “my beauty is all they see.”

“If I could change that, what do you ask?”

The idea inspired her, as she gushed her long thought desire. “I no longer wish to be beautiful. Nothing good has come from it.”

Stheno and Euryale cautiously entered the room observing Mehdi cupped in the lap of Athena.

Mehdi looked over at the sisters. "Make me like them."

"Them?"

"Yes, I saw your true form," she said to the sisters. "No man would dare touch me again if I looked like that and if they did, I would be strong enough to fight them off."

Athena frowned.

"Do you think we are hideous?" Stheno asked.

"No," she said with reverent awe. "I think you are terrifying, and I want that same power. If a man even attempts to gaze upon me, I want the power to stop his heart and turn his blood to stone."

The three exchanged glances and conversed silently, before nodding in agreement.

Athena spoke, as she brushed away Mehdi's tears. "It appears fate has revealed itself and I will grant your request. However, you, Priestess of Athena, have people waiting for you to lead them in mourning."

"Mourning?" she asked, confused.

Athena looked at the sisters, "She does not know?"

Stheno shook her head.

"Know what?" Mehdi asked.

Euryale sighed. "When Poseidon attacked you and shook the earth...he caused a tidal wave."

"What?!" Mehdi croaked.

"The town was flooded."

"The infirmary," Mehdi blurted, recalling the full beds. "How many were injured, are any lost or...dead?"

Stheno's face wrenched in sorrow. "Yes, there are many missing and others confirmed dead."

Mehdi covered her mouth in horror, admonishing her selfishness. As she wallowed in self-pity a tidal wave struck the island leaving wreckage and carnage in its wake. Damage of her doing. Fearful, she entreated, "Danae, Perseus? Are they okay?"

Euryale swallowed hard. "Yes, but Dictes is missing."

Relief washed over her to know they were safe, but she saw no reason for the honor. She tried to sit up again. "Why am I leading them? I am the cause of this."

Athena's fingers delicately brushed Mehdi's face. "Because I have chosen you. You know their suffering and more. Represent me. Show them Athena mourns with them. Afterwards, the sisters will show you the answer you seek and then you can be my wrath."

CHAPTER 16

BATTLE SCARS AND TWO COINS FOR CHARON

Mehdi stared into the polished mirror. Adorned in the full regalia of an Athenian priestess, Mehdi tugged at her himation strategically draped to display her bruises. The vestments empowered her, but her wounds showed her weakness.

"Those are battle scars," Stheno's voice cut through Mehdi's thoughts.

She turned to find both sisters watching her.

"Battle scars?" she asked, grazing a hand over her bruised wrists.

Stheno nodded. "Would you look at them with such shame if you had gotten them on the battlefield?"

"She would not. I remember her first scar. She still wears it proudly." Euryale snorted, brushing her hand over the fine line on Mehdi's arm.

Gripping her bicep, she rolled it outward to examine the

scar on the inside of her arm in the crease of her armpit. "I won my first skirmish. Of course, I am proud of it."

"Then why are you not proud of these?" Stheno motioned at the mirror.

Mehdi looked back at her image scanning the purple splotches, and bandaged gashes in her flesh. "Because I lost."

"But you lived." The sisters hugged her from each side, as Stheno fixed a curl. "We learn as much from our losses as we do our wins. I taught you that long ago."

Mehdi agreed but looked away from her visage as her throat clenched and her chest panged with failure.

"Come," Stheno encouraged. "The city awaits."

They met up with the other priestesses and began the journey down the hill. The funeral procession would end at the burial grounds, but it started at the beach. Mehdi worried her fatigued body would not make it back up.

Tana and Myra swooped to Mehdi's side, looping their arms around hers, providing support. Surprised they did not ask her about her injuries, then she remembered them at her bedside, taking away the bloody rags and soothing her with gentle words.

Myra lightly squeezed her arm. "We have something for you."

Mehdi looked between them in confusion.

Tana produced a boat, woven out of grass and inside lay scallops and two coins.

Baffled, she stared at the funerary gift, then back to them.

"For Alexios," Myra replied, "They are listing him

among the dead and," she gulped hard, "we found your offering in the temple, so we thought..."

"We thought," Tana continued, "that if this was your special connection...if he is dead, the boat could find him, and he would know it is from you."

Mehdi swallowed hard, overwhelmed by their kindness, but also trembled at the terrible thought that Alexios was dead. If Poseidon wanted her, why would he let Alexios live? Maybe that is why he never came back.

She choked on her tears and took the boat. "Thank you."

As they approached the main market, a trail Mehdi avoided for over two years, her worries of everyone staring at her reemerged. Despite being the victim and Athena's assurances, she feared their accusations and judgment for invoking Poseidon's anger. Was she in the wrong for refusing him? Any that did stare at her, dipped their heads in reverence, eyes darting about looking for danger. Her beauty once again condoned her as an outsider.

As she ventured past the village, the shoreline came into view, stirring concerns for Perseus and Danae. Excusing herself, she broke apart from the procession and limped down the ravaged path to their home. Or she tried. The shoreline, contorted and reshaped by Poseidon's anger, was no longer recognizable. Nothing in the same place and obscured by flotsam and jetsam, she used the deeply embedded jutting rocks as a guide, as she stumbled over a dune and gazed in horror.

One wall of Danae's home stood, and all of their belongings lay strewn and scattered about.

Bent over, Perseus picked through the remains. Scrambling over the debris, she called out. "Perseus!"

His head perked up at her voice. Dropping the random keepsake in his hand, he rushed to her.

As his strong arms embraced her, Mehdi burst into tears.

Perseus stroked her hair and cooed. "I'm okay. Mother is okay."

"I'm so sorry. I'm so sorry," she repeated.

"It is not your fault," Perseus assured her.

She lifted her head from his shoulder, "But it is," shaking her head violently, she asserted. "I tried to run away as promised, but he caught me and...and," she buried her face into his shoulder again, sobbing, "Perseus, I am so sorry."

His fingers stiffened, flinching away as they brushed across her gashes and bruises and sorted out her meaning amidst the choking sobs. Another wave of shame and failure washed over her, but then his body softened and curled her tight in his arms.

"Mehdi, you have nothing to be sorry for. Not then. Not now."

The dam broke again, and her tears soaked his chiton. He held her, not letting go, even when her knees weakened, holding her up and letting her bawl. Mehdi's tears eventually ceased. Gulping in a few fortifying breaths, she lifted her head to gaze at her friend.

A jumble of emotions fumbled across his face; anger, sadness, love. All hiding behind a mask of offered strength.

Brushing away her tears, he straightened her gold diadem of woven olive branches and owl wings and put out his hand. "Come with me, I found something that is yours."

She swallowed unsure how long he let her cry and eeked out, "We should get back. I know they are waiting on me."

"It won't take long." Holding her hand, they stumbled over debris and headed back to where he was when she saw him. Bending down he fetched a silvery object out of the sand.

It was her girdle.

Mehdi clasped her mouth.

The girdle wasted no time, flitting to life and wrapping around her waist.

Perseus chuckled. "I think it missed you."

Mehdi coughed a laugh and wiped her nose, "Can we leave, before I start crying again."

HEADING the procession to the burial grounds, Mehdi focused on keeping her pace strong and steady. Professional mourners wailed in her ears and bodies clung close, threatening to tip her over. Perseus joined Danae at the front of the city mourners as Mehdi led them all up the hill.

Glancing here and there, wondering if onlookers gazed at her with sadness of loss, or hate.

Body aching, legs weak, grief immense, each step towards the empty grave embedded guilt deep in her soul.

Reaching the tomb, she knelt and held out her offering, but it did not seem complete. Setting it down, she retrieved her dagger and sliced a lock of her hair from the nape of her neck. As the coil cascaded into the tiny boat, she knew that if the scallops were not clue enough, then her hair would be.

Her hands trembled as she lowered the offering into the grave and for a moment she wondered if he could still be alive, and if not; could he see her from the afterlife?

Upon standing, pain shot through her stomach again, but she hid it, bracing on the altar and using it to rise to her feet. Moving to the side, others stepped forward to leave their gifts.

As the tomb filled with gifts and coins, she attempted to slip anonymously into the crowd, but came eye to eye with Alcibiades and his new wife.

She was young, pretty, and clearly meek. The most significant details that caught Mehdi's eye were the bruises around the girl's wrists. They matched her own.

Anger surged within her as she grabbed Alcibiades by the throat and lifted him into the air. Stunned by her strength, he clawed at her hand and wriggled violently trying to get free.

Seething with anger, Mehdi glared at the girl. "Did he hurt you?"

The woman stumbled backward terrified by the sudden violence.

"Did he hurt you?" Mehdi demanded; barely aware she was strangling Alcibiades.

The girl backed into the crowd, disappearing from

Mehdi's sight. Turning back to Alcibiades' deep crimson face, she realized what she was doing and released him.

He crumpled to the ground, coughing and choking.

Shocked by her own actions, she stumbled backward. Stheno and Euryale came to her side, and drew her away from the disgruntled mob.

CHAPTER 17
THE DEATH MASK

Inside the temple, Mehdi paced back and forth, "Bruises. There were bruises on her wrists."

"I understand that, but you can't just attack him in public," Stheno pleaded.

"Why not? Better that, than in some secluded place where no one sees like he did to me, or he's obviously doing to her. How often does this happen? Do men just hurt women as they please?" She stopped and looked at Stheno and Euryale, "It's not just me, is it?"

The sisters looked at each other, then back to her, and said in unison, "No."

She stared at them for a long time with a stunned expression. Compiling realization formed, she was not alone. Other women suffered as she did. How many? How often? And why was she so self-centered to believe that she alone bore this affliction? A resolution resolved into her demeanor as she decided. "We have to do something."

"Well..." Euryale stated and looked at Stheno as she scratched the back of her head, "That could be the purpose."

"Perhaps Athena feels it is time to go on the offensive," Stheno agreed.

"The purpose of what?" Mehdi asked.

Stheno took in a deep breath. "The mask."

"The mask?"

Stheno nodded. "You asked Athena for the power to turn men to stone. Well...there's this mask."

"Like the girdle!"

"In a way..."

"It is a powerful object," Stheno warned. "It should be used with caution."

"It turns men to stone, but why?"

"It can turn anything to stone, looking straight into their eyes and judging the soul."

"Where is it?"

"Here."

"I want to see it."

The sisters looked at each other with apprehension, then Stheno walked over and pulled out a carved stone box. She pried the lid open with ease and inside lay a plaster mask.

Mehdi looked at its terrifying visage; bulging eyes, a tongue lagging out of a tusked mouth and what looked like wild curly hair, much like her own, was not hair but snakes.

Mehdi took a deep breath, her finger trailing across the tendrils, "The first man who touched me did before I lost my first tooth. He was kind, and gentle, and asked me if I liked it." Her voice shook softly, "I would say yes, and he would keep rubbing me. And it felt...nice." Inhaling deeply her breath came out in a soft shutter. "I didn't know it was wrong until I asked my father to touch me in the same way. Mortified by my request, he didn't say anything and his friend never came to the house again." She gazed at them, baffled. "Was it even about my beauty then? I was a child, but all my life people stared at me. At first, I didn't know why. For a long time, I even thought I was ugly."

The women shared a small bittersweet chuckle.

"But it didn't matter. No matter where I go, or where I hide, the lust of man is there." She lifted the mask out of the box. "And now I know it isn't just me who suffers. I'm not alone and that...that is worse." The mask's power pulsated in her hands, emanating an immense desire to put it on.

Stheno stayed her hand. "It is powerful. If you didn't have the humors of a god in you I don't think you could wear it and you should limit your time using it."

"Humors?" Mehdi asked.

Euryale bit her lip trying to find the right words. "You are not simply human."

"What do you mean?"

Euryale continued, "You remember the story of Metis and I told you the snake had other work to do?"

Mehdi nodded. She adored that tapestry.

"Your mother came to us when she could not get pregnant. She had tried and failed. After promising that when you came of age you would serve Athena, we helped."

Mehdi shook her head, "I don't understand."

"You are the product of your mother and one of the last

vestiges of Metis. Just as she sacrificed a portion of herself to bring Athena into the world. She, as the snake, slithered into your mother's womb and made you."

Aghast, Mehdi stared at them both.

"I'm like Perseus?"

Stheno gave her a bemused grin. "Yes."

"And my father?"

"Is not your father by blood, though he never knew. You were still promised to the temple, but he saw no reason in honoring the promise when your mother died."

She chuckled. "Then I wandered in of my own accord."

They chuckled with her. "Your father was livid, but we assuaged him with what most men desire. Money and honor."

Mehdi sat with the mask in her lap, taking everything in. Her birth, the actions of her father, and the actions of most men. "Honor," she snorted. "Men don't want honor, they want accolades. My father got the accolade of his daughter being chosen to serve Athena. Men receive accolades for marrying women of value. That is not honor."

Turning the mask in her hand, she decided what to do with this gift. Before relenting to the compulsion to wear it, she hesitated. "Will it turn you two to stone?"

They shook their heads and Euryale said, "No, this is the death mask of our sister. That is all that is left of her."

"I have not had time to ask, but are you also gods?"

They nodded and Stheno spoke, "In a way. We are deities of the old world, before Zeus and the Olympians. Metis was our sister."

"Then why are you here? Why do you hide as mortals and follow Athena?"

Euryale replied sadly, "Because there was a war and we lost. We have little power now, stolen by the Olympians, so we live and stay near Athena, she is our niece after all, as are you."

Mehdi put the mask on her face and felt it adhere to her skin. Energy surged through her body as she grew taller, more substantial. Something slithered across her collarbone and the flesh of her back tore open, expanding behind her. Her long luxurious hair transformed into writhing snakes with tiny glistening eyes and mouths that snapped and hissed. Wings protruded from her back, and with a thought she caused them to flap and lift her off the ground. Her legs morphed into the body of a giant snake. Twisting her torso, her tail whipped and smacked the ground with powerful might.

Stheno and Euryale, standing now with her in their true forms, gazed in approval. Her bond with them deepened, permanently tying her to these two amazing women.

Removing the mask and returning to her natural form, she announced, "I want to go visit Alcibiades' wife."

MEHDI KNEW WHEN ALCIBIADES' wife would be alone. She knew this because he was a creature of habit. Morning breakfast in the market. Conversations over business in the

Plaza, afternoon meal, then the bathhouse with friends. He spent most of his day away from the house, so she had plenty of time between lunch and late dinner to meet.

Throwing a himation over her head and body to blend in with the other villagers milling about, Mehdi made her way to his home. Taking in a deep breath, she walked up the path to his abode thankful that it was not hers, but mournful for the woman that took her place.

As she approached an older woman swept the entryway.

"Hello," she said, "is the Mistress of the house home?"

The woman nodded and motioned for Mehdi to wait, as she walked inside.

Alcibiades's wife and a male attendant shadowed the entryway, when she saw Mehdi she jumped a few steps back.

"Please," Mehdi implored. "I mean you no harm. May we speak?"

The male attendant stood in front of her defensively, but Alcibiades' wife relented and tentatively waved for Mehdi to follow.

Guided into the inner atrium of the home consisting of stoned pathways and a beautiful array of plants and trees with sitting areas for eating and relaxation, she motioned Mehdi to sit on a bench in a small garden.

Alcibiades' wife sat across from her with the male attendant standing at her side. She glanced at her servant, "After your attack... Alcibiades' is concerned for my safety."

Mehdi immediately surmised the irony, as she confirmed the woman's bruising. "I am sorry I scared you. I...wasn't trying to hurt you."

"You attacked my husband!"

She grimly nodded. "I did, but it was because," she wrung the edge of her himation nervously. "It was because of your wrists."

The woman gaped, glancing down at her hands. "My wrists?"

Mehdi nodded. She looked at the male attendant and then back to her. "May we speak in private?"

The woman seemed unsure.

"It is something rarely discussed in front of men."

She nodded and politely asked her attendant to step away. Obeying his mistress, but following his orders, he remained in the atrium, out of earshot.

Leaning closer, she softly spoke, "He gave you those bruises, didn't he?"

"Who?" She asked, feigning ignorance.

Mehdi's voice intensified. "Alcibiades. He pins you down so you can't fight."

Clutching her wrists, she turned away revealing additional marks on her neck.

"He isn't gentle, is he? I know how terrible his temper is."

"It isn't so bad. You just need to know—"

"How to not make him angry?" Mehdi replied.

Whipping her head back, their eyes locked in the shared experience.

Clutching her hand, Mehdi insisted. "He shouldn't hurt you." Mehdi noticed the flush of youth gone, replaced by dark circles under her eyes and sadness in her soul. Recalling the night she stared out the hole in her thatched roof as her father sold her, she asked. "How old are you?"

"It is not yet my fourteenth summer."

Mehdi's hand curled into a fist certain Alcibiades did not wait long after she broke their betrothal. "You know who I am, yes?"

"Yes." She replied, "He speaks of you often. He makes me." Her hand shot to her mouth to stop her quivering lip.

"He makes you what?"

She stuttered a few times before choking out, "He calls out your name." Her personal fury manifesting, she hissed, "These bruises are your fault!"

"Mine?" Mehdi replied in shock.

Resent filled anger forced her honesty. "He holds me down and calls out your name. Cursing you, blaming you. I blame you too." Hot tears rolled down the woman's face and she spat at Mehdi's feet. "I pay for your freedom."

Mehdi shot to her feet. "I'm sorry. Please. I came here to help."

"How can you help?" she snapped.

"Please," Mehdi beseeched, drawing a scroll from her belt. "Let me help."

"How?"

"If you wish for him to be judged for what he has done to you, then put this on your door tonight."

Curious, the woman unfurled the scroll. It contained a drawing of the death mask. "What is this?"

"She will protect you."

"How?"

"Just... If you want her protection, put this on your door." Mehdi squeezed the woman's hand, her voice crackled with dammed tears. "I'm sorry he hurt you. Let's make it so he never does again."

~

THE MOON HUNG high in the sky when Mehdi and her sisters returned.

"Are you sure about this?" Euryale asked.

"Yes," Mehdi replied. "When it was just me, I could bear it, but," her certainty resolved. "No woman should suffer, because of men and I have the power to change that." Merging from the shadows, she extolled. "Look! The image is on the door. She is asking for help."

The sisters shifted into their snake forms; a visage more eel-like than snake and lifted her over the house wall.

Landing on the other side with practiced silence, she surveyed her surroundings. Using her knowledge, she stealthily slunk across the atrium to the room casting light into the darkness.

Alcibiades sat alone, sipping an evening drink. His brow glistened and his chiton was damp from sweat, indicating he had taken the girl again. The thought stoked the anger she needed to justify her actions. Pulling the mask out of her pouch, she stepped into the doorway, allowing the light to cast on her and her purpose.

He saw the shadow of her movement pan across the wall

and turned to look. His brow furrowed in confusion. "Mehdi, what are you doing here?"

"Judging you," she replied, her tone cold and seething.

"Me?" He snarled, rising from his seat. "For what? It is you who attacked me."

"For what you did to me." She jutted her chin to his bedroom. "For what you are doing to her and for any other woman you have harmed."

He let out a haughty laugh. "You caught me by surprise at the funeral. Don't think that will work again."

"Oh, I think this will be your last surprise." Holding her ground, the glimmer of a grin danced across her face before disappearing behind the mask.

Alcibiades rushed her, attempting to grapple her, but his jaw dropped in horror as her body shaped into the visage of her aunts.

He froze, arms outstretched, as the mask activated and paralyzed him. Unable to move, he cried out in pain as his flesh cracking and groaning solidified into stone.

The sound turned her stomach and she wanted to lurch, but Mehdi's mind learned the side effect of her powers was worse, as images of all his cruelty flashed before her eyes.

Horrified, she watched her assault from his eyes. As he threw her to the ground in the grotto and demanded to ruin her. Her mind reeled, as he raped and beat his wife over and over again. After every violent and spiteful act he committed played out in her head, her body gave in and crashed to the ground.

Heaving, she pried the mask from her face, returning to

her human form. All the atrocities he committed locked into her mind as she sobbed uncontrollably. Collecting herself, she stood and discovered Alcibiades' wife hovering in the other doorway mortified by the scene.

Mehdi studied the petrified Alcibiades, fingers grasping at nothing and nodded, satisfied. "I told you. He will never hurt you again." Slipping the mask back into her bag, she turned to leave.

Leaning against the doorframe for support, she stammered, "What do I tell people?"

She stared at the young widow and then glanced at Alcibiades. "That he was judged and paid for his crimes."

The girl trembled in fear, staring at the fury etched into his face.

Mehdi braced her arm and assured. "He can no longer hurt you, me, or anyone ever again. And no man shall as long as I have the power to help."

She exited through the front door and found her sisters waiting for her under a tree. Euryale clutched Stehno's hand anxious to know what happened.

Somber and still, Mehdi uttered, "It is done."

CHAPTER 18

THE RISE OF MEDUSA

News of Alcibiades' demise spread quickly. His wife claimed a monster had slipped into the house, attacking and turning him into stone, before fleeing. What remained a terrifying mystery among the men, became a secret hope among the women of the island when Alcibiades' wife spoke to other wives, telling the story of Medusa, the Protector.

Mehdi returned to her duties as priestess except for fishing, which hurt too much to do without Alexios and she worried that Poseidon would attack again.

She chose to join the harvest in Olive Grove. The trees were ripe, and the women of the village congregated there to gather, sort, and prepare the fruit for storage.

She lifted the forked stick in her hand and shook the branches showering herself and the netted ground with olives. A woman walked over and helped shake the tree. The olives thudded to the ground filling the air with a soft rumble.

Moving closer to Mehdi, the woman spoke. "I am told that you were the one that called The Medusa for Jacinda."

"Jacinda?" Mehdi asked.

"Alcibiades' wife."

"Oh," Mehdi said, ceasing in the rattling of branches. "Why do you ask?"

The woman hesitated then said, "My sister...her husband beats her."

Mehdi shook another branch listening to the olives pummel to the ground, the noise reminding her of when Poseidon made the earth shake. Her breath stilted as she gripped the handle tighter.

The woman's voice shook with worry. "She is pregnant, and I fear for the child."

She shook another branch vigorously, focusing on the falling fruit. Undeterred, the woman waited for her to respond.

Mehdi lowered the stick, and replied, "Tell me what he looks like and where to find him alone." The woman divulged the details, as they cleaned the net of fallen twigs and leaves, then they gathered it up and took the olives to their next destination.

As dusk fell, Mehdi headed for the road that the wife-beating husband took home. As described, there was a crook in the path where you could not see ahead. Sitting on the obscured side of the path hidden among the trees, she put on the mask, and waited. Curled in a spiral beneath her torso the tip of her tail flicked impatiently. Alerted by footsteps crunching up the road, she peered through the foliage to confirm it was the husband. Certain he matched the description, she stepped out of the trees, blocking the path.

He instantly stiffened seeing her horrifying visage. Mouth agape in surprise, arms raised in defense, but nothing stopped his fate.

Mehdi shuddered once again seeing a man's violence and atrocities. Tearing off the mask, she wrenched to the left and puked into the grass. Wiping her lips with shaking hands, she drew her symbol in the dirt at the statue's feet. Satisfied that her actions secured another woman's safety, she staggered away.

The next day she returned to the olive grove and went about her tasks, as the attack wagged on tongues of those around her. Two men turned to stone. Was it a monster? If so, what did it look like and where was it hiding?

She tried to calm her racing pulse as a wry smile tugged at her lips. Instead, she focused on the harvest. Twisting the wheel of the olive press with great vigor, the fruit groaned, and seeds cracked expressing vital essence into the basin below. Pungent vapors filled the mill, making bile to rise up her throat and forcing her to step away from the press. Outside, she gulped in fresh air and stretched her back, wincing lightly. The aches and pains from Poseidon's attack no longer bothered her, but the recurring nausea worried her.

The breeze gently washed across her face, carrying the salty air up her nose and a longing into her lungs. Sadness washed over her. She missed the sea but feared going near it. The thought of crashing waves brought both good and bad memories that swirled in her chest leaving an unending sadness.

Sighing, she tried to return to the press, but one whiff of the crushed olives made her sick. She excused herself, heading back to the temple.

Stheno met her on the path, calling out. “I was coming to find you.”

“Hello,” she replied, finding little energy to converse.

“You look pale. Are you well?”

Mehdi shook her head. “I keep getting nauseous.”

Stheno mothered her, checking her face, neck, and hands, examining for signs of illness. “You should rest. You are still healing.” Crooking her arm around Mehdi’s, she guided her back to the temple.

The two walked in silence, winding out of the grove along a well-tread path. The sun dappled light through the trees caressing Mehdi’s skin, but the chill in the air reminded her that summer was gone and fall fully entrenched.

Stheno brushed Mehdi’s arm warming her goosed flesh and asked, “Do you know anything about the man turned to stone while walking home?”

Mehdi shrugged. “Maybe, he shouldn’t have been walking alone.”

Stheno mulled over that phrase and the sarcasm that delivered it. “Is that your plan? Any man that you choose will suffer and die?”

“Why not? We’ve suffered long enough. Forced to

remain silent and take it. Perhaps, they need to feel what it's like."

"In my experience, men don't respond nicely when threatened."

She stepped ahead of Stheno and raised her arms. "Let them come."

Stheno frowned, "This will only lead to more suffering, Mehdi."

Mehdi grasped her mentor's hands. "But think of all it will free! And they were bad men. The world is safer."

"Do you feel safe?"

Mehdi scoffed. "This isn't for me." She swayed slightly feeling another wave of nausea.

Stheno braced Mehdi and examined her face again. "Saving others is for later. Bed. Now."

UNABLE TO LIE around waiting to heal, Mehdi took charge of the peplos being made for Athena's new statue. She, with help from the other priestess, pulled the loom from storage and set it up for the great undertaking.

Mehdi unraveled a skein of fine spun wool and laid it down the warp, fastening weights to the threads. They hung as taught as bow strings. The tradition was to weave Athena's role in the battle of Gods and Titans. But as Mehdi wove the shuttle vertically in and out of the warp she could already feel the muses tugging at her hands and knew this year's peplos would be different.

The job was not possible alone, so as expected, women from the village volunteered to help with the gift. Mehdi was beating up the weft of the first layers of the peplos when a woman entered to assist. As they wove in the intended pattern, the woman expelled the story of her husband's infidelity. While not illegal in the eyes of the law, it wounded the woman.

"He is not the man I wanted to marry, but as the eldest son, he had the right to choose me over his brother."

"You love his brother."

She drew in a hard sniffle. "Yes." Like Mehdi, and all other women of Seriphos, she had no say in choosing her husband. Her heart ached to be with the brother, but she was bound to an adulterous feck.

"Is he cruel?" Mehdi inquired.

"In that he does not hide his philandering, or his lack of affection for me."

As the woman told the story, Mehdi noticed they were weaving it into the cloth. The first panel was Zeus and his paramours. Going from one to another with no care of the destruction left in his wake. At the end of the panel was Hera, Goddess of Marriage, weeping in a chair. She wore the hair and clothes of the woman helping.

"And the brother? By law, you will be his if he chooses. Is that what you want?"

"It is what we both want, but he can't take action against

his brother, or the new marriage may be called into question. My husband has made sure of that."

"But a monster attack..." Mehdi suggested.

"Yes, If Medusa attacks. It can't be connected to him. That is how they see her, a violent beast. They do not see the lives she saves. But we do."

Mehdi stopped her actions and took the woman's hands into hers. "Put the symbol on your door and she will come."

The next day she finished the panel of Zeus, weaving the shuttle in and out and tugging the wefting thread taught, then wove the shuttle in and out in the other direction.

Euryale wandered in and pulled Mehdi's loosened hair back into a braid. Hair secured, she lifted the tamping stick and beat the thread into place. "Another man was turned to stone last night."

Mehdicontinued her task, shrugging. "I hear he was a rather unfaithful husband."

"I find most husbands are unfaithful." She surveyed the panel. "After all, they do not have a great role model."

"It is still adultery and if the wife were to do it she would be divorced or worse, killed for the same actions. Why shouldn't he face the same punishment?"

"I agree, but how many more statues will there be?"

Mehdi stepped back, lacing thread for the next panel, "How many women are abused, mistreated, and discarded? That many." Her fingers deftly pushed the shuttle with precision. "If they come to me, I am going to help."

"And when you get caught?" Euryale implored.

Mehdi jerked at the weft; eyes focused on her task. "Let them come and stare at the monster they made."

~

BEYOND AIDING the women of the Island, Mehdi had another secret that was beginning to show. Her wounds had healed, but her belly swelled. She realized this after the first month but had kept the revelation to herself. Being unwed and pregnant was unacceptable, but the father possibly being a god was dangerous to her and Seriphos.

A young woman approached her at the loom and by the bulge in her chiton Mehdi suspected she suffered the same affliction. They worked in silence as the girl struggled to speak.

Her lip quavered and her fingers trembled as she choked back a sob. "He promised me we'd marry. I was foolish and believed him."

"But you were with him by choice?" Mehdi inquired.

"I thought he loved me. He said he loved me," she spat.

"He knows about the child?"

"Yes." She began to weep. "He refuses to marry me."

"Why?"

"He's already arranged to marry a woman from a better house," she croaked.

"He was already betrothed, but he promised he would marry you?" Mehdi asked, struggling to understand the girl between heaves and rattling breaths.

The girl's head bobbed as she blew her nose into a rag.

Mehdi put down her tools and stroked the girl's arms, assuming the common scenario. "He persuaded you into conjugation, though he could not marry you."

She nodded again.

"Did you know?"

She shook her head.

"And now you are..."

The girl choked a bawling moan and dropped her face into her hands.

"But if he dies." Mehdi queried, "What about the child?" In her new position as protector, she learned to make sure that her actions would not lead to another's desolation.

"He rejected me," she answered with anger and spite. "He is of no consequence to me or my child's future."

WITH CONTINUED USE, Mehdi discovered the nuances of the mask's power, including the ability to transform into anything she chose. Slipping on the mask, she transformed into a giant snake, and slithered toward the false lover's house. The lump in her belly bulged the sides of the snake looking like a meal waiting to be digested rather than the anticipated child soon to enter the world.

Spying the sigil scrawled on the doorway and the noises coming from inside, she wound up a tree and peered into the home from above.

Inside the atrium, a family happily ate and conversed. She could see the patriarch, the matriarch, aunts, uncles, grandparents, children, and a couple. He matched the description down to the chiton embroidered by his secret paramour. The young man afforded kindness to his betrothed, but both remained civil and polite with little love or connection between them.

Patriarchy dominated the gathering as the men talked and enjoyed their repast, while the women catered to their needs. As the light in sconces guttered and the servants took away the last dishes, he stepped outside to relieve himself directly under her tree.

Moving along the branch, she lowered her form till her head hovered behind him. The tip of her forked tongue flicked out of the mask and tickled his ear.

Absently scratching the itch, he finished peeing and turned around, forcing him to face her.

All of his transgressions passed before her eyes, but the story differed from the one the young woman had told.

Yes, he was betrothed to another woman. Yes, he did not tell the girl, but it was because he was in love and did not want to be with his betrothed. Yes, he got the girl pregnant, but the girl did not tell him.

His story revealed his family forcing him to honor the agreement and the poor man's heart breaking as he could not be with the woman he genuinely loved. He was foolish to keep seeing her, but choosing between family honor and love was a terrible choice.

The young man stood paralyzed as his skin hardened

into smooth alabaster. A punishment for the evils of men, not the bad choices of the fool hearted.

Decision made, she shifted back to her original form, falling out of the tree in an ungraceful clump. The young man's body returned to normal, crumbling to the ground; unconscious, but not dead.

Sounds from the household started moving towards them.

Mehdi picked herself up, clutching the mask in one hand, and hurried away. Her heart pounded as she ran, but the night enveloped her before anyone could see,

THE NEXT DAY the young woman returned to the loom, upset and angry. "He isn't dead."

Medhi's fingers worked the shuttle through the hanging threads causing the stone weights to knock up against each other, tinkling softly.

She stomped her foot. "I said, he isn't dead."

"I know," Mehdi replied, tamping up the weave.

"Why?"

"He wasn't guilty."

"He lied to me!" she shouted, hands curling into her chiton and stomping her foot again.

Mehdi sighed. She made the decision not to kill him because he was not guilty of intentionally hurting her. "Yes, he lied, but not to hurt you."

“He betrayed me,” she croaked, anguished.

Mehdi stopped weaving and looked over her shoulder, “No more than he did to himself.”

The girl’s eyes darted in confusion.

Her heart ached for Alexios when she said, “He does love you. He just can’t be with you.”

The young woman choked back her tears. “But he...lied.”

Holding back her own tears, Mehdi turned and gathered the woman into her arms. “He didn’t want to hurt you, but he succumbed to his father’s demands. And,” she pushed them apart enough to look at the girl, “he doesn’t know about the baby.”

The girl looked away.

Mehdi pulled to her chest and stroked her hair. “A man shouldn’t die because he was stupid. I’m sorry he hurt you, but he’s a good man that made a hard decision.”

The girl sobbed into Mehdi’s shoulder, leaving a trail of tears and snot.

Her eyes drifted in the direction of the sea. “We can make bad choices. It doesn’t make us bad. Especially if we learn from it.”

CHAPTER 19

EMBRACING THE POWER WE HOLD

Mehdi sat under an olive tree stretching her bare feet out of the speckled shade into the sunlight. The days were getting warmer again, and the sun felt good. Eating an olive while watching her toes wriggle, she looked up when a shadow fell over her. "Hello." She said to Stheno warmly.

Stheno lowered herself next to Mehdi and took the offered cheese, "Feeling well?"

"A little tired."

"How is the peplos coming?"

"Beautifully," she said with a grin.

"I am told you have no lack of assistants."

She unconsciously rubbed her stomach. "Athena has given us a great gift. She deserves a worthy garment."

The two women leaned into each other and closed their eyes taking in the drowsy day.

Half-asleep, Stheno asked, "So, when are you going to tell me?"

Mehdi yawned. "Tell you what?"

"Your own gift from the gods. Well...a god in particular."

Mehdi took in a deep breath and let it out long and slow. Despite her best effort, hormonal induced tears welled up in her eyes. She brushed one away and said, "Once I accept it's a gift and not a curse."

Stheno pulled Mehdi into her arms and stroked her hair. "It's not a curse."

She sniffed. "Then a punishment."

"For what?"

"I don't know...being."

"Being?"

Mehdi pulled out of the embrace. "Being too pretty, too desirable, just...being."

"It wasn't your fault."

"Then why does it keep happening?" She sniffed. "Why can't I walk down a street in peace?" She pointed in the direction of the ocean, "I can't even go fishing without a god deciding to rape me! Tell me how it's not my fault?"

"Being who you are should not cause others to hurt you."

Mehdi scoffed. "Men die for kings because they were born in a certain place. Feuds among family houses never end. Men beat their wives if they refuse to obey. Simply being, seems to be a completely logical reason for someone to hurt you."

Stheno sighed. “You are right. I say it shouldn’t, but it does happen.” She stroked Mehdi’s hair again. “But we can fight back. Whether directly, or by choosing to be ourselves and not how others see us.”

Mehdi looked slightly confused.

Stheno continued, “Euryale and I...do you know where we come from?”

Mehdi shook her head, “The ocean. It is our home. It is where we were born, but we live on land because we chose not to be ruled by Poseidon. He is violent. He is cruel and he killed our sister, so we refused to live in his realm. Making that decision has made us his enemy, but helped us hold on to who we are.”

“He killed Metis? I thought Zeus did?”

Stheno nodded, “She escaped Zeus, but was weakened. Zeus sent Posiedon to finish the job. He would have killed us too, but Athena gave us refuge. We have served her since.”

“It’s so strange hearing that gods serve other gods.”

“Mortals serve other mortals.”

Mehdi’s head quirked. “I never thought of it like that.”

Stroking back Mehdi’s hair, she reflected. “There is so much happening in the world beyond these walls. Beyond this city. I wish you could see it.”

“Little chance of that.”

“Perhaps someday you will. For now, let us go to the market.” Stheno stood, but Mehdi hesitated.

“I don’t really think I should.” She touched her stomach.

Stheno smiled. "I think their response will surprise you."

The two women headed down to the market and a wave of memories washed over Mehdi. She remembered people staring, men ogling, and her insecurities in coping with it. Today people did stare, and men did look at her, but it was different. There was a reverence, an additional kindness that perplexed her.

"You are with child," Stheno reminded her. "And right now most are realizing whose child."

"But shouldn't that scare them? I know it scares me."

"Maybe, but they dare not harm you for fear of angering a god."

Mehdi felt slightly empowered.

Stheno patted her arm in assurance. "That's right. Use it."

MEHDI DID. She resumed her old morning task of fetching items from the market. As her belly swelled, the attitude of the people changed. They would part for her when she passed in a crowd. Offered her extra treats when she collected items from her list and a seat to rest if she became flushed.

She had not stopped weaving and watching over the creation of the peplos, or her visits to places that put up her sigil, but she enjoyed the trips to the market because there she could see the results of her actions.

Men were visibly scared of the gorgon that plagued the

city and would turn ashen if they saw the symbol on their threshold. They quickly learned the type of actions that summoned the terrifying creature and vowed to reform.

Mehdi noticed her sigil appearing in places she had never been. Affixed as a ward of protection denoting her influence growing beyond her actions. She was the monster that terrible men feared and she liked it.

Waddling through the market one morning, she noticed the table that Alcibiades used to sit at was empty. Remembering how he lounged there, his rotund belly stretched, as he sipped wine and watched her shop.

Sitting down in the spot, she claimed it as her own. Stretching out her belly, she exhaled taking in the moment of bliss, a little glimmer of peace washing over her.

"May I sit with you?" came the voice of Perseus.

Her eyes fluttered open and she smiled. "Of course. How are you?"

He nodded and sat.

"And Danae?"

He frowned slightly and then tried to hide it.

She touched his hand, "What is it?"

"My Uncle."

"The King? Are you still living there?"

He hesitated then sullenly nodded.

"What is wrong?"

"He wants to marry my mother."

She sat up straight, but the being inside her objected and kicked. She carefully leaned back again. "Your father is still missing?"

"Yes, it has been months. The King wants to declare him dead, but my mother does not. She has stalled him so far, but he grows impatient."

She snorted. "Impatient. Men!"

He nodded. "I would say not all men, but no, you are right, as a whole we are pretty deplorable."

Laughing, she withdrew a fig from the basket and took a bite. "Good thing that gorgon is keeping men in check."

Perseus eyed his friend, suspiciously. "Went after Alcibiades first, lucky you."

"Me?" She coyly asked, "He was no longer my problem."

"Accept you did attack him the day before."

Feigning distraction, she looked out into the market and mused. "She does attack abusers and he was an abuser. It's why I attacked him that day, though doing that in public... probably not my wisest moment."

"And lifting him off the ground. It was almost... godlike," he slyly replied.

She snorted and then leaned in close. "But I'm not the one with the blood of the gods running through my veins."

He leaned conspiratorially. "I'm not so sure."

"Well...maybe you are right, but no matter what blood runs through mine I would have always bested you."

"It is why I admire you," he approved. "Your will and determination are unbreakable."

Brushing away his compliment, she rubbed her belly. "Unfortunately, I am, like any other woman, just their plaything."

His demeanor changed. "So that rumor is true?"

Eating another fig, she focused on the people as they milled about relishing in their normal lives and affirmed his query.

He gently took her hand. “Mehdi...if you wish...like my father... I could.”

Gazing back at him, moved by his gesture, she smiled. “Perseus your kindness knows no bounds, does it?”

“The child needs a father and the gods, as I am proof of, never help rear their progeny.”

She cradled his face, considering his offer. She could, in a heartbeat, have a happy life with him.

They knew each other. Though their relationship never moved beyond familial, she saw no reason it could not. She saw it all. Quiet lives, demi-gods raising a demi-god. Perhaps it could be a happy ending, but something told her, pulled at her, that this peaceful path was not for them.

She sighed. “Part of me wants to say yes, but...”

“But?”

Glancing away, she sighed, “You and I both know this is not our fate.”

“Let us make our own fates.” He gently implored, “I already love you. Most marriages rarely have that to begin with. We can learn the rest.”

His argument was persuasive. “Perhaps...”

Jumping from his seat, he enthused, “A maybe, is a start. Let me obtain permission and I promise I will be the father the child needs.” He held her hand tightly for one last moment. “And the husband you deserve.”

Before she could say anything else he was bounding

down the street and out of sight. She weakly called after him, a bit dazed. *Did he just propose?* The idea no longer seemed abhorrent to her, especially this proposal which did not feel like a lifetime of oppression.

"Marry Perseus?" She didn't hate the idea, she almost liked it.

CHAPTER 20

THE MONSTER THEY MADE

Battling a flurry of thoughts and emotions Mehdi's eyes darted around and fell on an adolescent boy in a threadbare chiton. Lithe and tan from long hours in the sun, he hocked bundles of sticks to passing villagers. A man approached his small section of the market and the boy perked up offering the customer a stack. They conversed, but the patron did not seem interested in the offered bundles.

Mehdi sat up quickly when she saw the man stroke the boy's cheek affectionately and offer a large coin. The boy's eyes dimmed as he took the coin and went with him.

Her stomach twisted in anguish. He was so young and desperate. She had to do something, but what? Her feet were moving before she fully realized that she was following them.

They wound down an alleyway to a bathhouse. A men's only bathhouse, so she couldn't enter. Standing across from it, she sat down and contemplated what to do. More time than she liked passed when the boy finally exited. He was clean, but his skin was dull and his eyes downcast.

She approached and asked, "Are you okay?"

He looked up at her, shocked to be noticed. "Yes."

"Are you sure?" she insisted.

He studied her face, confused at her questions.

Perhaps it was the months of righting wrongs that emboldened her to directly ask, "Did that man rape you?"

He looked stunned but replied, "He paid."

"But you are so young."

"They like us young."

"Us too." She replied, relating to the young man's lack of status. "Would you do it if he didn't pay?"

The boy scoffed. "With him? No, but I need the money."

She reached into her coin purse. "This is for the rest of your wood, and from now on gather all you can, every day, take it to the temple. We will buy it." She put the coins in his hand and touched him on the shoulder. "Your body is not for others to use unless you choose it."

The boy eyed her strangely but took the coin.

"I mean it." She reinforced, "Take your wood to the temple and we will buy all of it."

He nodded and left.

Mehdi turned back to the bathhouse and stared at the ominous structure with billows of steam floating out the top. Underneath, stokers fed the fires that warmed the baths where men languished, relaxed, and participated in conjugal pursuits if they wished.

So focused on protecting women she forgot that men also prey on small boys. Grooming and raising them to accept the advances of their elders as a natural thing. Mehdi did not abhor the coupling of men but did not accept the act of molesting children.

Moving to the side of the building and obscuring herself from view, she removed the sack off her shoulder and drew out the mask. She weighed the dangers of coming out during daylight, but worried the man might leave and find another boy to molest.

Hands trembling, she slipped on the mask and formed her body into a serpent. Ensuring no one saw, she coiled her way up the side of the building and slunk inside.

Mehdi slithered among the top of the columns watching the men below move about in the warm baths below. Some men soaked in the water, letting the heat seep into their bones, while others got massages, and a few partook in more carnal pleasures.

Mehdi ignored the men consensually enjoying themselves, as she scoped the bathhouse for the man who had harmed the boy and anyone else taking advantage of others. Hanging on the edge of a private bath, head down on the stone surface with his eyes closed, he did hear her descent.

Months of wearing the mask and seeing a lifetime's worth of atrocities hardened her heart to horrifying acts, so with an eerie calm, she coiled herself down towards the molester. Submerging into the pool, she altered her form to the upper torso of a man and swam towards him.

Sliding her body behind him, she cooed, "So you like young boys?"

He turned his head to look at her, but she gently pushed his head down and rubbed up against him. Her other hand moved across his hip and around his groin.

He groaned in pleasure, "I seek pleasure in many forms."

"What is it about young boys that you like?"

"Their innocence, of course," he replied with no guilt.

He reached for her, but she grabbed him, forcefully pinning him against the edge. "Ah," she said, still rubbing his cock feeling it harden. "Do you like robbing them of that?"

Her actions hindered his ability to speak, so he moaned, "Not robbing, teaching. Like someone taught you. They taught you well."

"Oh yes, I was taught, and I have learned much. Would you like to know the most important thing I learned?" she replied.

"Yes," he grunted, ready to explode.

She gripped him hard and flung him around to face her. He cried out in pain and then screamed in horror upon seeing the mask's visage. "Consent."

He pushed at her masculine chest, but she held fast, feeling his body turn to stone. Mehdi, numb to the horrors playing across her mind, felt no remorse when she ripped his penis off and tossed it against the wall. She smiled with satisfaction as it shattered into a thousand shards.

His screams alerted others, who rushed to the private bath in alarm. Transforming back into her half-snake form and rose from the water. Using her mask's powers, she turned to stone anyone who was guilty of harming women or children. Cries of horror peeled through the bathhouse and out the door, as half-naked men fled in terror.

When the only men left were made of stone, Mehdi coiled her way back up the columns and onto the roof. There she stayed, recovering from the great effort until her clothes dried. Below she listened to a crowd gathering and wondered how to get down unseen. It was still day and a long wait til dark, but there was no easy way off the roof in her condition. She contemplated flying away, but never used her wings for flight and would be seen.

The town guard arrived to investigate and disperse the onlookers. Peering over the edge she could see the soldiers were moving inside giving her a chance to escape. Taking her moment, she snaked back down the wall and pulled off the mask. Glancing around again, she grabbed a piece of burnt wood and marked the building with her symbol. Waddling back towards the marketplace, she rubbed her belly and thought about how good the day turned out to be.

MEHDI and the other priestess were preparing for Panathnaia when Stheno and Euryale came in. Fear and concern hung on their faces.

"What is it?"

They ordered the other women from the room before speaking.

Stheno wrenched her hands. "We need to talk about what you did at the bathhouse."

Of its own volition, a smirk spread across Mehdi's face.

Stheno admonished. "The elders have demanded the head of the monster."

"Haven't they already sanctioned an order for that?"

Euryale added, "This is worse. They have ordered all the men of the city to force their women to tell them who the monster is. They know we know."

"No one has revealed me, yet. I protect them."

"They have threatened that if any house brandishes the symbol their women will be punished."

"What!"

Euryale nodded. "If anyone calls for you, they can be punished or even put to death by their husband."

"They can't do that."

"They can. You know that a husband can cast away or even kill a woman that has dishonored him. They see the women using the monster as a threat against them."

"They should. Why should men have the sole right to determine our fate? Why can't we defend ourselves?"

"We can as long as it doesn't threaten them."

"You know that makes no sense," Mehdi spat, placing the laurel on her head.

"But that is how it is."

Mehdi's eyes narrowed. "Not anymore."

Stheno demanded, "Mehdi, this must stop. You are no longer protecting them but putting us all in danger."

"We are always in danger. Every day, every breath, our

fates are determined by their whims, and we always will be until we say NO MORE."

"They will kill you!"

"Not if I am wearing the mask," she said with pride. "They can't get near me without turning to stone. And you two are gods, start acting like it. Man does not have to rule you." Pivoting away from her sisters, she picked up the peplos of Athena.

"What are you doing?" Stheno asked with a tremor to her voice.

Mehdi coolly replied, "I am going to present Athena with her gift. As is my honor."

Stheno and Euryale gaped as Mehdi walked out of the room to join the procession. As she exited the temple the other priestesses followed behind her trekking to the great statue of Athena; resurrected in her honor, after she defended the city from Poseidon.

Despite the tension and looming fears, throngs of people from all over Seriphos waited for the ceremony to begin. Cheers filled the air when Mehdi appeared with the peplos draped across her arms.

She carried the woven garment up the Parthenon and to the statue. At the feet of Athena, Mehdi unfolded the garment and handed the edges to the priestesses. They stepped to each end of the dais, stretching it taut and displaying the full length of the peplos for all to see its story.

Like the garments woven before, it depicted the history of the gods and Athena's role. This story, however, played out a little differently.

Hera bound in a faithless marriage powerless to stop a philandering husband. Persephone kidnapped and forced to live in the land of the dead, leaving the world barren half the year.

Aphrodite, forced into marrying Hephaestus because her beauty was too great.

And Athena, born out of Zeus' head after he ate his pregnant wife. She sprouted forth fully armed and ready to fight.

The violence and destruction of the male gods versus the strength and power of the female goddesses provided to the world.

Awe fell over the audience as a full understanding of the peplos sunk into their collective consciousness. Mehdi used this moment to draw the mask from its pouch and put it on. Her body shifted and grew into her winged snake-like form. Taking the peplos from the surprised priestesses, she flapped her wings and draped the gift around the statue.

Behind her, she heard people shouting and the unsheathing of swords. Laying the last bit across Athena's outraised arm, she turned her gaze onto the crowd.

The men rushing toward her froze in their tracks as granite filled their veins.

Today she was angry and did not bother to judge them. If they attacked and caught her wrath, she sealed their fate.

Slithering down the steps and through the parting audience Mehdi picked up a discarded sword and shield, felling any who crossed her path. Undeterred, she filled the road to the sea with fallen bodies and broken statues. Leaving only the wise who averted their gaze or ran away.

She traversed the rough path down to the sea and to the cove she had not seen in nine months. Unsure why she came here, she stopped and stared at Alexios' island. Was it to remember him or to call up Poseidon and see if she can turn a god to stone?

Euryale and Stheno broke from the path and onto the beach. Breathless, they rushed to Mehdi's side.

Stheno grasped her arm. "We must leave. They are coming!"

"No," Mehdi refuted, her voice absent of any feeling. Then months of anger roiled in her chest and burst forth as she cried out. "Poseidon!"

"What are you doing?" Euryale shrieked.

Shirking off their grasps and pleas, Mehdi slithered towards the water, "Poseidon! Face me."

The waves swelled and crashed against the shore with growing violence, creating the words. "What do you want, Child?"

"I am no child!" she shouted. "I am the consequence of your actions. Men die because of you."

"It matters not to me if men die."

"What does matter to you?" Mehdi needed to provoke him into human form. She thought about what she could say that would appeal to his selfishness. She knew one thing from her few encounters: he was possessive. "What about me? Or your child?"

A giant wave rose and smashed against her body, but she

did not flinch. As it bided, Poseidon stood before her. He wore the guise of Tavros, but older with a salt-and-peppered beard. He stood inches from her, his entire presence bearing down on her with crushing intensity. Placing his hands on her stomach, he smiled.

Infuriated, Mehdi struck his hands away and grabbed him by the throat. Holding his gaze, she activated the mask. But looking into a god's mind was not something mortals should do; even demi-gods.

As his flesh hardened under her grasp, her psyche fractured. Willing to lose her life to take his, she refused to look away.

Poseidon wished otherwise and fought against the mask's power. His limbs crackled as they broke free grabbing her by the shoulders and tossing her to the ground. He cried out in rage and pounded towards her but found Euryale and Stheno blocking his way.

Striking them away with little effort, he bared down on Mehdi. Ready to fight, she caught his gaze again, stalling his attack. The ground shook violently, and the sea rose into a giant wave ready to crush the women.

Mehdi cried out, barely able to handle the mind of Poseidon. His volatile rage was all-consuming, all his violence, the countless lives he had taken, she saw it all. In the middle of this cacophony was Alexios. She sobbed seeing him step off the tiny island into the sea, tears streaming down his face. He was alive but trapped in a cave. Poseidon had refused to let him go and now kept him prisoner, to suffer for daring to defy him.

Mehdi held onto the memory, seeking to learn more, but Poseidon broke free of the psychic bond, and his fist headed straight for her face. She blocked defensively, flinching when she heard his fist crash and release an echoing clang, but felt no blow.

Looking up, she saw the backside of a shield braced to the arm of a giant glowing Athena. The shield's brilliant reflection caused Mehdi to look away, but she heard Athena speak. "Twice you have attacked my charge and on my land."

"She attacked me," snapped Poseidon.

"With good reason. This fight didn't start today, but the day you raped her." She stepped fully between Mehdi and Poseidon pushing him back toward the sea. "You are a god. You are the greater being, start acting like it."

"And take what I wish? Agreed." Trident appearing in his hand, he cracked it against Athena's shield. The reverberation turned the sand beneath them into glass.

"She is not yours to take. You do not own her."

"Not yet, but those greater than her have succumbed to my will. Besides," he said, landing another strike blocked by the shield, "The child. It is mine."

"No!" Mehdi yelled, striking him in the thigh with her sword, "I have borne this, not you. And you shall have no control over me or my child."

Arrogantly, he stared down at Mehdi, allowing her gaze to catch his once again. His body stiffened. Pulling the sword out of his thigh, she aimed for his head, but before she could strike Athena took the advantage and thrust Poseidon back into the sea.

"No!" Mehdi yelled. "I could have killed him!"

Athena pulled her back, "No," she said firmly. "You would have only killed his avatar and died in the process." She watched the ocean to see if he was coming back, "Pick your battles wisely."

Mehdi tore off the mask and crumpled to the ground, screaming in anguish and anger.

Euryale and Stheno scooped Mehdi into their arms and looked up at Athena with confusion and fear.

"They are coming. What do we do?" Stheno asked.

Athena glanced at the pathway. "You need to leave."

"But where?"

Athena leaned down and touched Mehdi's belly. "To the island of your Grae sisters. They are the only ones that can help with the birth."

"An island?" Mehdi choked out between sniffles. "He will still surround me. Is there somewhere he cannot reach?"

Athena grinned. "It is an island above the sea not in it."

"Then how do we get there? We still must sail."

This time, Euryale smiled. "Not exactly."

Mehdi looked at her sisters. "I am too weak to fly."

Euryale brushed away Mehdi's tears. "Just hold on. I have you."

The sisters helped Mehdi to her feet.

Stheno nodded to Athena and said, "Thank you again for your protection."

"You all have served me well, but your battles are not done." Athena looked at Mehdi. "There are numerous ways to defeat someone rather than killing them. Do not lose hope."

Euryale opened her wings and coiled her tail tight underneath her. She pulled Mehdi and Stheno close and with sudden force shot into the air, blinking out of sight.

As they ascended Mehdi, the mob of villagers entered the beach, but stopped in awe observing Athena draped in Mehdi's peplos, before she disappeared in a flash of light.

CHAPTER 21

MYTHS IN THE MAKING

Exhausted, Mehdi's labor started soon after she arrived on the island. Met by three older women who seemed to have anticipated her arrival, they ushered her into a room prepped and waiting for a birth. Her stomach tightened, sending whipping pain across her back and down her legs. Struggling to stay aware and perform the simple act of breathing, the older women encouraged her to walk around.

She limped onto the connecting balcony to behold a breathtaking horizon laying before her. Carved out of the mountain, the building sat among jutting rocks and blended into the landscape. Blue sky hung above them and a sea of clouds encircled the island obscuring anything beneath.

Remembering Athena mentioning this island hung between water and sky, she wondered, "Are we floating?"

The three older women chuckled in unison creating a

sound like tinkling bells. "No," One replied, but she was unsure which.

"But you cannot get to the top of this island unless you can fly."

"Or, you know the path up as well as you know yourself."

Mehdi nodded, having little strength to do more. Her labor continued through the night but didn't progress. Mehdi spent the last 4 hours pushing and pushing but to no avail. Weak, and unable to eat or drink, she writhed in unbearable pain. Huddling in a corner, the three women discussed options with Stheno and Euryale.

Mehdi sensed their apprehension, but could barely think through the pain. Accustomed to listening to the women speak as one she didn't try to follow who was speaking when they approached.

"The child is too big."

"It can't come out on its own."

"We could cut you open."

"But then you could die."

Mehdi looked at Stheno with abject horror. "I don't want to die."

Euryale gripped Mehdi's hand. "We have an idea, but..."

Stheno grimaced. "The mask."

Mehdi looked at them in bewilderment.

"You've used it to shapeshift. Perhaps you can change your size so you are big enough."

"Like what?"

"Perhaps the Serpent form could work?"

"It would stretch," a Grae sister agreed.

"Okay," she tentatively agreed.

Stheno gave her the mask and Mehdi put it on. She willed her serpent form up her body and over her belly. Falling limp to her side, nature took its course as the snake-type vulva opened and the baby emerged. When a snout and hooves appeared, Mehdi bit her pillow and bawled in pain and horror. Stehno wrapped her arms around Mehdi in consolation as the Grae sisters helped bring forth her child, a horse with wings. It quickly stood and clattered about the room tumbling over its legs and wings. One of the Grae sisters worked to wipe the blood and fluid off the child.

"A horse," Mehdi bemoaned. "My baby is a horse."

"A horse with wings!" one of the Grae sisters said gleefully.

"We are not finished," another sister added.

Her body contracted, forcing her to push again, this time the small cry of an infant filled the room.

"A beautiful golden boy," a Grae sister cooed. Cleaning him up, she placed him in Mehdi's arms.

Embracing the baby, she touched his head, grasped his feet and sobbed with joy when his little hand gripped her finger. This was her child, the other was an abomination. Glancing again at the winged horse clopping about on wobbly legs, his blue roan coat triggered the memory of Poseidon's hot horse breath on her face and she shuddered.

MEHDI SAT in a meadow watching Pegasus prance about. His happy trots, and wistful ninnies invoked no motherly joy or connection. He was a reminder of who helped in his creation. Guilt panged in her chest for feeling that way, but there it stayed forever a reminder of his violent act. In her arms, she held the perfect child. Plump, and happily suckling. His voracious appetite challenged her body to keep up, but she did not mind. Lost in his tiny curls, wiggly toes, and that special little sound he made when catching his breath between gulps. She fooled herself into thinking Poseidon had nothing to do with this beautiful child.

Pegasus ran up to her and attempted to nuzzle, but she ignored him. He whinnied for attention but received no response. Disheartened by the lack of affection, he trotted off.

"Mehdi," Stheno spoke from behind.

Mehdi looked over her shoulder and raised her brow.

"It is your child."

She glanced at Pegasus, agreeing with Stheno's statement. She gave birth to Pegasus, meaning he was no less her child than Chrysaor. She made him and should love him. Conceding this truth did not resolve one issue. "I can't feed or hold him."

"Sure you can," Stheno encouraged. "With the mask."

"A horse?"

Stheno nodded. "Why not? You know you can change shape."

Mehdi stared at the foal desperately seeking attention

then back to Chrysaor asleep in a milk-induced stupor. Standing, she gingerly handed her son to Stheno.

Slipping on the mask, she focused on turning into a horse, but only half formed, becoming a winged centaur. Pegasus whinnied excitedly and pranced around her. Mehdi wobbled on her hooves, but her stance steadied. Pegasus darted and jumped as Mehdi trotted about, working to not step on him.

Reading his moves, she pranced and played with her son. Pegasus ran to and from her, nudging her to chase him. He took off and she followed. First on the ground gaining great speed, then both expanded their wings, taking flight. They flew in and out of the Cloud Sea, laughing and neighing with delight. When they landed, Pegasus nuzzled his mother. His soft fur stroked her torso and love fluttered in her chest. Wrapping her arms around him, she let him suckle from her breast. As her fingers stroked through his mane, sorrow lifted from her heart filling with the joy and peace of motherhood.

AS MEHDI NURTURED HER CHILDREN, she discovered herself healing. Not only physically, but mentally. The other women assisted in rearing and feeding, giving her time to relax and repose.

The Grae sisters offered patience and wisdom that they

freely shared with Mehdi. She admired their tenacity in overcoming the disabilities of old age.

Sipping a cup of tea, she watched them as they mashed a poultice and evaluated its consistency between toothless gums.

"Why must you do that?" Mehdi queried.

"How else are we to eat?" they replied.

"I also noticed you use a polished crystal to see."

They tittered amongst themselves. "We do but thanks to your children we are down to one."

Mehdi sat up slightly. "What?"

The old women giggled showering the room with tinkling peals of laughter. "Chrysaor was playing with one, and before we could react, he had hurled it so far it fell off the side of the mountain."

"And the other?"

"Cracked under Pegasus' foot."

"Oh no. I am so sorry. I can find the one that was thrown."

They shook their heads. "Don't get lost in the space between the clouds. It is dangerous and designed to confuse any who pierces it."

"So how do you leave this place?"

"We don't have to, but if you wish, your wings can guide you straight up or down. It's the winding paths that will drive you mad."

Chrysaor toddled in and Mehdi gasped at the sight of her month-old walking. A horse she understood, but Chrysaor was also growing exponentially.

"What is happening?" she asked, scooping him into her arms and undoing her chiton.

He hungrily latched on and she winced, when his new teeth bit at her nipple. Sensing his mother's pain, he relaxed his jaw and settled into long deep suckles.

"They have the blood of gods in them."

"God," Mehdi snipped.

"Gods," they replied as they continued to crush and mash their dinner.

"I forgot that there is a remnant of Metis in them, but it's knowing that Poseidon is, too."

"We cannot choose our parents, but as a parent, you can help them both grow strong and wise."

Mehdi's hands slipped causing Chrysaor to break his hold. He grunted and latched on again. She ran her finger over his brow and studied his features wondering what he would look like as a man. More importantly how he would act as a man.

They walked over and tapped Chrysaor's chin. He opened one eye and looked at the old women warily. Stroking his chin again, they made him reflexively break the latch and offered him some of the poultice. He sniffed it, then one of the sisters shoved the spoon in his mouth. He played around with the mash for a minute before swallowing then asked for more.

Mehdi watched the women coo over Chrysaor. As they fed the boy, they spoke, "Metis was a great goddess. Powerful enough to challenge the King of the Gods, before he was known as such. In fact, she was too powerful, so this god and his brothers fought her and the other older gods."

Mehdi remembered the tapestries at the temple. Metis chose to marry Zeus in the hope of an alliance but was eaten by the jealous god. She knew little of what happened to Metis before or after the birth of Athena because her story was not important to the patriarchy. It was also dangerous.

Like when Mehdi exposed the horrors of the male gods upon the female gods. Even in godhood, the women suffered. Mehdi wondered what Metis was like before Zeus and how such a powerful being kowtowed to a demonstrable god.

They nodded as if reading her thoughts. "In the end, she sacrificed herself in order for many of the older gods including her sisters Stheno and Euryale to be safe, but she was also cunning."

"Cunning?"

"She divided her power so when the new gods took on their roles they would not have too much. Some of her essence became Athena, while much spilled onto the earth slithering out into the world. And some of that slithered into you."

"I know that. That is why I can use the mask."

"But why stop there?" one asked.

"What do you mean?"

"You have Metis' same courage and cunning. Perhaps, you can find a way to finish what Metis started."

"Which was?"

"For women to no longer be subservient to men."

"But she lost."

"The battle, but the war is not over."

~

There was freedom in this place, especially when she flew with Pegasus in and out of the clouds. She felt at home in the sky, though she still longed for the sea. One day she ventured to fly below the cloud line. The barrier was thick and deep, but thinned into fine wispy tendrils that parted and revealed a beautiful landscape below.

The mountain jutted down, cutting here and there giving space for buildings. It broke violently into a valley scattered with jagged rocks making the entrance difficult. Mehdi heard a whinny from behind her and as Pegasus caught up with her.

Scanning the surface below, Mehdi spotted a grand open air temple in disrepair that seemed familiar. Guiding her son, they alighted on the ground and approached.

The opening was large, easily allowing her to enter in centaur form, inside was a long passage that ended in an altar and throne. It wasn't exactly a throne, but a chariot turned away from the altar so one could sit in it or turn around and stand to guide whatever beast could carry this massive vehicle.

Mehdi brushed her fingers across the rays of a breaking dawn.

A woman riding the chariot drawn by horses of fire

pulled the sun from the dark filling the world with light. The woman's hair resembled her own thick, wild, and full of curls that cascaded behind her ending in flickering red tips. She touched her own hair in awe. Something that she always associated with her love for the sun and sea seemed to have a greater meaning. She pranced to the other side and saw the chariot again flying over the seas, below mermaids leapt to greet her while sirens flew in a protective formation around her.

Pegasus let out a warning whinny drawing Mehdi's gaze to three women entering the temple.

"See, Calliope," said one of the women to another, "I said she would be here."

"Yes, Clio, as usual, you are correct."

"And so is the child!" proclaimed the third woman, Thalia. "Look at him. He's magnificent."

Pegasus' trepidation immediately melted away and he pranced up to the woman enjoying her cooing.

Mehdi was hesitant, shifting her hooves back and forth in uncertainty.

Calliope caught Mehdi's gaze and approached. "It is okay. You are safe. We know who you are."

Mehdi locked eyes with Calliope and pulled off her mask transforming back. "Who I am?" she asked.

Clio nodded. "You are more than just a girl from a nameless village. You are a Priestess of Athena and Medusa, protector of women."

Mehdi shook her head. "Surely, you are mistaken. I'm no one of importance."

"No one of importance?!" Clio declared. "You are the cherished one of Athena. You are the coveted one of Poseidon. You are the priestess who lifted the veil that hid man's cruelty toward those they called daughters and wives. You can see into the hearts of men and turn them to stone."

"How do you know all this?"

"It is my duty to know these things and to record them."

Mehdi felt uneasy and looked upward when she heard wings flapping in the sky. It was Stheno and Euryale. They landed next to her and then knowingly embraced Calliope and Clio.

Stheno turned to Mehdi, very concerned. "Why did you leave?"

"I don't know," Mehdi replied. "I wanted to see what was below."

"Where is Chrysaor?" Clio asked.

"With the sisters," Stehno assured.

Mehdi's gaze flitted between them, confused. "What is this place? Who are these people?"

"This was our home. Her home. It is a solace from men, both mortal and immortal."

Mehdi stared down at the mask still in her hand and stroked the snake-like tendrils, "I've dreamt of such a place.

"Well, here it is," said Calliope. "This land is hard to find and harder to enter. You can stay here if you wish or up in the clouds."

The tightness in her chest eased and she looked at Pegasus. "The Graes sisters' home is nice, but," she looked around, "I can see the sea from here."

"There are others who live here, do you wish to meet them?"

Mehdi agreed.

Calliope and the others guided her down stone stairs that wound down to the sea below. She hesitated, feeling a torn longing to be in the water and an unnerving sensation to protect herself from Him.

Clio placed a reassuring hand on her arm. "Just like the temple this place is protected."

Spires of rocks shot violently out of the water causing the incoming tide to thrash violently sending up sprays of water and filling the air with that delicious salty taste she missed. The crashing waves seem to take on a song that calmed her soul.

Taking in the scene, she noticed there were creatures sitting on the spires. They were winged women both old and young. The younger ones had feathers that glistened gold in the sun and they appeared to be the ones singing. The older ones stood watch with steely gazes and gray bodies that ended in silvery tips.

One of the older women noticed her arrival and lifted into the air. She was followed by a younger one and they landed on the cliff before Mehdi, dipping into a bow.

Mehdi gaped in awe at their majestic splaying of wings and drooped heads; stunning creatures to behold.

"Welcome," said the older one. Her voice was raspy with age but attaining great strength.

"We have sung about your arrival for so long," added the younger with a tantalizing voice that beckoned attention.

"Who are you?" Mehdi asked.

"We are the guardians."

Mehdi tipped her head forward seeking further explanation.

"We protect this island from those forbidden to come here."

"How?"

"When we are young," the younger one answered, "we are known as Sirens and we call to our sisters in the sea who bring the waters to the shore. With their help, we control who can enter or leave." She nodded to the older one, "When we are older, you call us Harpies and we take to the sky and bring down water to the land and sea below."

"Sisters of the sea?" Mehdi asked.

"The nereids, of course," answered Clio.

Pegasus, seeking attention, nuzzled under his mother's hand and she stroked his mane. The motion soothed both mother and child. "What is this place? Why do you protect it?"

"It is an Isle of Refuge."

The Harpy added, "A place created for those seeking solace from the horrors of men."

"Men? But you are all magical, some of you are even gods. Why hide from man?"

"Not just mortal men, but all men."

"Well," Clio quipped, "at least the ones we cannot trust."

"So who else lives here?"

"Perhaps we should go up to town."

The group, now flanked by harpy and siren, guided Mehdi back up another path and into a beautiful city carved into the side of the mountain. People moved about their daily lives tending small gardens, drawing water, mending clothes, and preparing food. Mehdi noted that they all seemed to be women both young and old and there was a peacefulness that radiated from it all. She immediately felt at home.

Despite Athena's temple always feeling safe it was like visiting the home of a friend. Here, here she felt grounded. The walls themselves seemed to respond warmly to her touch.

She smiled hearing Pegasus clatter up and down the stone paths and greet everyone.

The residents looked up from their daily tasks and beamed at their arrival. Mehdi was surrounded by warm hellos and welcomes. Some of the women reached out to touch her as if to make certain she was real. The reverence put her at unease, so she moved to create space between herself and the townspeople but remained polite.

Tables were wiped down and food was gathered as all the women ate and conversed, much in the manner the priestesses would in Athena's temple, but Mehdi realized that some of these women were more than just mortals.

Many had lived long lives, and seen harrowing battles, but still managed to smile and carry on with ease. The muses shared stories and when they stopped speaking their stories invoked others to talk and reminisce. Stheno and Euryale also seemed at greater ease among these women than they ever did in Seriphos. They laughed and touched each other affectionately, finding no need for reservation.

As they ate, an excited Pegasus clattered up to Mehdi and whinnied for his mother to come. She put down her cup and followed him to a section of the city that looked out over the sea and the setting sun. As the sky turned orange, she saw movement in the horizon draw closer. They were horses adorned with wings of flame.

She stepped back in awe reaching out to protect Pegasus, but he was already in the air and flew around them as they approached the cliff and landed with thunderous clattering. Their wings disappeared with the sunlight allowing Mehdi to approach. Without hesitation, she stroked their beautiful manes and marveled at their fiery hues.

They did not flinch at her approach, completely at ease with her presence. "Hello there."

Pegasus pranced alongside and happily romped with the herd. The mares responded kindly to him with gentle nuzzles and allowed him to be among them.

Stroking one, she curiously asked, "What are you?"

"Fire Mares," said the Harpy.

"Fire Mares?"

The woman confirmed. "They drew the chariot that sits in the temple. Once long ago, they helped bring light to the sky."

"Once?"

"That is no longer their duty. I believe it is Apollo?"

Mehdi nodded. "Yes, it is he who carries the sun across the sky."

The woman stroked one of the mares. "He apparently doesn't need a chariot and horses." She patted the horse's neck, "Too bad. It was a beautiful sight."

"You've seen it?"

"Yes... long ago," she replied, but did not elaborate. Falling into a recollective silence, she guided the horses back to the stable.

Mehdi returned to the dinner, as more of the sirens and harpies entered the hall. Sitting among the other women they feasted on caught fish and game. Though these monsters ate raw flesh with their claws and sharp teeth she did not fear them. Monsters, she realized. She was surrounded by gods and monsters and yet was safer than she had ever been among mortal men.

~

MEHDI CHOSE to live below the clouds and was given a fine home in the center of town. Over time she learned how each of the women ended up on this island. Most fleeing terrible lives. Mehdi noticed that there were few mortal women among the refugees and surmised that was because of how hard it was to get to the island. For a woman to get to sea, she would have to take a boat sailed by men and get to an island that was protected from men. The Sirens and Harpies helped many and one woman spoke of being spirited away by a nereid when she attempted to drown herself. Still, Mehdi thought so many women could use a place like this and many more could use her help. Once again, she was safe but felt a burden to protect others.

“Mehdi, this is madness,” Stheno pleaded as she watched Mehdi buckle a bag across her centaur torso. “You are safe. Your children are safe. Why do this?”

“Nothing has changed. There are still others out there who need help. I can’t let my fear of Poseidon keep me from helping others.”

Euryale clamped her mouth stifling a shocked gasp. Fear filled her eyes as she glanced desperately at Stheno.

“They will come after you again.”

She tightened a strap. “Let them.” Exasperated, she stared directly at Stheno. “I have a way to fight back. Can you say that for the others?”

“You can’t save them all!”

“No, but I can save some and give others hope.”

CHAPTER 22
THE CABAL

Flying high into the sky, she looked down at the sea below. The sun above reflected off its bright blue-green surface and sped below her with alarming speed. She was so fast in this form that she caught sight of land quickly. Not wishing to be seen in this form, she skimmed in and out of the cumulous masses until she found a secluded place to land.

Returning to human form, she pulled a shawl over her head and headed into the village with little clue what she was going to do. It was eerie how similar the place was to her town; the streets, the market, the people. She bought bread from one vendor, and fruit from another. Despite her cowled head and attempts to go unnoticed, admiring glances followed her, but no one dared to approach. It was liberating. Savoring each bite, she strolled the foreign market with relaxed ease.

Then there above the doorway of a shop, crafted in clay

and colored glaze, was her emblem. The one she drew on the walls, and in sand. The one she handed to Alcibiades' wife. The death mask. She entered the pottery shop moving past brightly painted pots, plates, and jars to a woman painting images onto an amphora.

The woman's gray eyes smiled up at her. "How may I help?"

"I was curious about the symbol on your doorway."

"Ah." She put down her brush and wiped her hands. "The Gorgon."

"The Gorgon?"

The woman nodded. "Medusa, the protector. She guards us against men who seek to harm us."

"Do you need her protection?"

The woman nodded again. "My husband passed. This was our shop, but now..."

"You can't own your husband's property."

She dropped her head and sadly affirmed.

"But how will a symbol help?"

Lifting her head, the woman's eyes glinted with admiration. "They are afraid of her."

"Really? Why?"

"Because she can turn them to stone!"

"But," Mehdi motioned to this village, "here?"

"All know who she is and what she will do, since she disappeared men fear that she could be anywhere."

Mehdi was stunned. Here she was feeling guilty for being safe and racked with an overwhelming need to do more, while her reputation alone became enough to freeze men's hearts. A smile of pride spread across her face.

"Was there something you needed?" the woman asked, filling the awkward void.

Mehdi's thoughts returned to the shop, and she perused for something to purchase. After looking around she saw her visage in snake form emblazoned on a pot. Picking it up and turning the vase, her story played out in the ash and clay in her hand.

Gazing at Medusa turning men to stone, she grinned, then rotated the pot to when she made the peplos and placed it on Athena's statue. Shifting it again her eyes fell on herself as an Athenian priestess and Poseidon's attack.

Seeing the sea god bear down on her helpless form caused her to shudder. The pot slipped from her grasp and shattered. "I'm so sorry," she said, her voice trembling.

"No, my fault. I should have warned you, but since you were so interested in the symbol. I thought you knew."

"I do..." Mehdi replied, "but it was just...startling to see."

"I believe all stories should be told, not just the ones that favor the gods."

Mehdi nodded and stooped to help clean it up. "Let me pay for it."

"No need to worry. A broken pot can be made into something new." The woman put a hand on Mehdi, "People too."

"Do you think the symbol is enough?"

"For?"

"Protecting you," she uttered, staring at Poseidon's broken face in her hand. "Eventually, they will come."

The woman dusted off her hands and poured the pieces into a bin. "Yes, but the ward will give me a little time."

Mehdi jumped when a thunderous crash from outside, caused by the displays getting knocked to the ground as a group of young men ran away. She rushed after them, but the woman grabbed her wrist.

"Don't."

"They should pay for that."

"I'm sure they were paid well to do it."

Mehdi was fuming. "Who is it? Brother-in-law, Uncle?"

"Brother-in-law. He also wishes for a marital union."

"Where can I find him?"

"Why, what can you do?"

"Make him fear The Gorgon."

The woman hesitated, but after Mehdi pressed for the information, she received the name and location of her brother-in-law. Heeding caution, she tried to encourage Mehdi that the symbol alone is protection enough, but Mehdi argued that it was only a matter of time before she was forced to concede through loss of income from the destruction or actual force.

Mehdi found the man at his residence, languishing in his garden eating dates and drinking wine and that is how his servants found him frozen for all of time in stone. As she slithered over the atrium wall, she heard the screams of terror resound behind her.

When she returned the next day to the woman's shop,

she saw apprehension and terror in the old woman's eyes. "You do not have to fear me."

"But it was you," her voice quivered.

Mehdi pulled out the mask, showing it to the potter and said, "But I can't do it alone."

"Obviously, you can."

Shaking her head, Mehdi explained, "I can't be everywhere, but perhaps my reputation can." She walked over and lifted the symbol off the door and put it in front of the woman. "Use it, not just as a symbol, but to help each other. Let them know they are not alone. I am sure you know who here can help."

"But what can we do? There are laws and the simple matter that they are stronger and in control."

Mehdi gripped her hand. "But we are more cunning. We already speak in a network they know nothing about, as we wash the laundry, harvest the fields, and weave cloth. We pass herbs in quiet to prevent or stop pregnancies. We gather and pass on our knowledge of how to survive our monthly cycle and the change. Why not use these places, that network, to help women flee terrible husbands and abusive fathers? Why not use that network to pass herbs to sour men's stomachs and teach them that any woman they meet could hold the power of the gorgon?"

Swept up in the excitement, the potter, Iole, offered, "I can make tokens with your emblem that can be used to identify and move along the network."

"Yes, but how can we get them to the island? It's not feasible for me to carry them one at a time."

“So, you can fly,” Iole muttered with awe.

Mehdi affirmed, “But we need a boat.”

Iole’s face lit up. “There is a woman I know who has her own ship and an all-female crew.”

“Will she help?”

Wrapping a scarf around her head, she exited her shop. “Only one way to find out.”

Mehdi’s chest pounded and her confidence waned as they approached the ocean, but she set her own fears aside. The dock bustled with activity as men loaded and unloaded ships trying to beat the change in winds and tides. Down at the end of the pier the worst slot of the port sat the ship they sought.

The rest of the dock ignored their sailors as they prepared the ship to sail.

A woman with hair plaited like a man’s and wearing a short chiton for ease of movement on a ship met them at the plank. “Iole! What brings you? Do you have an order needing transport?”

Iole embraced her friend. “Hello, Adrasteia. No, not today, but my friend needs assistance.”

Mehdi gave a curt nod. “I wish to speak to the captain of this ship.”

“You are speaking to them,” the woman said with a smirk and waited for a shocked reply.

Mehdi was pleasantly surprised and continued her inquiry. “I require a ship for passengers.”

“When?”

"I wish to retain you for safe passage of women when they need it."

"I am not a ferry."

Mehdi nodded. "This is not mere transport from one port to another. This is something more."

Adrasteia looked back at her friend.

Iole dropped her gaze and with a serious tone suggested. "We should talk below."

Dipping down below into Adrasteia's quarters Mehdi disclosed their plan. Adrasteia did not seem convinced until Mehdi presented the mask and transformed just enough for the snakes to come to life. Eyes closed she heard their audible gasps of horror. Both Adrasteia and Iole leapt to defensive positions, but their shoulders relaxed when Mehdi removed the mask and put it away.

"If you are her," Adrasteia began. "Why do you need us?"

"Because I am one, but we can be many. Let them fear the monster and be blissfully unaware that my eyes and ears are everywhere."

Iole pulled out a coin sized image of The Gorgon. "I was thinking we can use these to help identify each other. If we only give them to those seeking help or those willing to help we can have a way to identify each other."

"It could work," Adrasteia considered.

"Do you think you can help women escape?"

"Escape where?"

"Wherever they wish and if they have nowhere to go, I have an island of refuge."

"How can we communicate with you?"

Mehdi contemplated. "I suppose the Harpies can help. I will look for a discreet way to get messages back and forth. To do that I need to get back."

"You're leaving?" Iole asked.

"I need to arrange things on the island. Do not worry, I will send messengers to continue communication." She looked to Adrasteia. "And instructions to get to my island."

"I can provide you passage and you can show me yourself." Adrasteia offered.

Mehdi shook her head. "I fear I tempt fate too much if I sail his waters. I have my own means."

Adrasteia nodded though unsure what Mehdi meant. "Then until we meet again."

MEHDI'S SISTERS were not as keen about her plan as she was, but it took little effort to convince them. The Harpies did not hesitate to assist and revealed that they can communicate with other birds and send them to places they cannot easily fly. When Mehdi mentioned the ship, Stheno said it was time she met the nereids.

They escorted her down a path cut into the mountain that led to an inner cave and lagoon. Languishing among the jutting rocks were women, half-woman half-fish, or so Mehdi thought at first and then she noticed some appeared in full human form and others giant fish.

Euryale leaned over. "They are limited shapeshifters, like us."

Stheno slipped her hand into Euryale's and added, "But more importantly they help control the tides and currents. If you want your friend to have any hope of getting here, she will need them as a guide."

Mehdi looked at the water with longing and sadness, but fear kept her feet on the rocks. She appreciated that she could gaze out at the crashing waves and smell the spray in the air, but being in the water was dangerous. Too much was at stake to risk him finding her.

A nereid sensing her emotions stepped forward and took her hand. "Come."

Mehdi shook her head. "Poseidon."

"This water is within the island. You are safe."

"It's safe?" Tears of relief rushed forth and spilled from her eyes. Choking back a nervous laugh, she tentatively touched the sea again. The water lapped at her toes and made the island truly feel like home. The nereid beckoned her in further. Waist deep and sensing no sign of Poseidon or his minions, she submerged her body under the water. All her tension washed away, soothed by the salty lagoon. Waves of emotions swelled in her chest forcing her back to the surface. As gasped in the salty air, tears poured forth and did not stop. Unable to hold back the crashing sobs, she leaned against a rock and released her pent-up worry and fears.

The nereids grouped around, soothing her with delicate touches and began to sing. The song was different from the Sirens but beautiful, coaxing the sorrow from her body and replacing it with peace. She cried and cried, letting her salty tears join the sea. After a long moment she felt a little more complete.

Lifting her head and looking around, she saw patient, gentle faces looking back with warm gazes. "Hello," she choked, embarrassed by her breakdown.

"Hello," one replied, her hair was the color of the sea varying in shades from brilliant teal to the deepest blue. It was wild and curly with streaks of white that looked like cresting waves in her raucous mane. "Stheno says that you need our help."

Mehdi looked around to find Stheno. She and Euryale were also in the water in their natural forms. Mehdi had never seen their tails in the water and smiled at how they shimmered under the surface. Glancing back to the one who had spoken, she asked, "The Sirens say you control the channels and tides, yes?"

The blue-haired woman nodded. "Yes, I am Thetis, Goddess of the Sea."

"But I thought... Poseidon?"

"Is King of the Sea. I am the sea," the sea personified firmly stated.

Mehdi grinned, instantly liking Thetis. "I have a ship that at times will want to come here. Is it possible?"

"You can only get to this island if we wish it, and even then, you cannot land. They will have to be guided and stay off the coast."

"Then how do people get here?"

"The Sirens can fly them in," Euryale chimed in.

Mehdi glanced over at her sister entwined with Stheno, bobbing in and out of the water.

Thetis squeezed her hand. "That is settled then. Come swim with us."

"What?"

She gently took Mehdi's hand and drew her deeper into the pool, "Come swim with us. You want to."

Her body hungered for the long-forgotten joy. "I do."

The Nereids motioned toward the pouch slung at her side and beckoned her into the sea.

Shifting her body into any form was becoming second nature. Mask on, she concentrated on needing to breathe and move underwater. The tail was the first to form black and slick like an eel. When the fin fanned out she grinned at the red tipping like her hair. Focusing on her gills, she submerged her head underwater, and instinctually drew in the sea.

The moment, both terrifying and exhilarating, as bubbles rushed out of her mouth and water filled her lungs. For a moment she thought of Alexios then she thought how for a normal person this would mean certain death, but she was far from normal. A protective film congealed over her eyes as they adjusted to the low light.

Fully formed she undulated and through the water with great speed, hitting the rocky walls on the other side. Giggling, the nereids coached her until she navigated around the small pool on her own. Then they motioned for her to swim beyond the cave and into the open water.

Mehdi swam through the opening and towards dancing

streaks of light before bursting out of the water to the sky above. She arched her body and plunged back into the water, diving deep below. Urging her eyes to adjust to the murky depth, the world below came to life. Fish swam through waving seaweed, crabs scurried on the floor, and an octopus snatched at his prey drawing it back into his lair.

She spiraled up and around a rock an octopus called home, before breaking the surface again. The mask adjusted to the new environment, forcing her to spit out water and take in air. Wondering if she could think of a way to breathe both water and air, her chest lurched as gills grew on her sides. She chuckled at the odd sensation of breathing both air and water simultaneously.

Clinging to one of the rocky spires, she gazed up at the steep path crawling up to the city and took in her island from the sea.

"You should see it when the sun sets," Thetis said as she joined Mehdi, leaning up against the rock.

"Then we will," Mehdi stated, settling into place and taking a rare moment to simply be present.

She thought about Alexios and how he always seemed to be that way. Absorbing each moment like it was precious and temporary, with no rush, just simple enjoyment. She recalled the calming sound of her net flying into the water with a swish and plunk and felt a brief moment of peace.

Glancing over at the nereids who were sunning, she asked Thetis, "Do you know all the waters?"

Thetis smiled. "Anywhere the sea meets the shore, I know."

A sliver of hope grew inside as she wiggled closer to Thetis. "I am looking for someone Poseidon is keeping prisoner."

Thetis tensed slightly. "What do you mean?"

"I only saw it for a moment, but there is a man, maybe not a man anymore. He is blind and trapped in an underwater cave."

Thetis appeared apprehensive. "If Poseidon is keeping him prisoner there is a reason."

"There is." Mehdi glowered. "To torment him. Why else would he not let him go or kill him?"

"There are so many things about the Gods that you do not understand."

Anger singed Mehdi's voice. "I know they can be cruel and petty."

"But also kind and benevolent," Thetis noted.

"Poseidon benevolent?" Mehdi scoffed.

"When our protector fell, and Poseidon became King of the seas he took us in. He became our King."

"Protector or Benevolent Tyrant?" she fumed.

Her face contorted with conflict as she refrained from answering.

"How did your protector die?"

Tossing her hair back, she sighed. "She sacrificed herself and gave up her power to protect us even in death."

Medhi's brow furrowed. "The same protector as the Sirens and Harpies?"

Thetis nodded.

Mehdi touched the mask on her face. “Metis... How did a goddess so powerful and loved become defeated?”

Thetis tenderly placed her hand on Mehdi’s. “Because she loved. Her compassion was greater than her need for power.”

“But without power, compassion is merely a wish. I’ve seen that.”

Thetis pursed her lips. “No, it is seen in smaller acts. Metis was wise and cunning. She reigned and ruled knowing that dawn comes after darkness and that life and death are interconnected. She died so that others could live and she would live on in other ways.” Mehdi touched the mask and Thetis nodded again. “What is left of her is in there and in you.”

Thetis reached out and stroked her hair. “I think you know what I am saying.”

“But how?”

“Metis gave a piece of herself to bring you into being and then her sisters waited. They waited and watched until you were ready.”

“Ready?”

“Ready to reclaim what you once had?”

Mehdi pushed away from her. “Once had? But I am no god.”

“Don’t you see, but you are. You have all the powers of one.”

“No, I have a mask. It has the powers. Only a sliver of Metis was used to make me. I am no god.”

“No one but you can wield that mask. To everyone else

it is but stone. Don't you see? Just like her, you protect. You protected the women of your island and now you continue to protect others."

"Because they deserve protection."

"I am not disagreeing with you, but I think it is time you realize how strong you are and what you can do with that power."

~

IN WINGED CENTAUR FORM, Mehdi circled the incoming ship. Willing her wings to close, she landed on the deck. Mask removed, she transformed to her human form and embraced Adrasteia. "You have guests for me?"

Adrasteia smiled, motioning to a mother and daughter. "Yes."

"Cassia!" Mehdi declared in utter shock.

Cassia, no longer the youthful beauty Mehdi spent a summer exploring, stood before her with the same look. Her once tan skin sullen and her sparkling eyes dull and sunken. Though barely in her mid-twenties, her hair already showed signs of gray. Mehdi gaped wondering what had life done to her.

Clutched in her arms was a young girl of six or seven. Stroking the girl's hair, she stammered, "Mehdi?"

Mehdi stared at Cassia, a million thoughts and memories flooding her mind, including the fact that if Cassia was here, she was in serious trouble, danger, or both.

The girl in Cassia's arms screamed in fright when the Harpies landed on the ship's deck. Their wings rustled and fluttered close as their clawed feet dug into the deck's wooden planks.

Mehdi rushed to her. "Sshh, shhh. It is okay. They will not hurt you."

The young girl peered out from Cassia's chiton but looked unsure.

Keeping her eyes on the child, she beckoned for one of the Harpies to approach.

As she came closer, Aello cupped her clawed hands behind her back and did her best to smile at the child.

Mehdi stroked one of Aello's silver wings. "See how pretty they are? They are going to fly you to the island."

The little girl shook her head and pointed at Mehdi. "Horsey."

"Would you like me to take you in?"

The little girl nodded.

Mehdi looked to Cassia for approval.

"I trust you," Cassia replied, her throat ragged from a long journey.

Giving the little girl a smile, Mehdi pulled out her mask and transformed into her centaur form. The little girl giggled with glee. Cassia helped her daughter onto Mehdi's back, then allowed a Harpy to pick her up.

"Come eat with us, Adrasteia," Mehdi requested, prancing into position to take flight.

"I'm afraid I cannot."

Mehdi's brow furrowed. "But why?"

"Because the Island and the Nereids see me as a man today."

"Really?"

He nodded. "It was a rough ride in. Their songs are quite beautiful. Luckily, Thetis knew me and stopped us before we crashed."

Mehdi's front hooves shuffled with agitation. "Oh no! I'm so sorry."

Adrasteia shrugged. "It is well. I had always wondered myself, now I know."

"No matter, you are a friend and ally to me and all who dwell here. I am sure we could carry you in with no harm."

Adrasteia touched her arm. "The offer is appreciated, but..."

"I could invite Thetis."

He raised his brows in interest.

Mehdi gave him a wry grin. "Come, eat."

"Very well, I will attend to my crew and follow."

"I will see you then." Taking a few steps back, she instructed the child. "Hold on."

The little girl clung to Mehdi as they launched off the ship, her hooves scraping the surface of the sea before her wings flapped in strong heavy strokes, lifting them into the air.

Wanting to delight the young girl, she swooped past the nereids sunbathing. They waved and sang with the Sirens clinging to the craggy rocks above. Wishing to stretch out the journey she flew past the village, the groves, and the stables, giving the girl an aerial tour of her new home. Tour complete, she landed and galloped to a stop at the feasting hall.

Pegasus pranced out to greet her and Chrysaor followed, dancing with joy seeing another small child. Aging around a year a month, he appeared five to six years in age.

The two children chattered, as they wandered back to the table.

Pulling off her mask, she headed inside, when delicate fingers touched her elbow. Mehdi turned to find Cassia staring back. Her heart beat wildly gazing into those eyes again.

Despite being worn and tired they stared back burning with curiosity. "Mehdi, you are Medusa?"

Mehdi gazed at her old friend and lover. "I am."

Her fingers flew to her lips, as she uttered, "How, when...why?"

Motioning for her to follow, she guided Cassia to sit down and eat. Cassia's daughter was already happily munching away, next to Chrysaor.

"How did you hear of Medusa?" Mehdi asked.

"Among the women servants after..." Cassia touched her eye and looked away.

Mehdi could see the remnants of a bruise fading. "Your husband beat you?"

Cassia sniffled back tears. "Only when I am being impudent, or he caught me helping with tasks and chores."

"What?" Mehdi asked confused.

"Daily life is beneath me," Cassia recited with venom. "Mehdi, I should have never left. I should have requested sanctuary as you did. Oh, how many times I wish I had defied my brother and my family." She grabbed Mehdi's hand, "Then you and I could have stayed together and invented things with no one telling us we couldn't."

Mehdi's eyes smiled, but it was weak and full of pity because Cassia's words were not just a fanciful wish, but pure fantasy. If Cassia had stayed, would she have ever met Alexios or caught the eye of Poseidon? No... Poseidon made it clear that he was watching her long before meeting Alexios. A twinge of longing for Alexios danced across her heart.

And still, she savored Cassia's hand as it intertwined with hers. There were new lines, but fewer calluses, from years of not swinging a sword or pulling back the string of a bow. Cassia's fingers trace over Mehdi's calluses and then ran down the center of her wrist. Her skin sang at the old familiar touch.

Drawing back her hand, Mehdi cleared her head of inappropriate thoughts and asked. "So your servants helped you find the network?"

Cassia nodded, biting her lip, "But it wasn't for me that I fled." Her eyes darted toward her daughter then back to Mehdi, "He sold her, just like my brothers did to me and the brute was unwilling to wait for her to mature!"

Mehdi's jaw dropped. "She can be no more than seven!"

"Aeneas felt allowing me to grow up outside his household is why I am so...difficult." Cassia's eyes rimmed with tears, as she choked. "Melina was to leave and move into the man's house before she could be corrupted any further."

Mehdi's fingers flew up and entwined into Cassia's curls. "I'm so sorry."

Cassia welcomed her touch by cupping her hand against Mehdi's.

She smiled. "But that is why I made this place accessible, so people like you and your daughter could escape their oppression."

Cassia looked around. "All these women?"

"Fleeing the cruelties of man."

Admiration for Mehdi's accomplishments shone in her eyes, then her nose creased curiously. "You still haven't told me how you became Medusa." Worry raced across her face. "Was it Alcibiades? Did he try to attack you again?"

Mehdi withdrew her hand and rubbed the weariness from her face. "I wish it was that simple. I wish I was that simple."

Cassia squeezed her hand. "There is nothing simple about you Mehdi."

"I'm aware." Inhaling sharply, Mehdi deflected the inquiry and offered Cassia a cup. "Eat. Rest. You and Melina are safe here. And don't worry," she promised, sipping from her own cup. "There will be plenty of work for you to help with. We will work those calluses back in no time."

Cassia chuckled as her shoulders relaxed. Seeing Melina still happily chewing, and chatting away with the young boy, she ate.

Mehdi's eyes drank in Cassia hoping for signs of the person she knew, but then she noticed Thetis walk in with a sour face. "What is it?" Mehdi asked with great concern.

"Adrasteia was followed." The joyful chatter filling the room ceased as all eyes fell on Thetis. She continued, "The ship was stopped and destroyed but it means they are trying to find us."

"That is not surprising," Cassia replied. "The reputation of Medusa is well known and has sparked retaliation."

"What do they plan to do?" Mehdi asked.

"Find you, kill you."

She scoffed, "Let them try. We are no longer their victims." Sensing fear ripple across room, Mehdi stood and addressed the women of the island. "Everyone is here because some man decided they were better than us. That they could use us, beat us, and throw us away when we no longer gave them pleasure." She shook her head and squeezed Cassia's hand. "But we are strong. Perhaps stronger than them, because we know how to endure hardship and still find room in our hearts to love and care for each other. Let us remind our oppressed sisters that we have powers men can never possess and offer them ways to fight back. Let us all become the monsters they fear. Let us become gorgons, defending those who cannot defend themselves."

The room swelled with hope and a murmur of excitement.

"And if," Mehdi uttered, then adjusted her phrasing. "And when they come, may they tremble on our shores, falling to stone at our feet."

"We would be in so much trouble at the temple!" Cassia gleefully declared as she locked the mechanism into place.

"Yes, but now I'm in charge!" Mehdi replied, stepping back to pull the length of rope in her hand taut. "Ready?"

Cassia ran to her side, squeezing her arm. "Ready!"

Mehdi pulled, releasing the latch and sending the missile barreling through the air and into the rocky spire.

It struck with tremendous force sinking deep into the rock and sending debris flying. Shouts of frustrated nereids floated up the cliffside to the two women peering over.

They clung to each other fighting off a fit of giggling.

"Sorry!" Mehdi apologized.

Cassia's fingers dug deeper into her chiton and rub along the curve of her waist. Mehdi's heart raced, wanting more, but she also wanted to give Cassia time to heal before starting anything new. Mehdi understood the struggles of trusting someone after being hurt. Even though Cassia was not any of the men that hurt her and not even a man, intimacy with anyone came with fears.

Cassia spent the first night telling Mehdi about the hardships she endured in her marriage. Her marital duties and obligations. Sex became a chore, no longer a pleasure, or a desire. Even while her heart beat wildly for her old lover, she refused to cross boundaries until permission was given.

Instead, the two resumed their friendship and love of inventing, leading them to this cliffside with a giant contraption sending cross bolts into the protective rocks that surrounded the island and Cassia's fingers brushing the underside of her breast.

Taking a chance, Mehdi lifted her eyes to Cassia's lustful gaze staring back. Her throat tightened, but she fought her fears and pulled Cassia closer. Just as she was about to chance a kiss, their large arrow fell from the sky and sunk into the ground at their feet.

They bounded apart, staring up at an incredibly angry Harpy.

Aello closed her wings and landed firmly on the ground, her claws digging deep into the earth. The scowl on her face said everything, "My duty is to guard this island and you, Your Majesty. I was unaware I would need to protect the island from you."

Cassia cupped her mouth to hold back a giggle, "Your Majesty."

Mehdi jabbed Cassia playfully in the side. Because of her heritage and natural leadership the residents of the island saw her as their queen. Even the name Medusa not only meant protector, but also ruler. She carried the title as a formality and with great humility, rarely seeing herself placed any higher than any other on the island, but the title stuck. Especially among the Harpies and Sirens who swore an oath to protect Metis and in their eyes, Mehdi was Metis reborn.

"My apologies Aello, I did not think about the rubble. Just wanted to see if she would fire."

Aello nodded, "Might I suggest another part of the island that is not inhabited?"

"Of course."

Cassia frowned, "We still need to work on mobility. It was rough getting this up here."

"Allow me," Aello offered, launching into the air and with a few wing beats, she hovered over the contraption. Digging her claw into the frame, she flew towards a rockface further up the mountain.

Cassia snickered, "Did she do that to be nice or just to get us out of her feathers?"

Medhi laughed, yanking the cross bolt free. "Either way, she is right. It is very secluded over there."

A wicked smile spread across Cassia's face, "Is it?"

"Mmmmhmmm, Much like our favorite tree."

"The one by the creek?"

Mehdi licked her lips and nodded.

Cassia slipped her hand into Mehdi's, rushing toward the spot. "I can't wait to see it."

CHAPTER 23
STAKE YOUR CLAIM

Chrysaor, fully grown, approached his mother. "Pegasus and I have returned with the reports."

She beamed back at her son and stretched to the tips of her toes to kiss him lovingly on the cheek. "And?"

"The network is still working, but retaliations are occurring. Public images of your visage have been banned, but Iole's coins are in full circulation. Some cities now have curfews forbidding women to walk unescorted after dark, so most information is being passed in the washing areas, the market, and the fields. Adrasteia is being overworked, though, and asking to purchase another ship and train new crews."

Mehdi nodded listening as she reviewed the other information strewn across her table. Including maps, reports and tiny pieces of paper, transported by winged messengers, and other correspondence spilling out of waterproof vials carried by nereids. "Give Adrasteia anything she needs, but women only."

"Mother," Chrysaor began.

Mehdi lifted her head hearing the concern in his voice. He looked so much like his father, with the same strong jawline, same eyes, and that one untamable curl, just like Alexios.

Two years and fully grown. It was hard to fathom, but there he stood. His mind matured just as fast, wearing out all his teachers, including the muses. Thankfully, his rapid aging slowed as he entered adulthood, and now he gazed at her with worry in his eyes. "You know I am a man."

She grinned amused, "Of course."

"And you can trust me."

"Of course."

"Then why do you hate men?"

Her brow furrowed, "I don't...hate...men."

"Your actions would say otherwise."

She sighed, "I hate how men, as a whole, treat women. I hate how society allows them... gives them the legal right to abuse and mistreat women. We are not property."

"I know. I don't see you that way."

"Because you were raised here, among women, and not under a patriarchy that tells you that you are better than us."

"But sometimes when you speak against men, it hurts me."

She took her son's hands. "That is never my intention. I know there are good men. I've met them, known them, trusted them, but they...you are still the exception and not the rule."

"So how do we change that?"

She cupped his face. "By raising our children to know better, so they raise their children to know better. But until then we must right wrongs and save who we can." She released him, motioning to the table, "We need to shake the very foundation so that those who think it is okay to treat women like property will have to change their minds. Show them that their pillars of justice and virtue are built on the sands of inequality."

"I believe in you mother, but what you propose goes against an entire way of thinking. People don't like change."

Mehdi rubbed her brow. "I know it isn't easy, but we have to start somewhere, or we will go nowhere."

"Have you considered brokering peace?"

Tilting her head, she inquired. "Peace? How?"

"You say you want them to change, but you have made no proposals, no demands."

She sat back down. Her son was right. She wasn't changing anything, just bypassing their laws. "I have been too busy saving them that I never thought... Do you think we have such power?"

Chyrasor stepped toward the door and motioned to the bustling village outside. "Your number is great and because of who you are they are trained not just to defend themselves but fight." He turned back to her. "You are more than their protector. You are their Queen and they will follow you.

Stake your claim and demand the respect of the other Kingdoms. Declare they change or pay the consequences."

"Claim Sovereignty? They will surely demand my head rather than respect my power."

"Then let them try. I know no man, nay, no one that can best you."

She knew one, but that was before the mask. Could he beat her now?

"I will consider it." She promised and dismissed her son to other duties.

Sighing deeply, Mehdi leaned back into the curve of her chair and closed her eyes. The sounds of the village safe and content soothed her mind, and she did not stir when Cassia padded into the room and hover over her. Delicate lips fell upon hers pressing a soft kiss. Mehdi sighed into the kiss, slipping a hand into Cassia's hair.

Draping her arms over the chair and down Mehdi's chest, she queried. "Arguing with Chrysaor again?"

Mehdi snorted, "That would imply one of us won."

"Oh heaven forbid either of you lose an argument!" Cassia laughed.

Mehdi opened her eyes and smirked up at Cassia's beautiful face. "I play fair."

"Ha!" Cassia scoffed, "You most certainly do not! Nor should you."

"That was his argument," she retorted, gesturing to where he earlier stood. "He feels it is time to go on the offense."

Cassia's mouth pursed lightly, but she did not answer.

Mehdi contorted in the the chair to get a better look at her lover's face, "You agree with him?"

Stepping around to the front of the chair, Cassia kneeled in front of Mehdi.

Mehdi leaned forward to face her eye to eye.

Swallowing Cassia began, "Too often we react rather than act. The island is safe, but the rest of the world isn't and no matter how many we help,"

Mehdi grimaced. "Not everyone can come here."

~

MEHDI STOOD on the prow of the ship and watched the foreign kingdom grow closer. Maintaining a stalwart appearance, her stomach churned at her audacity to cross Poseidon's domain. A confidence grown from creating a refuge and challenging the laws of the Patriarchy, but fear of retribution lingered.

Thetis lifted from the waves crashing into the ship and slipped onto the deck next to her. Lightly gripping her wrist, she assured, "Don't worry. I promise you are safe."

Mehdi smiled at her weakly. "You defy him in protecting me."

"He was not my first ruler, nor will he be my last. Gods come and go. Water is forever."

"Then why let him rule you?"

"You know as well as I that it is a delicate dance and he knows that a ruler is only as great as his subject's loyalty.

Something you should remember and remind these kings you go to confront. They rule not just the men, but the women, too, and if they lose the faith of their women their society will crumble."

"Then why is He...why are they so cruel?"

"Because in their rise to power, they have forgotten how they got there." Thetis squeezed Mehdi's hand. "Remind them."

~

MEHDI STEPPED off the ship and onto the dock. Behind her floating in the harbor was the rest of her fleet, awaiting orders. She wore the full regalia of a warrior queen complete with her winged helm gifted to her by the muses specifically designed to hold her death mask so she could lower it at a moment's notice.

She tucked it under her arm like a head without a body. People shuddered when they glanced at the stony visage. She herself wore a red himation over her golden armor and white tunic presenting a sense of pureness and power.

The city parted and stared in awe as she and her entourage of warrior women walked to the palace. There she stood before the King awaiting his response.

"Mehdi, Priestess of Athena, and slayer of my men. You dare seek an audience with me."

"You will call me Medusa, The Protector. I have only punished those that have deserved it."

"I have a garden of stone men whose only crime was to dare fight you."

"Their crime and yours was to allow the women of your kingdom to suffer. They were guilty of complicity."

He stood barely able to hold back his rage. "You were the monster who roamed my streets killing. Not them."

She coldly stared back, unphased by his pomposity. "I punish only those who carried cruelness in their hearts."

"How can you claim to know such and judge them?"

"A gift from Athena and Metis herself, the fallen goddess of wisdom. I can see into the very soul of men and what I have seen would turn you white as stone. Care to look?" She lifted her helmet and smirked as terrified gasps filled the chamber.

The King raised his hand requesting she stay her action. In one simple act, he acknowledged her power and his respect for it.

She gently nodded and put the helmet back under her arm.

"You have requested my audience for a reason. State it."

"Simple. I want you to give women the same rights as men."

"What?"

"You heard me and I know you understand. Give women the same rights as men. The right to own/sell property and not be property. The right of daughters to choose their mates, rather than sold off like sheep to the highest bidder. The right to defend themselves if they are dishonored. Simple rights men have that women do not."

"And what makes you believe women should have these rights?"

"I know men often pontificate that they rule because Zeus is King of the Gods, but there were gods before him and the first to exist was Gaia, Mother Earth, if she had not born children and those children had not born children then none of us would exist. There would be no men without women."

The weight of her words settled on the crowd, as the king lowered back into his chair.

She stepped closer. "I believe men have forgotten the power women have. I know women have forgotten too, but I am here to warn you all. Treat us as equals or suffer the consequences."

The king's anger spewed out of clenched teeth, "You speak of equality, but threaten. I warn you, my men know how to fight and will happily go to war."

"Do you think women shirk at the thought of violence? We have suffered from it for far too long." She was now within threat range and leaned forward locking eyes with him. "And we know how to endure it, do you?"

He swung his arms gesturing for his guards, "Remove yourself from my land, before I expel you."

"Wait." A woman's voice spoke from the shadows.

The King turned startled to find his Queen speaking.

"Medusa is right. Women who bear rulers, should not also be the objects of men." The Queen took the king's hand tenderly into hers. "Perhaps if men treated us with respect and fairness, we could find it in our hearts to love and marry them not through force, but by choice."

The king's demeanor changed as he studied his wife's countenance. Love flowed between them, but also the remnants of a previous spat.

His desire for forgiveness becoming Mehdi's advantage. "Perhaps," he spoke, stroking his thumb over the Queen's hand. "We will consider your offer, but this is my land and my people."

Taking a step back, she bowed. "Then I suggest you listen to your wife and change the rules of your land or watch it all turn to stone and ash."

The eyes of the crowd followed her in silent awe as she exited, not daring to threaten this new queen and her army.

CHAPTER 24
FATE ARRIVES

Mehdi slept peacefully in her chambers when her body woke sensing something before her mind was fully awake. She remained still, listening to the clap of feet on the stone floor. Her eyes opened to slits, but nothing moved in her periphery.

Vacant space filled Cassia's side of the bed. Up to administer a dose of comfrey to Melina for her cold, which meant someone was in the room.

The distinct sound of breathing tickled her ears, as warm body hovered over her, but nothing was there. Hearing the sharp inhale of someone readying an attack, she quickly rolled away.

As she retreated, she snatched up her helmet, slipped it on, and changed form hoping her supernatural sight allowed her to see the invisible attacker. It did not.

Picking up her sword, she carefully slid across the floor,

lifting her body higher to better defend and strike. A rock crunched under a sandal near the door.

Bolting toward the sound, she flinched back when the door slammed shut. Using the action to locate its position, she struck where she thought her attacker stood. An invisible blade blocked her blow and cut through her toughened hide. Wincing, she pulled back her arm. Stunned by a blade able to slice her, she gauged his location and prepared to fell her attacker before he could strike again when a voice called out.

"Mehdi, wait it's me." Her opponent appeared, pulling a cap from his head and revealing himself.

"Perseus! What are you doing here?" she shouted. "Why are you attacking me?"

He put down his sword while averting his gaze. "I was not attacking you. I was trying to wake you, but forgot I was still invisible."

Blood dripped from her cut. Dropping her sword, she tried to staunch the wound. "That still doesn't explain why you are here."

He moved to aid her but jumped back when the blood hitting the floor moved. The blood transformed into a snake and struck his retreating form. He hissed in pain, "What was that?"

Horrified, Mehdi crushed the blood snake with her tail, killing it. "I don't know."

Perseus wobbled.

Fearing more snakes would appear, Mehdi wrapped her wound with a sheet and helped Perseus to the bed. "What is happening?"

"Your...snake...bit me." He struggled to say as his eyes filled with fear. "I think I'm dying!"

Cupping her mouth in fright it smashed against the mask. Fearful for her friend's life, she tore it off and turned to get help.

Pounding crashed against the door as Chrysaor called out. "Mother! Are you okay?"

Still transitioning, she fumbled the door open.

Her son and others clamored to her aid including Cassia, Stheno and Euryale.

"Stheno, it's Perseus! He's dying."

Baffled to find him sitting on Mehdi's bed white as the sheets and dripping with sweat, Euryale blustered. "What is he doing here?"

"No time," Mehdi replied. "He cut me and my blood turned to snakes."

Stheno and Euryale's eyes widened.

"Give me your right hand!" Stheno commanded.

Mehdi obeyed without question.

Stheno struck her uncut arm with a small dagger creating a thin slice and hung it over Perseus' mouth. "Drink."

Perseus, delirious but still lucid enough to find the demand bizarre, refused.

"Drink or die, Perseus."

He opened his mouth and Stheno pressed Mehdi's arm to his lips.

They all waited in the eerie silence and then Perseus flopped onto the bed in convulsions.

Stheno helped Euryale pin him to the bed and asked. "Were you wearing the mask?"

"Yes, he came into my room. I thought I was being attacked and then he struck me with his sword and cut me."

"Cassia, grab the sword. Mehdi, put on the mask."

Both acted instantly. Stheno took the sword from Cassia and slowly slid it across Mehdi's transformed arm. Still convulsing, Perseus's mouth thrashed against her arm, but she fought the pain and then his body went limp.

Mortified by his clammy flesh, she slithered onto the bed and scooped him into her arms and coil. "No, please, don't die."

He wheezed and then coughed. "Not today." Wiping the blood from his face, he attempted to sit up, but continued to cough and wheeze lightly. "That did not go as planned."

~

STHENO TENDED to Mehdi's wounds in the infirmary as Perseus tried to explain his presence. but he was too distracted by Chrysaor. Each time he started to speak, his eyes flitted back at Mehdi's son until he stammered. "Alexios?"

Mehdi touched Perseus on the arm. "No," she smiled at Chrysaor, "his son."

Baffled, he refuted. "But you have not been gone that long."

She shrugged, "The power of the Gods." Seeing her son

glower at Perseus with caution and suspicion, she practiced introductions. “Chyrasor, this is Perseus. A friend. He knew your father.”

“But I thought my father was Poseidon.”

“He is in a way, but you look too much like Alexios not to be his. No one beyond this room should know that.”

Her son nodded in understanding and his stance eased. “If he is your friend then why does he have a weapon that can harm you?”

“That is a good question.” Euryale concurred, as she played with taking the hood on and off causing her to blink in and out of sight.

Perseus offered the sword to Chrysaor. “It is a gift I received during my quest. It can cut through the toughest hide.”

Her brow furrowed at Perseus, “Why are you here?”

“Your scene at the ceremony and continued disruption across Greece has infuriated the King. He is calling for your head.”

“I know that, so have many others, but...why have you come for my head?”

He shook his head, “The King did order me to come for your head, but I actually came to find you before someone else did. I quickly learned you are not easy to locate.”

Mehdi smirked with pride. The Nereids, Harpies, and Sirens protected this place well. No man could cross onto the isle by sea without them knowing. Recalling this fact, she inquired. “How did you find me?”

“I asked Athena, but even she was cryptic. See the

Graes," he recited in an annoyed tone. "I had to figure out who or what the Graes were and then get here." Weak and parched from his near-death experience, he quenched his thirst, then continued. "Grae is their name and they are also old."

Mehdi snickered. "You speak of Grae sisters who live on the mountain peak above us in the clouds." She imagined him trying to understand them as they spoke as one and recalled them saying that if someone tried to walk up the mountain to their home they would go mad. Her eyes trailed across Perseus's face and confirmed his sanity was intact. "How did you even get up there?"

He shifted his hip and bent his heel towards her to show off the winged shoes.

She shook her head in amazement, "A sword that can cut my flesh, a cap of invisibility, and flying shoes. You needed all that just to find me?"

"Athena also gave me this!" His hand touched the cowl covering his shoulders and chest. It was a hide of metallic scales that shined in the light and reflected back her image. Long snake-shaped tassels hung from the cowl, covering his torso.

It reminded her of her girdle. Touching it lightly, she gasped, "That's Athena's Aegis!"

He nodded, "I've been on quite an adventure. I finally made it here by flying up to where the Grae's live and they told me that you were just below. They warned me that men are not welcome so I stayed invisible as I searched. I finally found you, but you were not alone, so I waited. When," he turned to Cassia. "When you left, I took my chance." His fingers twitched towards Mehdi, wishing to take her hand, but he hesitated, "I was so excited to see you that I forgot I was still invisible."

Mehdi took his hand and asked, "If you didn't come for my head, then why are you here?"

"Because others are coming, and I hoped to get you out before they do."

She laughed. "Perseus, many have tried and failed. You yourself could not get here without godly intervention. We are safe here."

"They are trying and eventually they may succeed. You are not safe."

"If I was in danger, Athena or muses would warn me."

"We have warned you," everyone said in unison.

She rolled her eyes and grinned, "Fair point, but perhaps there is something more?"

Perseus leaned in closer, "If I fail to bring back your head then Mother has to marry him."

"That's absurd." Mehdi scoffed.

"You know he has wanted her hand for years. My father is still missing and by law, he has a right to her."

"No!" Mehdi growled, standing in defiance. "Why?! Why do men feel they have a 'right' to us? This is what I fight against. I will not let that happen!" Yanking her hand free of ministrations, she paced in anger and plotted. "You. No. We will go back, but this time Polydectes will face judgment and it is he who will lose his head."

MEHDI LEANED against the balcony banister, gazing at the water as the sun broke its horizon. The deep grays of dusk brightened in hue as streaks of orange and pink shimmered across the falsely calm water. As the sun rose, she thought of the little island and searched for any signs of a large black tail breaking the surface. A hopeless wish she failed to give up.

Eyes set on the sea, she jumped when someone touched her hand. Perseus flinched, not wanting to startle her. Happy to see him, she clasped his hand, as her head fell on his shoulder in a familiar way. All that changed since they last met vanished as they slipped back to a time of innocence.

Below them, the horses strode out of the stables and rushed off the cliff becoming a fiery blaze as they took flight.

Perseus' gasped in awe. "This place is certainly like no other."

She nodded into his shoulder and sighed. They clung to the silence for a very long time then Perseus tensed.

Swallowing hard, he wetted his parched mouth before asking with apprehension. "Why did you leave?"

Lifting her head, her brow furrowed. "Leave? I thought that was obvious. I was in danger. More importantly, I was a danger to the city...and to you."

He shook his head, dissatisfied with her answer. "Why did you leave without me?"

A proverbial dagger pricked her heart feeling his pain

and sadness. "Oh, Perseus. I'm so sorry. It happened so fast, and I never thought,"

"That it would bother me that you were gone? You were not the only one who lost people, who Poseidon hurt. And we," he encapsulated her hand with his, as his eyes hung low with regret. "I was going to help you."

Cupping his face with her free hand, she lifted his gaze to hers. "I know and the offer alone was enough. I'm sorry that," she halted her apology as they reminisced about the path not taken. If she had stayed they would be married. A friend turned lover for the sake of companionship and protection, but that was not their path. "I'm sorry."

He cast his eyes away again. "I thought if I did find you I could still help, but," he glanced inside. "He is already grown! And is that Cassia?" He shook his head. "It is not what I expected."

She chortled and grinned. "I also gave birth to a winged horse. Nothing is as I expected."

Exhaling hard, his shoulders slumped. "And now there is no reason to marry."

"There was no reason in the first place." Holding his hand, she led him down the winding trail into the village. "I promise women can and do have children without husbands and as you can see we are all well."

Disappointment clung to his voice. "It's just not what I had planned."

"Does anything ever go according to plan?" She wafted her hand across the horizon. Villagers milled about their daily duties, and the distinct clop of Pegasus hooves headed towards her. "I became a priestess of Athena to avoid the chains of men and still ended up raped and vilified as a monster."

"But you used that to fight, to save others." He gestured around the small village. "In my journeys, I have heard the stories. You have saved so many from horrible fates and made men think more keenly about how they treat the women in their lives. Yes, the stories are told with you as the monster, but that is because bad men must vilify those who try to stop them. Despite that, mothers tell their children to be kind and good or Medusa will see into their souls and turn them to stone. Your emblem hangs above houses as a ward against evil, not because you are evil, but because evil fears you. Gods and Kings want you dead because they are afraid. You not only avoided the chains of men. You broke them." Shaking his head, he stared at her with the same awe he displayed seeing the fire mares. "I came here to protect you, but I was wrong. You don't need protection and I could use your help."

"Danae..."

He nodded at his mother's name hanging in the air. "I need your help defeating my uncle."

"Of course." Mehdi replied without hesitation. "Did you miss the part earlier where I said 'We'?"

Medhi and Perseus met everyone at breakfast and discussed their plan with the others. Perseus dug into the bounty piling meat, cheeses, and fruits onto his plate.

Mehdi chuckled, wondering when he last ate. Turning to share the comical scene with Cassia her smile dropped.

Cassia glared at her. "Alone?"

Biting into a piece of fruit Mehdi rolled her eyes. "I am not going alone. I am going with Perseus."

"Just the two of you?" Stehno asked.

"We are demi-gods," she argued.

Placing her hand on Mehdi's knee, she pleaded, "Wait for Adrasteia to return. Take a ship. Allow your army to follow you."

Shrugging, she handed Perseus some bread. "Why, when both Perseus and I can fly?"

"You are a Queen," Eurayle insisted. "You have warriors you can send."

"Not this time. Seriphos is too far away. If I wait for Adrasteia and take my army it will take too long. We can't even sail in that direction until the seasons change."

"But so far?"

"We will rest along the way. I have not seen Iole in a while. She says Ethiopia is lovely this time of year."

Glancing over Cassia's shoulder, she saw Stheno tapping her teeth in a worried fashion. Euryale slipped next to her and squeezed her while looking at Mehdi, "We know we can't stop you, but we do worry."

"How is it you raise warriors, but worry when we leave to fight?"

"Because it is smart to know how to defend yourself, but wise to know every battle has the risk of death."

Mehdi gazed at them with love and let out a long sigh. "I know, but you have trained me well. This is the best move. Besides, Danae does not deserve to be forced into marriage any more than I did."

"She is likely already married. What is your plan? Simply walking up and cutting off his head?" Cassia queried.

Mehdi mulled the idea, envisioning his head tumbling down his lap to the base of his throne. The same throne he sat in, silent, as they persecuted her for a crime she did not commit.

Cassia frowned at the smirk on her face. "Tell me you have a plan."

Squeezing her hand, Mehdi chuckled, "We do. It's quite clever."

Perseus's hand dropped to the table mid-bite. "Married?"

Mehdi surveyed his worried countenance, as revelation spread across his face. Seeing his worry, she asked, "You said you have traveled for over a year?"

"Yes, but," he replied as his mind rolled over his travels and processed how long he was away.

"Time lapses when traveling. Days turn into nights as you stay focused on your goal. By the fifth kingdom we visited, I was unsure what month it was, except that Adrasteia insisted we begin the journey home before the currents changed. We lost more time revisiting the other kingdoms on the way back, razing three that refused to comply with our demands."

"But a year? Did he know it would take so long?"

Cassia brokered a morbid fact. "You were likely sent to fail or die."

He stared at her in shock.

"I doubt your uncle knows you are a demi-god."

"He does not."

"Either way. He got you out of the way and likely married your mother as soon as he could."

"But my father could be alive."

"And as king, he can declare him dead," Mehdi affirmed Cassia's point. "With you around to protest it would be ill-advised, so getting rid of you will allow him to act as he wishes."

His skin turned ashen as he pushed away his food. "I would like to leave as soon as we can."

MEHDI PACKED a saddle bag and draped it over Pegasus' back. She could hear footsteps behind her and knew who it was by the well-known sigh. She turned and found Cassia leaning against the stable wall with the same concerned face she gave Melina after an escapade with Pegasus.

"Are you going to talk me out of this?"

Cassia stepped over and slipped her arms around Mehdi's waist. "I'm not an idiot."

Sighing, her fingers knotted into Cassia's hair. "Are you mad that I did not ask you to come?"

She tugged on Mehdi's hips. "We are a team."

"But Melina is sick."

Glancing away, she agreed, but sulked. "Yes."

"I will miss you."

Cassia pulled her closer, "And we will miss you."

"How is she?"

"Her cough has improved, but you are right, we can't both leave her. She will not like that Pegasus is going and she isn't."

Chuckling, "She will not. Let her know I promise to bring something back for her."

"Do not give her the head of that king," Cassia chided.

"What?" Mehdi queried with a smirk. "Not a good gift for a child?"

"No, not even for a budding warrior."

Mehdi grinned and kissed her. "She is strong and intelligent like her mother."

"And cunning like her Queen Mama."

After all these years, Mehdi still shook her head in laughter at the name. Melina was as much her child as Chrysaor or Pegasus. She never asked to be called anything more than Mehdi, but Melina assigned her the name when she went looking for her one day and it stuck.

The thought made her think of Danae, her own surrogate mother, who at this very moment was forcing herself to submit to the king in order to survive. That was Mehdi's hope at least, that Danae would hold on and wait for her son's return. For her return. Surely, Danae knew Mehdi would come to her aid?

Brushing a stray tear from her lover's face, she beseeched, "Then for her sake, let me go rescue my Queen Mama."

Cassia released a long sigh and nodded. "Okay, but please return home."

With a strong kiss pressed against Cassia's lips, she promised.

Not finished with their goodbye Cassia opened her mouth for a deeper kiss. Mehdi's heart fluttered, as she inhaled sharply pushing Cassia into a stall. Cassia kicked the stall door shut and shoved her lover to the ground. They rolled in the hay, hands dancing up legs and under skirts.

Mehdi panted heavily, feeling both herself and Cassia climaxing when Perseus called out her name. Cassia almost stopped, but Mehdi braced her hand and kissed Cassia to keep their moans muffled. The intensity pushing them over the edge, they whimpered and shivered in each other's arms as Perseus entered the stable. Hapless, he called out for Mehdi again.

Silently giggling, they reoriented their clothes and tried to stay hidden.

They failed when Perseus's head peered over the stall door and down at them. "Should a queen be rolling around in the hay?"

"A Queen can do as she wishes," Mehdi quipped and stood with regality.

"Oh, can she?" Perseus retorted with a pleasing smirk, "And a King?"

Mehdi huffed and helped Cassia up, "Okay, fine. A ruler can do as they wish as long as it isn't harmful to her people and there is willing consent."

Cassia smiled, while picking straw out of Mehdi's hair. "This subject is very willing."

Mehdi quirked a smirk at Perseus. "See?"

Arms draped over the door, completely amused with the scene before him, he relented. "Fair."

"Besides," Mehdi added. "Cassia is my wife in all but right of marriage. We've been together long enough to claim that."

Cassia beamed at Mehdi, "If I could marry you. I would."

Mehdi stroked her fingers across Cassia's cheek.

"Well...Why not?" Perseus offered.

Mehdi stared at her friend with curiosity. "Why not what?"

"This is your queendom. You can sanction it."

Her mouth dropped open. She was queen and on an island full of women, why not? "Many of these women are still married. Including Cassia," she countered.

"You do not have to recognize another ruler's laws."

"There is a hypocrisy in ignoring another King's laws while forcing my demands on them."

"You are demanding women have the same freedoms. Can a man divorce his wife?"

"He can by sending her back to her father."

"Who are rarely better than the husbands," Cassia snarked.

"And wives have to have a man speak for them," Mehdi added.

"But no men are allowed here. And again. You make the laws."

Mehdi squeezed Cassia's hand, "I don't like to be reminded of that. I create laws that are good for the people."

"Will being allowed to marry who you wish be good for the people?" Perseus postulated.

She shrugged. "There is no need. We have no laws banning personal relationships."

"But no marriage laws? No union ceremonies?"

"Again, no need."

Cassia tugged on Mehdi's arm. "I'm not the only one that would enjoy the idea of being married. If old men can marry young men, why can't we marry each other?"

Perseus shook his head, "That is pederasty and temporary."

"Just another liberty men have and no better than marrying off girls," Mehdi sneered.

"One of my brothers still sees his former mentor. They are no longer officially joined, but have a more intimate relationship than he does with his wife."

Mehdi pushed back Cassia's hair, brushing away some straw. "Would you like that? To marry me?"

She smiled, "I would. I didn't get a choice the last time." Her voice caught in her throat, "I like the idea that I can choose. Would you marry me?"

Mehdi beamed. "I would."

Perseus clapped his hands. "Then it's settled. You can

decree that anyone is allowed to join in union in the manner they wish and you two can do the same."

Mehdi cupped her mouth, catching the joy that bubbled out of her throat.

Cassia grabbed Mehdi's hands and kissed her firmly on the lips. "Yes, let's do it before you leave!"

"I want to," Mehdi started. "But I want to give the people time to discuss the edict. You, Stehno, and Euryale should propose it to them and work out the details."

"And us?" Cassia asked.

Squeezing her hands, her chest swelled with excitement. "Upon my return."

"Then you better come back!"

"I swear," Mehdi promised and kissed her again.

With Melina in her arms, Cassia waved goodbye to Perseus, Mehdi, and Pegasus as they lifted into the air. Stheno and Euryale took flight and chased after them wishing them well with tears in their eyes.

THEY LANDED in Ethiopia just outside the main city and walked to Iole's shop. It was a good thing they stopped because the skies were ominous, filling with dark storm clouds and building winds. There was a strange sensation in the air and it made Mehdi wary. The marketplace was empty, but a murmur of voices rumbled up from the port. Just as she stepped up to Iole's shop, Iole appeared, her face long and gray with worry.

"Mehdi!" she cried out in surprise and threw her arms around her.

"What is it, Iole?" Mehdi asked.

"The most horrid thing." She grabbed her hand and started pulling her. "Quickly, I will tell you along the way."

As Iole rushed them through the streets, she spoke, "It is Andromeda. She is being sacrificed to Poseidon."

"What?" Mehdi exclaimed.

"Apparently, the queen declared her daughter Andromeda is more beautiful than the nereids. This apparently, made them jealous and they demanded Poseidon kill her."

"That's ridiculous." Mehdi spat.

"Ridiculous or not. She is, as we speak, being tied up and will be fed to one of Poseidon's monsters."

"Iole, I know the nereids and this doesn't sound like them."

"They lure men to their death all the time. Why not a woman?"

"They only kill men that try to capture them. Wouldn't you defend yourself if men were always trying to capture you?"

Breathless, they reached the oceanside as the skies opened and released torrential rain on the city. Iole pointed to a rock jutting from the sea where a woman was tied to a pole and grimly informed them. "Usually, that rock is for goats,"

"This doesn't make any sense." Mehdi declared. She glanced down at the base of the rocks and saw the nereids. "Let me go talk to them." Slipping on her mask, she slithered out into the water and towards the sacrificial rock.

There, she found the nereids, wailing and screaming.

Bracing herself against the rock, she shouted. "What is happening?"

Thetis swam up to her. "What are you doing here?"

"I could ask you the same. Why are you demanding the sacrifice of that woman to Poseidon?"

"We are not demanding anything." Thetis seethed, sending another giant wave to crash against the rocks. "Poseidon used us as an excuse."

"What?" Mehdi asked, while forming claws that clung to the craggy rock as another wave slammed against her.

"He wants the girl but has learned his lesson because of you. Now he just demands them as sacrifice and his minion, Cetus, takes them."

Horrified by Poseidon's tactics she demanded, "Then stop him."

"We cannot," Thetis replied in defeat. "We are his subjects."

Her fury grew. "Why is everyone so afraid of the Olympians?"

Thetis' eyes dulled. "Because we know the cost of defiance."

Livid, she snapped at her friend. "The cost of subservience does not seem any less!"

The nereids' wails grew louder as the water around them

surged. On the other side of the rock, a giant black scaly creature rose from the sea. In the shadowed skies and crashing waves, Mehdi could not make out its features, but he seemed familiar. Likely, another one of Poseidon's minions serving their god.

His claws sunk into the rocks drawing him up to Andromeda above. Mehdi's anger boiled as she surged towards it, confronting the creature. Minion or not, he was going to harm the girl and must be stopped. Hoping her power was strong enough to destroy the monster, she dodged his snapping teeth and blocked him from the girl.

Behind her, Perseus with Pegasus landed on the rock and frantically worked to free the girl.

Concentrating, she stretched her form as large and horrendous as she could. Her hair snakes snapped and hissed as her tail coiled deep into the crags for stability. Dodging another snap of the monster's teeth, she caught its gaze.

Mehdi was not ready for the life that passed before her. It was not of a creature, but of a man. A man with a happy childhood who grew into a kind person. She saw him as a young man getting caught in a storm and lost at sea. Floating on flotsam, starving from hunger, and dying from the heat of the sun. In his desperate hour, he prayed to Poseidon vowing servitude in exchange for his life. The god answered, and the price grim as he transformed into a creature of the deep. Bound to protect Poseidon's lair and do as the god wished, the man missed his home.

After years of servitude, he begged the god for another favor. Requesting to be a man once more. Poseidon agreed and the man joyously swam to the nearest island, walking on sand with two feet, but as he looked around his new home, his eyes burned and his vision vanished.

Unable to see, he cried out in pain, flailing and writhing on the ground. Poseidon had granted his wish but for a price. He blindly thrashed on the beach, refusing to give up, but knew all was lost.

Mehdi's heart skipped when a hand grabbed his forearm and steadied his feet. The next few memories were a haze, as the man built himself a new life. He learned how to live as a blind man, including how to fish. A newfound contentment filled his being as she listened to him cast the net with a swish, plunk...swish, plunk.

It was then that Mehdi realized that this man was Alexios.

Splitting her focus from his memories and back to the real world, she gasped seeing Alexios, as the sea monster turning to stone. His claw slipped out of their self-formed holes as his limbs cracked under the weight of his serpent form turning into rock. Mortified, she willed the mask to stop. The transformation ceased and his flesh reformed, but the encounter sapped his strength. His grip faltered and he plummeted to the water below. Horror ripped through her body watching him bump and crash into rocks on his descent. There was no one there to catch him.

The triumphant roar of the crowd hit her ears, as her heart sank with fear. Did she just kill Alexios?

She glanced back at Perseus, and the freed the girl.

"Are you okay? What is happening?"

"I have to go," She blurted, keeping her gaze askant.

He looked at her confused.

"I have to go. I can't explain," she squeezed his hand. "Take care of Pegasus and I will meet you in Seriphos. And I need this." She grabbed his sword, before diving into the sea.

Using her wings to control her descent, she plunged down into the depths. Adjusting her body she inhaled water instead of air and adjusted her sight. Frantically searching for any sign of Alexios, she saw the flash of a tail curl around a rock and darted after it. The currents around her shifted, pushing against her. Confused, she switched to a fish tail and thrusted forward, but Thetis and the other nereids formed around her. Unsure of their alliance, Mehdi readied her defenses.

Thetis spoke, "Why do you chase it?"

"It is Alexios." Mehdi spat. "He was here the whole time and you never told me."

"I..." Thetis stuttered in shock. "I didn't know."

"How can you not know? You are the goddess of the sea."

Her brow furrowed, "You mentioned a man, not a creature. Not Poseidon's pet."

"They are one and the same. How could you not know?" Betrayal crept into her heart, but Thetis' expression of shock and regret relinquished the thought.

"I am sorry. The ocean is vast and just like a body I do not know all its inner workings."

"And now? And now that you know, will you help me or stop me?"

Tension grew among the nereids at the idea of defying Poseidon to help her. "I know he is your king, but he is cruel and selfish. The only reason Alexios is here is because he had the audacity to love something Poseidon wanted for himself and I say something because in Poseidon's eyes, I am a possession. Not once did he care what others wanted or desired, only what he wanted, and because he is a god he is able to wield his manner any way he wishes. It is wrong, both he and Zeus take whatever they wish and the men that worship them feel they can do the same." Gazing at her friend with confusion, she implored. "Thetis you are the ocean, the ocean, but you let him rule you, Why?"

"Because he..."

"Because Zeus made him King of the Sea and all within, but you existed long before he did and will long after he is forgotten. He commands you, but he can do little without your obedience. So, stop being obedient, rather than fear his wrath, remind him that he is nothing without you, any of you. I'm not saying it will be easy, but together you are stronger than him."

Thetis smiled proudly. "You are the embodiment of Metis. I remember her giving the same speech long ago."

"But she lost," A nereid spoke.

"No," Thetis replied. "She relented, so we could live and fight again. I believe that time has come."

CHAPTER 25
DEATH TO TYRANTS

They swam deep into the ocean and into the underwater cave that she had seen in Poseidon's and Alexios' memories. Before entering, the nereids stopped, and all turned to her.

Thetis spoke, "What is your plan?"

Mehdi shook her head fighting uncertainty. "I will try to retrieve him."

"But he is a sea creature."

"When I saw him in Poseidon's memories, he was a man. He still has the gift to transform. Whether he abandoned me or is a prisoner, he does not deserve this. I will try to get him out and...go from there."

Thetis nodded, "We will wait here in case Poseidon comes."

"Can you not obscure his sight, like you did with the ships and me?"

“Yes, but he is expecting Andromeda. His servants abduct the girls and give them to Poseidon.”

Horrified, she croaked. “How many times has he done this?”

Thetis shook her head. “You don’t want to know.”

“That’s it!” Mehdi exclaimed. “When Poseidon comes, let him in. Let him think he is retrieving Andromeda, then once inside,”

Thetis affirmed, “We can trap him,”

Mehdi nodded and hugged Thetis tightly, before swimming into the cave.

The tunnel was long and deep, ensuring the only way in and out with the ability to breath water. Thoughts and strategies of her impending encounter played out in her head. How would he react to seeing her? Would he recognize her with the mask on? Would he leave? Her questions remained uncertain as she broached the underwater cavern.

The dark, dank cave with little to no light smelled of algae and must and under the one sunray piercing down through a crack in the cavern ceiling was Alexios. He sat with his arms wrapped around his knees and his head buried deep. He was not crying, but he was obviously broken by their encounter.

“Alexios,” she cried out, her emotions taking over her actions as she rushed towards him.

He stood alarmed, “Mehdi!”

“Yes,” She said between strokes, “I’m here.” Thrusting with her tail, she arched out of the water and toward the dry floor. As she descended, she willed her feet to form, landing near him. Breathless, she hurried to him. "I am here."

The sound he released was a guttural amalgamation of joy and relief. He touched her face and hair. "How are you here?" His fingers flinched, "What is wrong with your face? Are you wearing a helmet?"

"Oh!" she softly exclaimed, lifting the mask. "You don't know." She stroked his face, "I will explain when we have time."

"Mehdi you can't be here."

"And neither should you."

He shook his head, "I can't leave."

"Is that why you never came back?" She tried but failed to hide the pain that tightened her voice.

He turned away ashamed. "It is, but not why I left."

"I've thought about that so many times over the years. Poseidon forced you to leave?"

He bowed his head, "Yes, I chose my... our lives over my love for you. I'm sorry."

The confession hurt. *Our Lives?* Swallowing hard, she asked, "What did he promise you?"

"He swore he would not smite us if I left and served him once more."

Recollections of Poseidon's hands riding up her body made her shiver. "And what else?"

Turning back to her, confused, he asked, "What do you mean?"

"He didn't say what he wanted with me?" Poseidon's

violent words rang in her mind and her head ached feeling the echoes of pain.

"With you?" Alexios replied with alarm.

"Don't play the fool," Mehdi seethed, her anger towards Poseidon latching onto Alexios. "Thetis says that you bring him women. You would have today if I had not stopped you."

He clicked in his throat and grasped her arm, "But not you! I left so he wouldn't!"

She scoffed, "Then you are a fool. He raped me."

Alexios went limp, utterly stunned.

"I'm surprised he didn't come here and tell you all about it. Does he let you have your way with the other women before he takes them?"

He pushed away from her stricken with horror. "Never! I don't even have a choice!"

"Yes, you do!" Mehdi shouted. "Even if you thought you were saving me, which you didn't, you give him others!"

"No, Mehdi I swear. I don't know when I am doing it. I didn't even know today...when...Wait! That was you? You are the monster who turns men to stone." He paused, clenching his stomach, "I saw him rape you and I saw what you did to all those men."

"They are the monsters!" Mehdi yelled, her voice echoing off the cave walls. "They are the ones who rape, abuse, and murder. I give them the death they deserve."

He crumpled to the floor, curling into a ball again.

Mehdi knew the anguish on his face, he was trying to wipe away all the atrocities she had seen. A mortal mind would crack under the weight. Perhaps, he deserved it for leaving her.

Stepping back from her cruel thought, she cooled her anger. Mehdi saw Alexios' past. She knew his soul, he was not a monster. Part of her wished she had seen more, but that type of insight came at a cost. She placed her hand on his shoulder. "Why didn't you have a choice?"

"What?" he asked, voice choked with tears.

"Taking the girls. You said you don't know when you are doing it."

"I black out and wake up here again. Sometimes I wake up to a woman screaming for help. Others..." He shrugged and dropped his head back down between his knees.

Exhaling, her heart forgave him. He was simply a pawn under Poseidon's sway.

"I'm sorry I left, Mehdi. I didn't want to, but I know his wrath. I thought I was saving you from it."

Anger bloomed in her chest again, but directed at the god, not Alexios. "I'm sorry your action was in vain."

"But you still can't be here. Poseidon is coming and he will be furious."

Mehdi nodded. "Because Andromeda is not here."

He tensed. "Is the girl safe?"

"Yes, but he doesn't know that."

Clutching his chest, panic filled his eyes. "What do we do?"

Soothing his fear, she touched his face and announced. "I have a plan."

Mehdi listened as Poseidon rose out of the water and landed on the cavern floor. Without even seeing him, she could feel his swagger as he approached her. She remained huddled in a ball waiting to strike. To look more like Andromeda, she had willed her skin into black scales, it did not reflect Andromeda's complexion exactly, but it would be enough to fool even a god in low light.

Poseidon let out a shushing sound as he reached down towards her, "You no longer need to be afraid, my beauty. You are alive and I am here to give you a new life."

Mehdi seethed with anger. How dare he claim to be the savior of the woman he kidnapped? She wanted to attack him but needed him a little closer. Her fingers tightened around the hilt of Perseus' sword, Harpe. The tip curved and held a razor-sharp edge. Perfect for her looming attack.

Alexios' feet shuffled nervously, and she hoped he could play his part.

"Well done, Alexios," Poseidon cooed.

The warmth of his godly aura pressed against her skin as Poseidon kneeled. She felt his fingers twitching in anticipation and grinned when they flinched feeling scales and not flesh. That was her cue.

Mehdi unfurled and slashed out with the sword, slicing across Poseidon's throat. Blood gushed, raining down on her, soaking into her flesh. Shifting into her snake form, she hovered over his gasping body. The snakes in her hair hissed and spit, as her mouth curled into a vicious smile. "Not what you expected?"

Hand clasped at his throat, his eyes widened and his face paled with confusion when the wound didn't heal.

Euphoria surged through her, as she slithered toward him through his blood absorbing his pooling quintessence. "Slashing your throat was wise for two reasons. Watching you die quickly and not hearing your voice. Both are rewarding."

Hoping to retreat, Poseidon touched the water, but it did not yield to his will. His eyes darted around in panic, seeing no escape.

Mehdi snorted, "How does it feel to be trapped?"

Thetis and the nereids lifted from the sea in silence watching their King. He shot them a demanding plea, but they did not come to his aid.

"They won't help you." Mehdi replied. "They finally figured out you are nothing without them."

Poseidon tried to summon any power, but nothing happened.

"You are nothing without people to worship you, and others to do your bidding." She coiled her tail around his leg and pulled him away from the water. "You and your brothers bullied your way into rule and fooled everyone into thinking you were unbeatable, but I realized something. You have no real power. Only that which we give you."

Able to partially heal the gaping wound, Poseidon choked and spat, "It is still power."

"You are right, it is, but now you must choose. Do you

continue to take power by force and fear or do you change and use the power you are given for unselfish needs?"

He gawked. "You are sparing me?"

She locked eyes with him and felt his fear, "I won't lie. My life would be easier with you dead." His knowledge poured into her mind, and she knew that she had enough strength to turn him to stone. "And I will not wield this power with the same selfish cruelty you have wrought upon me and others." Energy surged through her body, and the ability to eradicate him completely from the earth made her salivate, but she chose to be better. Lifting her gaze from his, she exhaled, "Yes, I will spare you, but only upon your word that you will no longer act upon your selfish whims."

"And my kingdom?" He croaked.

"As for whether you will still rule the oceans. That is up to them." She motioned to Thetis and the nereids who stared back in awe.

"And you?"

"Alexios and I are leaving and he is no longer bound to you. Do not bother us ever again. If you do, I and all who are witness here, will consider your vow broken."

"But he is still a monster?"

She scoffed and looked at Alexios cautiously approaching. Mehdi embraced his hand, "A creature, same as me. What we look like does not make us monsters."

She brandished the sword back at Poseidon slowly lifting his chin. "Swear it. You will never bother us again."

He closed his eyes in consent. "I swear it."

"And if I sense you ever abusing your powers, I will bring you to your knees again and next time I will strike to kill."

He dipped his head in reverence.

Lowering the sword, she left a beaten Poseidon on the cave floor and escorted a tentative Alexios into the sea.

The nereids parted and Thetis allowed them to enter. Alexios transformed and his sight returned. She watched him take one look around the cavern and then back to her. Her mask did not react to his glossy black eyes. She had already peered into his soul and had judged him worthy.

MEHDI AND ALEXIOS stepped out of the waters where they first met and onto the shore of his little island. After the incident with the eels, she did not return to his home and was told the Tsunami had destroyed it. When she worriedly gazed up the hill, her jaw dropped seeing a new abode sitting atop the tiny hill. It was larger than the previous and the bleating of goats came from a small fenced-in area. Did this mean the garden in the back was also restored?

"Mehdi?" Alexios asked, grasping her hand. "Is everything all right?"

She squeezed back. "Um...I'm not sure."

"Are you afraid to go up? Is there something wrong? How long have I been away?"

Her brow furrowed, "You don't know?"

He shook his head. "After I returned to his servitude,

he caught me trying to visit you and locked me in that cave until I was needed. Refusing to be caged I would beat my body against the sealed opening until I couldn't. Still, he refused to release me, forcing me into long periods of sleep. Most of which I'd wake up and find half-drowned bodies in my clutches." His shoulders slumped and he released her hand. "I began to beg for sleep and ignorance to my actions in his service, but he made sure I remembered enough."

"Alexios," her voice cracked with agony. She took his hand again, "You are safe now. He can't hurt you again." Studying his face, she knew her words were a useless balm on the gaping wounds and vicious scars that latticed his heart.

He fell to his knees, tears flowing down his face, and overtaken by great heaving sobs, "It is not me I hurt for, but for those I was forced to hurt. Mehdi, there were so many." He choked back a wry laugh, "And he would always thank me for my service."

Mehdi kneeled next to him and cupped his face. "Those are not your atrocities but his. You fought against him so much he had to blank your mind and use you as a puppet. Making you see just enough was intentional torture to please his sick twisted mind." She gripped the back of his neck, gently massaging her fingers into his tense muscles. "You and I both fought his control and we may have lost battles, but we are here now. Free of him. We have won!"

He touched her face. "At what price?"

She let him feel her lips spread into a smile, "How much of my life did you see?"

Quirking his head, he replied. "I...can't recall...it is all a blur now."

Standing, she helped him back up, "Then we have a great deal of catching up to do, but first let's wait for Perseus."

"Is he here?"

"I doubt he has arrived yet."

"You would be wrong," Perseus replied.

"Perseus!" Both Mehdi and Alexios shouted in unison.

He came into view and upon seeing Alexios shouted in surprise, pulling him into an embrace. "You're alive!"

Hugs and kisses were exchanged along with hardy grasps and assessment of each other's well-being. He gave Mehdi a glance silently asking about the swollen red eyes of their friend. Mehdi shook her head, tabling the conversation for later.

Once they were all satisfied, Perseus motioned toward Alexios' old home.

"When did this happen?" Mehdi asked in awe.

Perseus tensed slightly, "Not long after the tidal wave. I just felt it needed to be rebuilt. I lived here after you left."

Alexios furrowed his brow in confusion.

"Poseidon destroyed your home in a Tsunami. Perseus has rebuilt it."

"Yes, and now that you have returned. I freely give it to you."

"How did you know I would come here?" Mehdi asked. She saw Pegasus eating from the garden and rushed up to him, showering her son in love.

"Where else would you go?" Perseus asked.

Mehdi introduced Pegasus to Alexios and laughed, "You have a good point, but I expected a crumbling ruin."

Alexios patted Pegasus' side then stepped back when wings flapped in his face.

A set of bright eyes peered out the doorway of the cottage, "Is this her?" Andromeda asked.

Perseus beamed and drew the strangers together, "Yes. Andromeda, meet Mehdi."

Andromeda studied Mehdi, "You are the Great Medusa? The one who saved me from Cetus?"

"Cetus?" Mehdi asked, "Oh you mean Alexios!"

Confused, Andromeda looked to Perseus for an explanation. He shrugged.

Alexios, bracing his stance as Pegasus nuzzled him, coughed. "That would be me."

Andromeda and Perseus stared at Alexios in confusion.

Mehdi squeezed Alexios' hand and nodded. "Poseidon forced him to do his bidding as Cetus, the sea monster."

"And now?" Perseus asked, expecting an explanation.

Mehdi chuckled, "Perhaps we can explain over some wine."

"And food," Alexios added.

Mehdi and Perseus swapped stories as they all ate. She learned that according to the people of Ethiopia, Perseus had rescued Andromeda and defeated the sea creature. Some of the viewers swore they had seen the monster turn to stone, so Perseus and Iole put together a bag that they claimed held the head of Medusa. He motioned to a bag lying still in the corner.

Perseus laughed. "We told them that even in death if anyone looked upon your visage they would turn to stone."

"You didn't." Mehdi laughed, dipping her bread in oil and spices.

He nodded and walked towards the bag. "We even put some snakes in it, so if anyone tried to steal it, it would move."

She watched the seemingly innocuous sack slightly stir and shuddered, "That's awful."

"Well, it was the best we could do, especially since you left."

Embarrassed, Mehdi motioned towards Alexios as her defense.

Perseus relented and forgave her sudden exodus.

Mehdi looked at Andromeda, "I think Perseus left something out. Why are you here?"

Andromeda smiled coyly and Perseus blushed.

"Oh!" Mehdi blurted.

"Actually," Andromeda spoke. "I requested to come with Perseus because I do not wish to live in a land willing to sacrifice me, so I asked him to demand me as his bride. My father capitulated, fearing that Perseus could easily turn him to stone." She touched Perseus' hand. "If something more happens that is up to us and no one else."

Mehdi nodded in approval, then asked. "What do we do about your mother?"

"Well, I don't think a bag of snakes will fool my Uncle. At least not for long."

"And now I'm dead," Mehdi declared.

Perseus weighed the statement. "Is that a bad thing?"

"Yes, how am I to continue doing what I do?"

"Who says you have to stop? Medusa is dead, but not her movement. They've tried to kill you before and your message lives on. Why not use that to keep going? And no one will come looking for you."

"That still doesn't help Danae."

Perseus reached over and took his friend's hand. "We go to the King and ask him to release my mother. If he refuses, you judge him."

She scowled, "You mean kill him."

He locked eyes with her. "I know I am asking a lot. We decide based on his actions."

Alexios smiled; eyes full of mirth. "You just spared a god. He may have a chance."

~

STEADYING HER BREATH, Mehdi along with Perseus, and Andromeda entered the home of King Polydectes. Sitting high on a grand hill, and stretching out in stacked stone walled squares, his wealth and power were on display for all to see. They were escorted to the inner atrium, where Polydectes waited. The opulence of his position shone in the mosaic-tiled paths and finely groomed fruit trees encircled by decorative bricks.

Hooded in a himation and wearing the clothes of a

servant, Mehdi walked a step behind Andromeda posing as her handmaiden.

The king's displeased eyes kept flitting towards the writhing bag in Perseus' grasp. At his side stood Danae, anxiously watching her son, but feet planted in place.

Around them, the atrium was filled with the king's court and sycophants. Perseus brandished the bag for all to see and declared, "I have done what you asked. Now release my mother."

Fear washed over the crowd as feet shuffled backward, and small shrieks of fright filled the air.

King Polydectes squirmed in his chair and scoffed, "A bag is not proof."

"Do you wish for proof?" Perseus asked, clutching the sack tighter, allowing the outline of the mask fitted in her helmet to press against the cloth. "I can draw the head out and all in here that gaze upon her will turn to stone."

The King's court grew uneasy.

"How do we know that will happen?"

"I am sure the stories of Ethiopia have reached your shores. Behold, Andromeda herself, who was chained to a rock and would have been a monster's feast if not for Medusa. A thousand eyes saw his stone body fall to the ocean below."

A murmur of agreement filled the room as they ogled the dark beauty.

"I, Andromeda, Princess of Ethiopia owe my life to Perseus and the powers of Medusa."

A grin tugged at Mehdi's mouth. Neither she nor Perseus were lying, just skipping certain details.

The terror filling the room was palpable and Mehdi drank it in. They muttered her name in fright and prayed she would not harm them. Her heart beat faster and her blood warmed with the same energy she felt when wearing the mask. She wasn't sure what was happening, but she enjoyed the power.

Polydectes' scoffed, "Merely stories. No man who has faced Medusa has survived. Why should I believe you did?"

"You still doubt me?" Perseus dropped the sack and unwound the tie. Snakes writhed and poked out as he reached in slowly lifting the helmet out.

A man screamed, "My Lord Please! She will destroy us all!"

"Stop!" The King commanded.

"Release my mother!" Perseus boomed.

Polydectes' eyes darted to Danae and back to her son.

He gripped the neck of the bag closed and lifted it again. "I have killed Medusa. Mehdi, Priestess of Athena. A girl of this Island that I love as a sister. That my mother loves as a daughter. I have destroyed who she is for you, upon the promise that you will release my mother from your claim. Are you not a man of your word?" Perseus demanded.

"You question my word?!" The King shouted, jumping from his seat.

Perseus stood strong and calmly replied, "I do when you have yet to honor it."

"Fine," the King blurted, throwing his hand in the air, and waving it toward Danae. "You are released."

Her stoic demeanor disappeared as she rushed towards her son.

Mehdi's shoulders relaxed in relief. The ruse had worked. She watched mother and son reunite, wanting desperately to also hug her.

Perseus and Danae remained in a long loving embrace before breaking to introduce Andromeda.

Danae whispered in a hushed tone, "Did you really kill Mehdi?"

Perseus patted her hand and said, "I will tell you all, but not here."

Danae ushered them to her room, so she could pack and leave.

Mehdi maintained her illusion as a handmaiden until they were inside, then she lowered her himation and called out, "Danae."

Danae, so distracted by the arrival of her son, did not hear her. Perseus touched his mother's arm and she turned her around. Dropped the scarf in her hand, she cried out. "Mehdi!" Embracing her, she showered Mehdi in kisses and sobbed. "I thought you were dead. Please tell me what has happened."

Mehdi grasped Danae's hands, choking back tears of joy. "In time, but let's leave here while we can."

"You!" A voice shouted. "You are not dead!"

Mehdi turned to find a furious Polydectes. He barreled

towards her with his massive frame, as his sword slid out of its sheath.

Danae tried to position herself in a protective pose, spreading her arms wide and bracing her feet, but Mehdi moved with lightning speed. Transforming into her snake-like form, she whipped between her surrogate mother and the king. Her body grew to an immense size and when she hissed her tongue lashed out slicing him across the face.

The transformation caught Polydectes by surprise causing a falter in his attack, and he stumbled back clutching his face. Mehdi took advantage of his weak stance, knocking him off his feet with the swipe of her tail and grabbing his arm as he fell. Lifting him off the ground she brought him face to face with her stony gaze.

He flailed in fright, clawing at her grasp, trying to break free and desperately avoiding eye contact. His actions failed and his body froze in terror.

She stared deep into his soul and it was one of the blackest she had seen. She saw his abuses of power, his habitual deceit, and many murders. He was not a benevolent king, but one filled with hatred and jealousy.

Among all this cruelty, she saw Dictes. Polydectes' envied his brother despite the fact that Dictes was not stronger, wiser, or more handsome than he but because Dictes lived a happy life.

When Polydectes murdered their father and took the throne, Dictes happily chose to live life as a fisherman. Polydectes lived high on the hill bedding any man or woman he wished, but somehow still felt jealous of his brother. Then

Danae arrived and Polydectes could think of nothing, but having her.

Mehdi saw his attempts to woo Danae and subsequent failures. Years and years of schemes and plots that always failed. Then the tidal wave hit and Dictes was swept to sea. Polydectes saw his opportunity. The law itself was on his side. If he was gone long enough Polydectes could lay claim to Danae.

Fate helped Dictes return to Seriphos, but Polydectes seized before anyone knew of his return. Fearing the portent of killing his brother, he instead trapped him in a cave. Keeping him alive with mere scrapes. Polydectes visited his brother to orate his consummations with Danae and his genius in sending Perseus off to die. He relished his choice in not killing Dictes, finding delight in torturing him over and over.

Mehdi's stomach twisted violently at his depravity and held nothing back as she judged him. Satisfaction filled her soul watching his body harden. Releasing her grasp, she watched him shatter on the bedroom floor. The sound of his stone form splintering into a million pieces sent a pleasing shiver down her spine, and a cruel grin curled along her lips.

She moved her gaze to the others in the room and they stood back terrified. Not wanting them to fear her, she returned to her human form and spoke. "I did not mean to frighten you."

Her sudden transformation shook Andromeda and Danae, both clutching to Perseus in stricken horror.

Perseus stuttered slightly, "I thought you said you could only change with the mask."

"Yes," Mehdi replied confused by his statement.

"You're not wearing it."

She touched her face in surprise and realized she was not. Her eyes flitted toward the bag of snakes and back at Perseus bewildered and confused. She used Metis' powers without the mask. Her thoughts flashed to the underwater cave and her body absorbing Poseidon's blood, then to the atrium and the power she felt when they prayed to her.

As the realization of what she was dawned on her, guards rushed in hearing the commotion. Seeing Polydectes' shattered body on the floor they all readied their weapons in alarm.

Perseus stepped forward brandishing the bag of snakes. "He attempted to attack my mother and go back on his word. I had no choice."

"Perseus is correct." Danae affirmed. "And by right of combat, he is now your King."

The guards worked to process everything that was happening and after a brief moment, the Head Guard tapped his spear twice and kneeled to their new King. His men followed his lead and room rumbled with the sound of armored knees hitting the stone floor.

CHAPTER 26
BEYOND THE MYTH

Mehdi's head reeled. Everything was happening so fast and she was not alone. Andromeda clung to Perseus reliving her recent nightmare as Perseus's eyes darted between Mehdi and Danae. Danae appeared to be the only one maintaining calm and decorum ordering the guards to collect Polydectes' remains and sending callers to announce Perseus as King.

In a matter of moments, the room was clean and quiet. Danae looked to the others. "Perseus I am sorry to thrust power on you so quickly, but it had to be done. Anything else would have meant discord and likely death."

"I understand, Mother," Perseus replied. Andromeda squeezed his hand to help ease his apprehension.

"Your father and I," Danae began.

Mehdi found her moment in the chaos to tell them about Dictes. "Your father!" she blurted. "He is alive."

"What!" Perseus declared.

"Polydectes has kept him prisoner since the tidal wave!"

"Where?" Danae asked, fingers steadying her lips as they trembled.

She grabbed Perseus' hand. "Follow me, I know where."

Mehdi rushed the group out of the room and down the corridors. Danae tugged at Mehdi's himation. Understanding her action, Mehdi hid her head deep into the cowl and hurried the group to the cave.

Large rocks covered the opening, carried by the tidal wave, leaving little to no way for a mere mortal to escape.

Mehdi scrambled up to the small opening Polydectes visited. "Hello?"

Right at her side, Perseus slid away additional rocks and shouted down below. "Father?"

"Perseus?" Came a faint cry.

"It is me!" Perseus declared, hugging Mehdi in excitement.

Danae crumpled to her knees and stammered. "But how do we get him out?"

Perseus and Mehdi exchanged glances devising a plan.

The two worked in unison taking advantage of their strength, lifting rocks and boulders mere mortals could not. Once the opening was large enough Mehdi used her tail as a brace to keep the rocks from collapsing and Perseus flew down, retrieving his frail father.

Dictes stumbled into the light and fell into his wife's arms. Danae's previous composure was gone, weeping openly and stroking Dictes in disbelief. Mehdi's heart ached to see the lovers reunited. They were a strange pair, this older man and his beautiful wife still wearing the adornments of a king's wife. Her thoughts drifted to Cassia and Alexios, replacing joy with confusion and dread.

Perseus carried his weak father back, intentionally taking the path through the city. He wanted all to see his father alive.

The onlookers swelled into a crowded celebration that carried Dictes all the way to Athena's statue. Mehdi tried to blend in and be forgotten, but Perseus dragged her into view allowing the villagers to see their priestess returned.

A moment of fear swept over the crowd. Athena was not the only stone statue on the sacred hill. Her victims were strewn about faces frozen in terror and their mute screams filled the silence. Mehdi's feet shifted, ready to run, when a priestess stepped out of the crowd holding the peplos she had woven for Athena.

The Priestess reverently adorned Mehdi in the peplos and kneeled. The women of the island released cries of joy and lifted Mehdi into the air, carrying to the feet of the golden statue. As they lowered her back to the ground, she stared out into the sea of onlookers with surprise and awe at their acceptance.

Perseus stepped forward, lowering to one knee. In his arms, he offered Mehdi her helm and the Aegis.

"What do I do with this?" She asked. "I no longer need it."

"But they do." Standing he adorned the Aegis across her shoulders.

Mehdi detached the mask from her helmet and affixed it to the Aegis.

The audience kept their eyes downcast afraid of the mask's power. Her power.

She straightened her shoulders and steadied her stance. "If you are true of heart and cause no harm you do not need to fear me. Gaze upon the mask of Medusa, Metis reborn, and know whosoever calls upon her, or wherever her visage is drawn they shall be protected."

ADORNED IN MAGICAL gifts and eating a feast made in their honor, Mehdi felt ridiculous sitting at the head table with the newly crowned Perseus. This was twice now she declared herself as Metis reborn. Was she truly a god?

The question left her mind when she saw Alexios being escorted in. In their time apart, he bathed and put on a fresh chiton. Grime washed away, his skin was pale from a lack of sun, but his cheeks were flush. Her eyes raked over his broad shoulders and lean muscles, happy to know he wasn't malnourished. Leaping to her feet, she rushed to help, sliding her hand under his elbow and guiding him to the table.

"I take it things went well," Alexios commented, before clicking in his throat and sitting down.

The sound sent a shiver down her spine causing her heart to lurch at him and her stomach to burble.

"Are you well?" Alexios asked.

She patted his hand, then pulled it away clenching it into a fist. "Yes," she lied. "A lot has happened."

"I'll say. Some stranger showed up on my island to inform me that King Perseus and Medusa requested my presence."

Her mouth turned down in a frown, but mirth filled her voice, "I'm sorry that I could not come to get you myself. Everything happened so quickly. How is Pegasus?"

"I'm pretty sure he has eaten half the garden."

Chuckling softly, she touched his arm and apologized. His flesh bristled under her touch, and she flinched her hand away. "Sorry."

Alexios paused a long moment, unmoving, and head bowed in thought.

"What is it?" Mehdi asked, fearing his response.

"What is to become of us?"

Her lungs froze and her heart beat so hard it hurt. "Us?" She finally forced out.

He nodded, keeping his arms folded in his lap, his fingers lacing and rubbing nervously. "I know I left, but I didn't stop loving you."

A sharp twinge pierced her chest. She still loved him, but like a wife that loves a widow. His departure hurt and even if his intentions for leaving her were justified the pain of abandonment seared scars on her heart.

And there was Cassia, whom she promised to marry. Mehdi had a life now. A good one with children and people to take care of, but could she just leave him here? Alone? "I... have a life..."

He raised his hand stopping her words, "I understand. I know how long I've been gone."

"No, Alexios." She stammered and grabbed his wrist. "You have been a prisoner too long! As a slave to Poseidon and cursed to live a life in limbo between man and creature. We can't get back the love we lost, but I won't let you remain alone."

His throat bobbed up and down as he swallowed hard. "Then what?"

"Come with me to my island. It is full of creatures like us. You'd be the only man, but...I am their ruler. If I say you are safe they will believe me."

"Creatures, like us?"

Mehdi scooted closer. "Yes, nereids, sirens, harpies, and even a few gods. We live there in peace, it is even protected from Poseidon, so even if the bastard breaks his promise it can be a place of refuge for you too."

"But your life?"

"Needs you in it," she said, shocked by her own confession.

He turned his head and clicked in his throat. "You do?"

Mehdi would have to explain things to Cassia and eventually tell him about Chrysaor, but her gut told her not to leave him. She touched his face with surety. "I do."

ABOUT THE AUTHOR

Cheryl L-G Trent is a queer dyslexic neurodivergent historian from Texas/Oklahoma. Despite limitations, her passion for writing never waned.

Cheryl loves to write about stories skirting famous events and specializes in Ancient, Medieval, American, and Clothing History. Additionally, she loves to tell stories of the interlopers and outcasts — the parts of history that were not written in books but did exist. Her goal is to share fun, adventurous stories that express the struggles of women, outsiders, and the invisible.

Webpage

clgtrent.com
linktr.ee/clgtrent

www.ingramcontent.com/pod-product-compliance
Lightning Source LLC
Chambersburg PA
CBHW070540310726
48982CB00010B/1415/J
9798989317059